THE
Adventures
OF
Long John Silver

ALSO BY DENIS JUDD

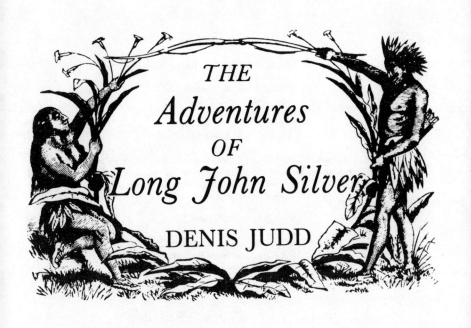

THE
Adventures
OF
Long John Silver

DENIS JUDD

MICHAEL JOSEPH
LONDON

First published in Great Britain by
Michael Joseph Limited
52 Bedford Square
London WC1B 3EF
1977

© 1977 by Denis Judd

ISBN 0 7181 1504 X

Printed and bound in Great Britain by
Billing and Sons Limited
Guildford, London and Worcester

Author's Note

This book does not seek to emulate Robert Louis Stevenson, and certainly not to mock him. The events described and the adventures related are merely designed to answer some of the riddles and unanswered questions in *Treasure Island* itself. The book is, above all, supposed to be fun.

DENIS JUDD

1

❧ The Sick Man at Tormartin ❧

I had not thought to take up my pen once more to recount deeds of blood and terror long ago. I earnestly believed that I had done with buccaneers, and buried treasure, and mutinies at sea. If the skull and crossbones was ever to fly again I imagined that it would be only in the worst of dreams. True, the memory of that bland, cruel, sharp and persuasive seafaring man with one leg had remained fresh within me. But I had come to believe that Long John Silver had gone to meet his irate Maker soon after the noble ship *Hispaniola* had sailed into Bristol harbour in 1766 laden with treasure.

Well, let me set it down in good order. It was in the latter years of the reign of our good King George III. I was doctor in a country practice in Gloucestershire. My calling did not make me the wealthiest of men, but the service that I performed in the hamlets of that rolling countryside, and the respect that was owed to me and my family, would have seemed riches enough to my poor dead father.

It was, I remember, just gone noon on a windswept day in April when I received the urgent summons to the sick man's bedside. Old Mrs Tomlin brought the message, huffing and wheezing, and looking as much in need of my attentions as any invalid. I took my bag and went to mount the horse that I called Ben Gunn in remembrance of those adventures that I have already chronicled. My patient wife Harriet watched me depart, before settling down to yet another meal without me.

The house at Tormartin, where the sick man lay, boasted fine mullioned windows cut from Bath stone. It was not quite a manor house, yet well set up, and superior in almost all particulars to any farm house in the neighbourhood. I had heard it rumoured that a gentleman with substantial interests in the West Indies lived there, a recluse with only a few servants. The door was opened by a man with coffee-coloured skin and with a crimson sash tied round his middle. He led me, with many gesticulations and grimaces, towards a heavy black door that swung noiselessly inwards.

On a couch by the side of a bright fire lay an old man. As I approached him he coughed fitfully and spat into a spotted red handkerchief. Ah, my friend, thought I, that cough bodes ill for you, upon my oath. Then, as I set down my bag upon the small table near the invalid, a tremor of recognition ran through me and, for a moment, a panic that I had not known since boyhood gripped me.

The sick man had only one leg, the other was cut off close by the hip! As he lifted his head and looked towards me I knew that I was not mistaken. The great round face of Long John Silver had been ruined by the tropical sun and by the passage of the years, and by God knows what else besides, but it was *his* face! His hair was white and wispy, and a rough, pale scar tissue disfigured his left cheek. But his blue eyes still flashed in a manner both commanding and beguiling. And he knew me, and smiled.

'Sit you down, Jim,' he said, motioning me to a chair beside him.

'Or maybe,' he went on, 'begging your pardon, I should have said Dr Hawkins. But we was shipmates once, Jim, and you won't be offstanding with old John now, as like as not.'

At this he winked and nodded, and the rank phlegm of his illness bobbled in his throat. Seeing I was still struck dumb with shock, he spoke again.

'It's like this, Jim. I've bided my time since I settled in this here house eight months ago. I've laid low and spied out the land, and kept myself to myself. But I can't get rid of this damn spittle in my chest or this cough that's tearing me apart.'

I nodded, and he continued.

'Then I discovered you and me was laid alongside, in a manner of speaking. So I've hauled you aboard to look me over, and maybe have a yarn for old time's sake, as well.'

I found my voice. 'But I thought you were long since dead, though whether at a rope's end, or in some fever swamp, I had no means of knowing.'

Silver threw back his head and laughed at this. It was not the hearty roar that I remembered, but it brought back to me in an instant the spruce cook's galley on the old *Hispaniola,* and flying fish and blue skies, and for a moment I heard again Captain Flint screech 'Pieces of Eight, Pieces of Eight' from his cage in the corner.

'Well, now,' said Silver, when his laughter ceased, 'if that don't beat cockfighting. You're a card, you are, and no mistake. Long John's too smart to hang like a pig at the end of a rope. But I've come near to it, by the powers, and I've seen such things as don't bear thinking of.

'I've seen men keel-hauled, I have, with their bellies ripped open by the barnacles on the ship's bottom. I've seen the savages on the Guinea coast a-sawing up young girls for sport. Plague, and bloody rebellion, and human sacrifice, and what not, old John's seen it all, and he's still here to tell the tale. And for why? Because you're a rogue, says you. Because I've known when to lay low and speak soft, says I. That's the secret, Jim, and you may lay to that.'

'That's as maybe,' I said. 'But what's to prevent me now from handing you over to be hanged at the next assizes? There are good men dead because of you, John Silver, men I've seen struck down before my eyes.'

For a moment Silver's gaze flickered. 'You'd not be persecuting an old cripple as is near to dying, Jim,' he said. 'No, not even Squire Trelawney and Cap'n Smollett, gentlemen both, would stoop so low.' He paused. 'Both gentlemen alive and well, Jim?'

I then told him, carefully measuring my words, that Mr Trelawney had been dead these eleven years, though he had sat in Parliament before the end, and had continued to shoot his partridge with unfailing accuracy until stricken with his last illness. Captain Smollett, recalled to sea by his nation's needs, had fought with Admiral Rodney against the French at the glorious battle of the Saints in '82. The French fleet had been scattered, and the British West Indies saved, but Captain Smollett had been cut in two by a cannon ball. At least he had died, as he had begun, in his sovereign's service.

Silver sucked in his breath at my words; he mumbled something about them being true Englishmen through and through, but I could see that in part he relished my news. After all, he had despised Trelawney, and his plans for seizing Flint's booty from Kidd's Island had foundered on the unyielding integrity of Alexander Smollett.

After a silence he said, 'But what of Dr Livesey? There was a man of honour, to be sure. Not dead too, Jim?'

This time I had happier tidings. Dr Livesey was indeed alive and well. He lived with his sister at Taunton, still practising his profession and much admired by Somerset society. It had been Dr Livesey who had invested my modest share of the treasure from Kidd's Island, and who had urged me to pass through medical school. In great measure I owed my present security to him, and not only in matters of finance, for he had also taken it upon himself to look with a father's eye over my education and welfare.

My talk of Dr Livesey reminded me of duty. I turned to John Silver as doctor to patient. He heaved himself into a sitting position, and together we pulled his shirt over his head. I was struck again by the breadth of his shoulders and by the two crooked scars across his ribs. I noticed once more the tattoo marks on his upper arms: one showed hearts entwined over the name *Annette,* the other one said, more plainly, *Damn all Excise men!*

But I saw too how Silver's great barrel of a chest had wasted, and how the skin hung pale and blotchy on his torso. A careful examination confirmed my first diagnosis of his condition.

'Well, John Silver,' I said, 'you may have escaped the hangman's noose and yellow fever, but you have consumption now, and I fear that your life has not much further to run.' As I said this, a little after the fashion of an avenging angel, I felt a strange and unexpected spasm of remorse.

To soften my words I added, 'But better men than you have staved off consumption with sober living and a sensible diet. If you should have a mind to do as I say, you may yet see more springs in Gloucestershire.'

Silver shook himself like some old bear at bay. 'Now see here, Jim,' he said. 'I'm bound for Davy Jones, and don't you tell me otherwise! I'm not afeard o' death. I've lived dangerous, as well you know. But I've also lived soft and sensible when I could. I'm no great drinking man, not me. Why, Flint and Billy Bones and others beside, they was real hard drinking men. I've seen poor Billy so soused with French brandy he could move no more than a babby, and Flint, well, he died of rum at Savannah, way back in '54. I'll knuckle under and obey doctor's orders, though 'tis only spittin' against a headwind for all the good as'll come of it.'

I was relieved at this response, but not surprised, for I recalled Silver's coolness and intelligence on board the *Hispaniola.* That he had survived so many untold perils was a tribute to his common sense, as well as to his cunning and bravery.

Yet the truth was that his illness had eaten deep into his lungs. As I saw his shoulders shaken once more with his terrible, racking cough, my feelings of compassion – almost regard – were again stirred. Liar, pirate, murderer, scoundrel and thief he may have been, but his crimes were of heroic measure. Set beside the dull virtues of lesser men, his bloodiest villainies marked him out. He was, I reflected, always a man to be reckoned with.

Silver broke in upon my musing. 'So, Jim,' he said, 'there's some comfort for an old seaman who sailed with Admiral Hawke, is there?'

'Now come,' said I, 'let us get this straight. You were a common pirate when I first clapped eyes on you. I'm not Squire Trelawney to be gulled with lies about service to King and country in the wars with France and Spain.'

I felt curiously pleased with my outburst, and heard again echoes of the righteous sentiments of Captain Smollett and Dr Livesey. But Silver had the last word.

'I can see as how you don't rightly trust me, Jim,' he said, 'and I've only myself to blame for that, I reckon. Well, seeing as how others have had the telling of the tale afore me, I wants to set the log-book straight, in a manner of speaking. I hear as you've already wrote down your adventures on Kidd's Island, and a tidy sum you've made out of it, or I'm much mistook. That goatsherd, Ben Gunn, he's been a-bleating, too, so I've been told, but I never took much heed of Ben Gunn aboard the old *Walrus,* and I ain't a-starting now, by the powers!

'But this don't signify. What's done is done, and I've but a short haul left, or I'm a Dutchman. I gives you my affydavy that what follows is the truth of the matter, or leastways how I sees it, which comes to much the same thing.

'I *have* sailed with Hawke, by thunder! I've fought under the King's flag I have, and scoured the Main for Spanish ships, and Frenchies too, along o' the Royal Navy! My poor old gal, that's been dead these thirty years, she bore me two fine sons, she did, and 'tis a pity there wasn't more beside. So just you hear me out, and don't go a-crying shame and traitor afore you know what's what.

'Of course, 'tain't the whole story. But I have a fancy to

talk of my early life, and how we come to bury the treasure on Kidd's Island, and how Billy Bones skipped off with Flint's cross upon the map. Some day, if I'm spared, I'd like to tell you how I see'd the voyage to the island from my point o' view. And then there's a good deal as happened after I quit the *Hispaniola* on the homeward run. But this is all talk.' He fell silent, as if exhausted.

For myself, I saw that I had no other course open to me than to comply with his demands. And so it was left that I would return the following evening, when he would launch upon the account of his life. I must confess that as I lay in bed that night my mind was filled with feverish imaginings of what I should have to hear, but the horror and the nobility and the sadness of what was eventually revealed to me far outran my dreams.

2

{C *The Apprentice Smuggler* }

S ilver seemed in good spirits when I called on him the following day at half past six o'clock in the evening. His lungs were still torn with fearful fits of coughing and he did not always breathe with ease, but he was as sharp and bright as his condition allowed. He was merry enough, too, over our supper, for he insisted that we ate before he began his recollections of his adventures.

By the end of the meal I was in a fine humour myself, for the food was well cooked, peppery fare, as befitted a host with such experience of the West Indies. Silver's coffee-coloured manservant was as attentive as could be desired, padding swiftly and silently over the stone floor. We had consumed a bottle and a half of claret, and had tasted the first drops of a rare rich port, before Silver turned our talk to himself.

'Well, duty's duty, to be sure, Jim,' he said, 'And I reckon you'll be wanting to understand a bit more about old John, before we gets much further.' He reached out a hand for his pipe and tobacco, but he saw my sudden frown and instead pretended that he had been about to drum on the arm of his chair with his great square fingers.

'Bristol's where we'll begin,' he said at last, bracing himself to his task. 'Bristol is where I was born, Jim, and my father too, and his father before him. It's a grand city, as you well know yourself, though I've heard it often said that the fine mansions and tall shipping offices there have been built out of the blood of black slaves, in a manner of speaking.

'For,' he went on, ' 'tis a cruel place as well as a grand one, Jim. I've seen the women weeping and caterwauling on the quayside when they've know'd their sweethearts was rotting beneath the African sun or maybe had been swept into the Main in one of them great blowing storms they have out there. There's many that come back to Bristol with a hundred guineas in their pockets, but there's others thankful to come home at all and to have 'scaped shipwreck, mutiny and yellow jack, and you may lay to that!'

He was now almost as animated as when I first saw him at the Spy-Glass Inn, hopping round the saloon bar, slapping the table tops with his heavy hand, and calling out Tom Morgan for associating with Black Dog. Indeed, so moved was he by recollection and recounting that there was little for me to do but listen to his flood of words, among which bobbed a great many choice oaths and blasphemies. I have a pretty fair memory for words, and a tactful way with blasphemy, so what I now set down is, I believe, a full and decent account of John Silver's life.

He was born in Bristol in the year of grace 1716, barely six months after the Jacobite rising against the House of Hanover had ended and the Pretender had scurried back to France after a brief and inglorious 'reign' as James III of England and James VIII of Scotland.

Not that Silver's family had any time for Catholic claimants to the throne who lived in France. The head of the house, Michael Joseph Silver, was a shoemaker by trade and a Congregationalist by religion. He hated the French, noblemen and popery intensely, and in that order.

Long John recalled the way his father would grumble and rant as he worked, bending over the cobbler's last and accompanying each thump of the hammer with a radical slogan. 'There (thump) is one in the eye for the French! And there (thump) is damnation to the House of Lords! That (thump) is a kick up the Pope's backside! And that is one for all bishops, may they be cast down as they were in Cromwell's day!'

Oddly, perhaps, for a man who hankered for the lost glories of the Puritan revolution, and who struggled to read Milton's poetry and Bunyan's prose by candlelight, Michael Silver married a girl brought up in the Anglican faith. It was in part, it must be said, a marriage of convenience. In the course of his business, Michael had dealt with Henry Broadrib, a shoe-shop owner from Bath, a bulky man with a hearty appetite and a loose attachment to the Church of England. Old Broadrib had two marriageable daughters, and seeing the advantages for his business in a family liaison with a skilled cobbler, he had pressed Michael Silver to marry his elder girl, Mary Hannah Broadrib.

Mary Broadrib was a young woman of spirit, tall and fair-haired, and Michael Silver, pale and somewhat stooped by reason of his trade, at first counted himself lucky to have wed her. She and Michael created a comfortable enough home out of the rooms behind the cobbler's shop in Sheep Street; they also produced three children: John, and two daughters.

John Silver was thus brought up in a home that wanted for little, except for greater harmony between his parents. Sometimes at night, as they all sat in the kitchen, with the wood fire blazing, Michael Silver and his wife would set the room crackling with their different views of the world. John recounted one such debate that seared itself into his memory when he was barely ten years old.

'Well, wife,' Michael said suddenly, 'And what papist nonsense have you been stuffing into young John's head today? More about the martyrdom of Charles I, I'll be bound!'

'Hush, Michael,' replied Mary, cradling her youngest daughter who dozed upon her lap, 'I'm no papist, but to have cut the King's head off all those years ago was wrong, no matter what they said he had done.'

'Wrong!' cried Michael Silver. 'The pity is they never

hunted down the whole Stuart brood and stamped on them like rats!'

He swung round to his son, open-mouthed beside him.

'See here, young John. Don't you ever think as how the world must always be as you find it! Men can change their circumstances. They can better themselves with the pen or the sword. Cromwell's Ironsides brought down God's annointed on Naseby field, and just before you were born we spurned James Stuart – that Frenchified pretender to the English throne!'

'That's as maybe,' said Mary Silver quickly. 'But men need order and tradition more than envy and rebellion. We need the feel of the old things, things of the past, things like an ancient church that goes back to St Peter – my church, Michael, not yours.'

'And what other things, pray?' sneered Michael Silver. 'A House of Lords, no doubt? Fat, stupid squires? Idle bishops, eh? Drunken justices of the peace? Let them all go hang, say I!'

'Duty, Michael,' said Mary calmly, 'Duty gives a meaning to all our lives. Duty and order; lose them and there's nothing left but a wasteland and the hellish pit.'

'Duty!' scoffed Michael. 'Chains and shackles, more like. But seeing as how you're such a one for duty, wife, let us take our only son here, with his eyes as big as saucers. Well, he's clever you say, and can read like a gentleman born – thanks to you. But I say it's high time he learnt his duty at my side at the cobbler's bench. Young man, it's an apprenticeship in the shoe-maker's gentle craft for you, and you may lay to that. We'll start tomorrow morning at six o'clock sharp, so off to bed, the pack of you!'

And so it was that John Silver learnt his father's trade. It was not work he relished overmuch, and he spent countless hours inwardly cursing the precision demanded by cutting, piecing, sewing, and nailing. His father's withdrawn moods punctuated by violent outbursts did little to reconcile him to his work. He looked gloomily ahead to a lifetime overhung with the smell of leather, subjected to the whims and rebukes of ungrateful customers.

Sometimes he talked with his father as they worked together. 'Father,' he would ask, 'There's other trades besides this one, ain't there?'

'Yes boy, there are. But it's a rare trade is this for training a man's eye and hand. It sharpens your wits, makes your thoughts and actions neat, like.'

'But there's not much fresh air in it, father. Not like a seaman's life. No sunlight and space. We're cooped up here like mice in the wainscoting, and no mistake.'

'There's money in the craft, boy. Not much, but enough. Enough to keep you free of Them – of landlords and squires and them as'll rule your life for you. It gives you your freedom, and then at night you can read and talk and think, and find God in your own way and steer your own course.'

At this John would fall silent. He knew that what his father said made sense, and yet he was not content.

It was small wonder, then, that when he reached the age of thirteen, John Silver was ready to kick over the small conventions of his craftsman's life. The opportunity was there for the taking. It began with a chance conversation with one of his father's regular customers, called Peter Dougan. Dougan was a man of middle years, thin to the point of emaciation, and with the smell of brandy often clinging to him.

He sometimes ordered a pair of stout sea-boots, or carried off dainty shoes for a female fancy of his. His manner was confident yet reserved, as if he held the key to many rich mysteries and could bask in an inner satisfaction. He always paid on the nail, and in good coin.

Young Silver was intrigued by this secretive, well-clothed skeleton of a man. One day their usual amiable bantering took a sharper turn. Dougan had remarked that it was not much of a life stuck behind a cobbler's bench from morning light to dusk, and Silver snapped back that at least it was respectable, and, by God, where did he – Dougan – get his silver coin? By cutting throats, as like as not!

At this, Dougan threw his boney arm over the counter and caught Silver by the shirt about his neck.

'You little leather-rat,' he hissed. 'If you were half as smart as me, you'd be rolling in money – not bowing and scraping to fat grocer's wives who come to buy your precious shoes. But you're like your father, all talk and nothing to show for it!'

John Silver was already big-boned and heavy for his thirteen years. He clamped Dougan's claw of a hand in his own broad palm and crushed it till the older man cried out with pain. Each let go of the other.

As Dougan wiped the sweat from his long face, Silver shouted at him, 'Show me how you gets your coin, then!'

'Why should I trust you, boy?'

'Because I'm as much a man as you, that's why!'

My God! I've done it now, Silver thought, he'll be out with his knife and stick me like a pig. He felt curiously calm, all the same.

Dougan looked keenly at him for what seemed like an age, then he laughed in his shrill way. Putting an arm round Silver's shoulder, he led him out of the shop.

He took him to an inn in the dockland of Bristol. There, amid the smell of tobacco and ale and rum, he let young John into some of his secrets. He was the leader of a smuggling gang, operating mainly in the Bristol Channel, but occasionally as far afield as Cornwall or the Hampshire coast. Tea, French brandy, gin and fine silks were Dougan's stock in trade.

The profits, he said, were enormous. Sometimes the tubs of spirits could be watered down by more than half and still sell easily. The custom-house officers were no great threat, and should they stumble upon a gang at work they could often be bribed.

'Well, young John,' Dougan said eventually. 'Do you care to join us? I could do with an honest-looking lad to run errands, and you've the face of a curate communing with the angels!'

Silver hesitated; he was both excited and fearful. At last he blurted out, shamefacedly, 'But surely there's real danger in it, smuggling and such? I don't fancy getting caught. My mother, she'd go on something terrible!' He fell silent, feeling a fool.

Dougan smiled. 'Well, of course, if you're a milksop still there's no more to be said. Crawl back to your home, milksop!'

'No!' cried John. ' 'Tain't that. 'Tis wrong to steal other folks' belongings!' As soon as he had spoken he felt foolish once more; foolish, and somehow adrift and out of his depth.

'Wrong!' laughed Dougan. 'Wrong to take a little from them as has too much already, eh? Wrong to rob the great ladies and gen'lemen of their finery and victuals, is it? Look, boy, your father's no lover of the wealthy and the high-born. Think as how you'll be denying a duke a bottle or two of brandy, or cheating some rich countess of a piece of silk. Your father'd be proud of you, and wish you God speed, he would!'

'Still' – he rose to his feet – 'If a lad's got no guts for a bit of adventure, that's an end to it. I thought you was smart as paint, I did, but seemingly I was wrong.'

He paused. 'However, if you should change your mind you know where to find me. Perhaps you ain't such a coward after all.' And with a shrill burst of laughter he left Silver and disappeared among the passers-by outside.

Young John made his way into the street. A fine rain was falling, but the thoroughfare was full of life. A scavenger's cart creaked by, loaded with discarded objects, its driver glancing keenly about him and every now and then ringing his brass handbell. Sparks flew from the wheel of a knife-grinder, dark-haired and bent to his task, but pausing occasionally to flash a brilliant smile at the serving-woman standing beside him clutching her mistress's knives like a quiver of arrows. A gingerbread-man waddled by, his tray, wedged on his belly, clearing his path through the throng like the prow of a well-laden East Indiaman.

Silver stepped carefully over the central gutter cut into the cobbled street; the dirty water trickled sluggishly beneath him, seeping round islands of rotting guts and other, nameless, items of refuse. Opposite him an old woman sat huddled, yet watchful, against the door of a draper's shop; the shop-sign, heavy with iron and lead, swung noisily above her head like the ill-aimed axe of a clumsy executioner.

Within minutes he turned, half-running, half-walking, into Sheep Street. The fine drizzle had become a downpour, and rainwater was cascading from the spout, or-namented with a dragon's mouth and teeth, that projected from the roof of his father's shop.

He pushed his way clumsily through the shop door and into the workroom. The rainstorm had shut out most of the daylight; the dark oak beams, fashioned, it was said, during the Wars of the Roses, seemed to swoop down menacingly over his head.

There was his father, hunched over his bench, peering at the sole of a bulky black boot. Too damn' miserly to light a candle, thought John, as he slipped into his seat at his own bench.

Suddenly his father spoke, his voice sharp and sarcastic amid the gloom.

'You been at prayer again, boy? Another of your mother's saints' days, I'll be bound. Sidling off like a pickpocket, more like! In the middle of the day, too.'

John stayed silent. Outside, the rain beat violently against the leaded windows.

'For all that you're my son, you're also my apprentice. Is

there aught in your 'prentice bonds as gives you leave to slip out o' doors when it pleases you? Well, boy? Answer!'

Silver replied, grudgingly, 'No, father, there ain't.'

'No, father, there ain't,' Michael Silver mocked. 'There is nothing of merit, I believe, in being young, is there? No Act o' Parliament passed, as I recall, elevating 'prentices to the House o' Lords?'

'No, father.'

'Well, boy, I'm passing a new law now, particularly for you. Given under the blow of my hammer this very minute. I, Michael Silver, forbid my apprentice John Silver to quit his place of work save with my permission. And, further-more, I do declare his weekly wage of one shilling and six-pence forfeit, from now on! Get on with your work, boy!'

John clenched his teeth, struggling to master his fury. He looked at his father's head, the hair thin upon its crown, bent once more over the black boot. For two pins he would stave it in! Crack it like a hazel nut with the heavy iron cobbler's last before him!

The minutes passed. No more words were spoken. John felt his anger slipping from him, to be replaced with sur-prise at the violence of his feelings, and also with a secret exultation. That was it! He'd run messages for Dougan after all! In the evenings. He was free from seven o'clock. Plenty of time, that! Very like he could stay out all night, too, if he locked his bedroom door and slipped back before dawn. Smuggling was work for the dark hours, in any case. Dougan would pay him. And a damned sight more than one shilling and sixpence a week! His mind was made up.

Within a week Silver had sworn a rambling and blasphemous oath of secrecy and joined Dougan's gang. He now began to lead a double life. In the daylight hours he sewed and hammered away at his shoes, and listened to his father railing against Jacobites and aristocrats. But at dusk, after his mother had fed the family, he would leave his sisters gossiping and wrangling, and slip out of the house to meet his new acquaintances.

Dougan had picked a pretty bunch to carry out his plans. Ex-gaol birds, drunken seamen, and brutal farm labourers composed his work force. Over this motley band he exercised a tyrannical sway which rested, in the last resort, on fist and pistol ball.

But Dougan could think as efficiently as he could dominate his subordinates. His ruses became, in time, a legend along the coasts and headlands of the West Country. One one occasion he dressed three of his men in shepherd's smocks. So disguised, they sauntered to the cliff's edge and proceeded to search for the eggs of sea-birds in the chalk face. A pair of customs men actually passed by, nodding and smiling, for it was commonplace to see shepherds leave their grazing flocks and go nesting in the cliffs.

The three smugglers boldly worked their way down the cliff in broad daylight. At the water's edge, they produced cutting tools from beneath their rustic smocks and dug out of the chalk a landing platform some eight feet by four. At night a rowing boat landed sixty-two tubs of best French brandy on the platform. Dougan's men often crowed over the memory of this piece of work.

On another occasion the gang had the luck to lay hold of a particularly active customs officer, nicknamed Hawk-eye for his peering and prying. They blindfolded him, tied his feet together, and cried, 'Throw him over the cliff, boys! Do it now!' The poor man shouted for mercy but they lowered him over the edge until he was clinging, desperately, to a narrow crevice in the cliff top.

For fifteen minutes Hawk-eye hung and bawled for help. Then his fingers and his arms could hold out no more and with a great scream of despair he fell. But the jest was that Hawk-eye had only three feet to fall! The villains had suspended him over the edge of a shallow chalk pit.

3
❧ *Escape* ❧

S ilver's smuggling career was cut short after ten months. The wonder of it was that his life was not cut short at the same time.

Two events conspired to put his life at risk. The first was that Peter Dougan broke an ankle after slipping twenty feet down a cliff face. This left the gang without a leader of sufficient guile and restraint. The second event was the appearance of two particularly active and daring customs officers along a hitherto unmanned stretch of coast.

It seems that the leaderless gang took it upon themselves to raid a customs house. This was a damned fool thing to do in England at the best of times. Quite a different matter from such sport on a wind-swept island in the Spanish Main or in the wilderness of Pennyslvania or New York.

At first all went well. The customs house was broken into, and the officers guarding it were smartly overpowered by the foolhardy rabble. The gang laid their hands on £2000 worth of tea and a little spare cash. But as they were making off, Jackson and Payne, the two new customs men, appeared. They managed to seize hold of Simon Curtis, a great, slow, lumbering fellow, and hauled him off to Major Rothsay, the local Justice of the Peace.

The rest of the gang got away scot free. But for how long? What should they do? 'Scatter.' That was Silver's voice in the debate. 'Scatter, and break up. Maybe for two months, maybe for good.' But nobody heeded young Silver that night. A less prudent spirit won general approval. This was Jonathan Turner, a tarry, sallow-cheeked ruffian.

'Lads,' said Turner, 'it's us or them, and you may lay to that. Them two bastards, Jackson and Payne, will have us clapped in irons before the week is out. Kill or be killed, that's my advice to you. We'll teach them such a lesson that giving evidence'll be the last thing they'll care to do.'

The rest of the men voted three to one to follow Turner. They were fearful of capture and conviction, and they were, at the best of times, a heavy-handed, cruel company.

That same night, Turner led the men to the customs officers' lodgings. Silver tagged along, fascinated and afraid at the same time. Jackson and Payne were asleep in bed when the gang seized them.

The two men were then tied onto the same horse. Jackson on top, and Payne hanging beneath the animal's belly.

'Whip them! Cut them! Damn their eyes!' screeched Turner, and the men crowded round to strike and kick the two unfortunates. For a mile or more this sorry procession wound its way through the coarse grass and bracken of the cliff tops.

By the time they reached the Dolphin Inn, which was owned by one of the gang, the two customs officers were dripping blood and crying for mercy. In the yard of the inn they were cut free from the horse, but Jackson plunged head-first onto the cobbles and lay there as if dead.

Silver, only fourteen years old, was sickened at heart by this brutality, but to protest might have marked him out for similar treatment. The rest of the gang swilled rum and gin and thus increased their fury and their daring.

At last they dragged the two officers into a field nearby. There they dug a deep hole for Jackson and cast him into it, to the accompaniment of vile oaths and blasphemies.

Silver swore that Jackson was still breathing as the clods of earth showered onto his bleeding head. Be that as it may, Jackson had found his final resting place.

A much worse fate now befell Payne. Besotted with rum, and exhilarated by his new-found authority, Turner pronounced sentence. Forcing Payne to kneel on the grass, he opened his clasp knife and said, 'Go to your prayers, you snivelling dog, for I will be your butcher.'

Poor Payne prayed with as good a voice as his parched throat and bruised lips would allow. Even as he was calling on his Saviour, Turner grabbed him by the hair and began to torture him, hacking him across the forehead, eyes and nose with his knife, while the others pressed in to kick the victim in the back.

Tiring of this sport at last, the smugglers hoisted the broken man onto the horse once more, resolving to drop him into Jonah's Well which lay close by.

On reaching the well, they forced Payne to crawl through a fence to the edge. Then, with shouts and huzzahs, they pitched him into the thirty foot hole. Still hearing him moaning deep below them, the smugglers gathered rocks and stones and hurled them into the well. At last Payne's voice was silenced. 'He's gone, boys!' Turner shouted triumphantly.

Before these barbarous deeds had been completed, Silver had slipped away, shaking with fright and consumed by guilt, his clothes drenched with sweat.

A few days later he sought out another of the gang, a hard-faced youth of seventeen years called Joshua Taylor, who lived but a few streets away.

'Josh,' said Silver, 'I'm sick with fear, I am. I never wanted no part in murder and suchlike. I'm not a villain, like some as I could name.'

Taylor pulled thoughtfully on his clay pipe. 'I see it this way, John,' he said at last. 'Our friend Turner's got rid o' all the evidence, like. Why, bless me if he didn't kill th'old horse as carried Payne and cut its hide into little pieces an' scatter 'em. They'll never track us down.'

'You're too cool, Josh Taylor,' said Silver urgently. 'Someone might blab, then we're all for it. It's griping away at me something terrible. I'd tell my mother for two pins, I would.'

'That's it,' said Taylor scornfully. 'Run to your mam! I'd forgot you was only a lad, though you're tall enough for a grow'd man. It'll be all over Bristol by tomorrow, I shouldn't wonder!'

'No, no,' said young John in desperation. 'I don't want that. I just wish I could rub it all out with a magic spell, and start again. I'd abide by what my father told me the next time, I would.'

Taylor said coldly, 'Well, you can't cast no magic spells, John. What's done is done. You keep your trap shut, or I'll bring friend Turner round to see you one of these days. He'll not stop at shedding a bit more blood, and you may count on that!'

So Silver slunk back home, cowed and resentful, and prayed nightly for deliverance with a zeal that gratified his mother and amused his father.

But within a month his world was turned upside down. One of the smugglers, convinced that the revenue men were on the point of seizing him, went to the authorities, offering himself as a King's witness and making a full confession of the whole affair in return for a royal pardon. Within a few weeks Turner and his chief confederates had been arrested. Silver was swept up in the search for accomplices and dragged from his distraught family to gaol.

The trial was decked up to terrify and confound any that should seek to emulate the accused men. A special assize was called, under three judges who, together with the mayor and aldermen of Bristol, attended divine service in the cathedral on the Sunday before the trial, when the dean preached a sermon of revenge and righteous indignation.

The trial itself was short and to the point. With three of the smugglers turning King's witness there was little that Turner and his fellows could do to save their necks. Turner presented a bold face throughout. He was insolent to the point of madness, announcing in ringing tones that he did not care a button for being hanged – which was just as well.

Silver was indicted with the rest, but acquitted of the charge of murder on the evidence of some of those less fortunate than himself. Three days after the trial had opened, the bench pronounced sentence.

Turner and seven others were to be executed. Five, including Silver, were condemned to prison. The public hanging of Turner brought the crowds flocking to the gallows and the sellers of hot pies did a capital trade. The corpses of the criminals were then hung in chains near their former dwelling places. Turner had said to the judges on sentence, 'Well, by God, I shall be hanging in the sweet air while you, my Lords, will one day rot under ground.' And hang in the air he did, while the crows pecked at his eyes and maggots dug into his disintegrating flesh.

Silver faced a more pleasant prospect than hanging, to be sure, even though the dirt and despair of his confined quarters were a sorry enough exchange for freedom.

Both his mother and his father visited him in gaol shortly after his sentence. It was almost more than he could bear to see his mother's grief.

'John,' Mary Silver said at last, 'I'm sure that evil men are to blame for your being here, men who have deserved the most terrible of punishments. But the law is the law, and if you have broken it you must bear the consequences. I pray for you, and hope that you will learn a good lesson. As a further punishment your father has forbidden me to visit you in this shameful place.'

As his mother left, accompanied by his father, who had remained withdrawn and silent throughout, John Silver bowed his head in despair. Long years of imprisonment faced him, he knew, and without the support of his family. What was more, he deserved the punishment – indeed his mother had said as much. He therefore resolved to act the model prisoner, hoping that he would find contentment and perhaps even salvation.

It is likely, I suppose, that he would have reached middle

manhood still inside gaol, but for a stroke of good fortune and an act of supreme daring.

His chance came after two years of imprisonment, when he and some dozen other prisoners were moved from one wing of the gaol to another. The turnkeys shepherded the convicts along, carefully locking one door behind them before opening the next. At one point Silver was halfway along a passage with the doors at either end of it bolted and locked.

Then he saw, to his amazement, that he would pass under an open window, left like that partly out of carelessness but chiefly because it was rare for prisoners to be taken along this route. Despite his size and strength the few steps that separated him from the casement seemed to be measured in miles not inches. But suddenly he was there! He leapt for the window's bottom edge, grasped it, hoisted himself on to the sill and swung his legs through to the other side.

Ignoring the pandemonium beneath him, he saw that the street outside was only a dozen feet below. He jumped! As he told me himself, that jump was the sweetest moment of his young life.

'It was no height to boast of, Jim. Why, many a time I'd leapt from trees and hillocks and risked more. But this jump, well, it was like patching up the broken part of my life again. A jump towards the light as well as towards the grave, by thunder!'

And there he was, sprawling among astonished citizens and laughing for the joy of it! A turnkey, frantic about the escape, clambered onto the window ledge and took aim with his pistol. But not daring to fire for fear of hitting some innocent bystander, he had to follow Silver down into the street, and by then young John had a good start on him.

Silver knew the streets, alleys and mews of Bristol like old friends. He weaved and ducked and doubled back, once even passing again under the window that had allowed him to escape. When dusk fell he was tucked away among some packing cases on the quayside, determined to quit Bristol and England at the first opportunity.

4

The Guinea Coast

Before dawn broke on the day following his escape, Silver had found himself a berth on a slaver bound for the Guinea coast. The *Osprey* sailed under British colours, and was captained by a tall, fast-talking Irishman called Desmond Feeney. Young Silver had responded manfully to Feeney's questions.

'What is your age, boy?' Feeney had asked.

'Seventeen, sir,' said John, pulling himself up to his full height.

'Ha-hum,' said the captain. 'And why should a lad like yourself be leaving home in such a damn' smart hurry, eh?'

Silver began to mumble about quarrelling with his father, but Feeney's next question thankfully cut him short.

'Can you sail, boy?' he asked, the words tumbling over one another. 'Can you reef a topsail with a head wind blowing? Can you drop a plumb line and gauge shoal water, eh?'

'You just try me, sir,' said young John. 'I've sailed with the best, I have. There's not much I don't know about a ship at sea, schooners, brigs and —'

'Ha-hum,' said Feeney swiftly, his grey eyes darting and cynical. 'Well, we shall see. But it's dirty work, boy, slaving. There's fever and treachery on the West African coast, and filth and stench and vomit on the Atlantic passage. It's no place for a weak-stomached child, as soon you'll find.'

'I'm not afraid of dirt and fever, sir,' said John.

'Maybe not,' said Feeney, 'but how do you fancy, ha-hum, a slave mutiny, boy, with a pack of howling savages lusting to cut your belly open, eh?'

Silver's hair prickled with terror at this prospect, but he

replied bravely enough, clenching his fists at his sides, 'Let them try it, sir, I'll knock their heads together and pitch 'em overboard!'

'Hah!' said Feeney. 'I don't believe a word of it. But still, I'll take you aboard. I'm shorthanded right now, since slaving ain't every seaman's chosen calling. The pay's good enough, but it's the yellow fever and the blood-letting as puts 'em off! Get below, boy. You'll learn quick enough, or end up as sharks' meat, one or the other.'

So the *Osprey* sailed with John Silver aboard. Although he had boated in the Bristol Channel it was the first time he had taken to the open sea, and afterwards he claimed that he learnt more on that voyage than in all the books he had read at his mother's side. For one thing he managed to conquer the paralysing discomfort of seasickness, though in the Bay of Biscay he would have gladly cut his own throat if he could have held the knife firm enough.

He also learnt the rudiments of sea-craft, helped a little by the rope's end which was wielded by a vigilant boatswain. His terror of climbing the rigging when the ship was pitching wildly in a heavy sea gradually subsided. In his early days aboard he was conscious of Feeney's quick grey eyes picking out his stumblings and failures, and imagined the captain's amused 'Ha-hums'.

Feeney was a tolerably good navigator but a poor disciplinarian. He drank moderately during the day and heavily at night, when the safety of the ship rested in the hands of Grierson, the first mate. Grierson was a tight-lipped Yorkshireman who had seen service in the Royal Navy. He believed in discipline, duty and God. Although Silver's mates spat behind Grierson's back and cursed him violently below deck, young John came to admire his cool judgement and his stolid bearing.

Silver had a generally low opinion of his fellow seamen. They did the barest minimum of their tasks, and no more. Gambling, gossiping, and quarrelling were their principal pastimes, and John tired of their bickering over rations and grog. Although at first he was put upon and victimised as the greenhorn of the crew, his quickness to learn and his obvious physical strength saved him from undue persecution.

By the time the *Osprey* put into the slave port of Anambu on the west coast of Africa, Silver was agog to see this new world of tropical forests, strange creatures and black heathen. The gorgeous flowers and lush vegetation that surrounded and threatened to devour the fortress and huts of Anambu seemed at first quite unreal to him. So did the flashing, bright colours worn by the Africans who flocked to the *Osprey*, offering fruit and choice victuals to her crew.

More wonders were soon to flood before Silver's eyes. Desmond Feeney shook off the taste for liquor that had characterised him at sea, and promptly got down to business. He put into Anambu in the jolly-boat with a sample of goods and half a dozen of the ship's crew. Among these latter was Silver, whom Feeney had picked out with the words, 'We'll have you, young cub, for a quick brain and a smart lie are as handy on this shore as a battery of five-pounders.'

So Silver was soon gazing in wonderment as Feeney clasped hands with Mongo Jack Andrews, the slave factor. Mongo Jack was a great flabby mountain of a man with soft white hands and an air of immense affability. He affected native manners and tastes, and his gaudy African robes were both showy and stained with sweat.

'Dear captain,' trilled Mongo Jack, 'We meet once more, but, damme, the times are harder than ever. I scour the rivers for strong black youths and handsome girls, and in dribs and drabs I get 'em, but the expense, my dear sir, the expense!'

At this, Mongo Jack flopped down on a cane chair that buckled under his weight, and wiped his sodden brow. Feeney sat down too, and bade his men display their

merchandise. This consisted mainly, so Silver recalled, of
tubs of brandy and rum, Manchester cottons, some braces
of pistols, fancy-laced hats, and iron bars.

Mongo Jack yawned. 'Nothing to set the Rio Orto alight
here, captain,' he complained. 'Upon my word, the
blackamore chieftains are already rolling in French brandy
and have eight cocked hats apiece. But,' he went on, stroking the smooth butts of the pistols, 'we shall see what we
can do, dear sir, we shall see.'

And that, for the moment, was that. Mongo Jack drew
Feeney into an inner chamber, plied him with wine, and
grumbled and complained. Outside, Silver and his companions received their share of refreshments brought by a
sinuous procession of African women.

John Silver was used to the girls of his Bristol boyhood,
but here, it seemed, were creatures from another planet!
Black, mulatto and quadroon, slender and buxom, brazen
and modest, they flitted before him, and their charms
stirred his young senses.

Amid the wine and the warmth, and the talk and the
laughter, Silver and his mates were soon dancing with the
women, who flew from man to man squealing with devilry
and pleasure.

'I could no more speak their damn' strange lingo, Jim,
than call a Frenchman brother!' he told me. 'But, by the
powers, I could dance a fine step when I was young and
strong and had ten toes.'

And so he danced, clutching the slim waist of a dark-
skinned mulatto girl with a wide mouth and oddly rosy
cheeks. We shall never know where this whirling and twirl-
ing would have ended had not Mongo Jack made a fiery
reappearance, heaving his great belly through the doorway
and loosing a pistol ball at the dancers' feet.

The women screamed and scattered, as well they might,
for it was their lord, master and husband who now stood
before them! 'By God,' said Mongo Jack. 'You have St

Vitus in your heels, I see, and you can sniff out a petticoat as smartly as my hounds track runaways. There's no harm in dancing, lads, but pray do not so weary my poor wives. You'll find sleep will best suit you now,' he added menacingly, 'for the sun of Africa will burn away your high spirits in the morning.'

Silver and his companions found out soon enough his meaning, for early on the morrow they set off along the Rio Orto to gather slaves. Feeney led them, leaving the dour Grierson in charge of the *Osprey*. Mongo Jack helped them on their way with an interpreter and effusive expressions of goodwill.

The river wound between densely forested banks, alive with the cries of unseen creatures and the brilliant hues of innumerable birds. Stripped to the waist, the crew toiled over their oars. At length they reached their destination, the trading post of Oba. There the King of Oba greeted them, and prepared to do business.

He lived in large airy rooms, and was surrounded with wives, servants, and slaves. His executioner stood leaning on his sword, ready to carry out his master's bidding. Even while Feeney, through the interpreter, was exchanging elaborate greetings with the King, the men from the *Osprey* watched openmouthed as two near-naked Africans were dragged from the throng and beheaded on the spot.

The King's violet gown was splashed with the warm blood of these unfortunate miscreants, but he heeded it no more than a few drops of rain. Silver soon saw why.

'The fact is, Jim, that old devil cared not a farthing for a man's life,' he said. 'Trading in human livestock was his work, and who's to say we had cause to sneer at him for that? His palace was a slaughterhouse, as you might say, but we were after the meat and no mistake.'

Indeed the King of Oba's prisons were packed with slaves, snatched from neighbouring tribes by his callous mercenaries or bought from other native traders. Feeney

soon set his men to work in sorting out the good bargains
from the bad.

'Look here, my boys,' he said. 'We've not come to collect
this old savage's leavings. I want tip-top goods and nothing
else. If you think a slave's too old, say thirty-five, or is missing teeth, or fingers and toes, or can't see straight, then
throw him out!'

So Silver, who not many months before had trembled for
this own life, now had the power of a high court judge over
these poor, witless beings. He struggled to mask his
squeamish feelings as his fellow seamen went among the
slaves, prodding and poking, kicking and cursing. Then the
slaves were branded with Feeney's own mark to prevent the
King of Oba, or Mongo Jack, from craftily substituting
bad slaves for good before they were safely aboard the
Osprey.

Branding was nothing new to some of Silver's companions, who plied the hot iron as casually as if dealing
with cattle. They chewed tobacco and told lewd jokes and
passed the time of day. Occasionally they would pause to
admire the beauty of one of their female victims before
pressing the searing metal onto the black flesh.

But for some time young John turned his eyes from the
sickening business and tried to stop his ears against the
wailing and whimpering of the slaves. Then, through a haze
of smoke and blurred images, he saw Feeney's sardonic
smile and heard him say, 'Here, boy, take my iron, I've
more important things to attend to.'

And there he was with the iron in his hand and two of his
mates hustling a half-grown boy, not many years younger
than himself, before him. For a second he stood irresolute,
blankly staring at the glistening black arm held up to him.
'Come on, you fool,' said Feeney smoothly. 'It don't hurt
them no more than a gadfly stinging an old goat. Why, the
worst thing is the smell of their burnt skin, but you must
think it's just a barbecue, boy, a barbecue!'

As Feeney's words rang in his ears, Silver was overwhelmed by feelings of revulsion.

'I won't do it!' he blurted out.

'Scared are ye, boy?' laughed the red-bearded seaman beside him.

Other voices rose around him, mocking, contemptuous.

'I'll buy your petticoats just as soon as we dock in Bristol!'

'My, what a pretty gal we have here!'

'Come on, green Betty!'

Silver's pride was stung. His arm shot out as if skewering a shoulder of mutton. The iron sizzled, the boy screamed, and it was done.

'Bravo, my bold Barbecue, we'll make a man o' you yet!' sang out George Thompson, an old hand who had taken kindly to Silver on the outward voyage.

The others laughed. 'Barbecue,' cried one of them. 'That's a rare name is that! Welcome aboard, Sir Barbecue!'

Hardly knowing what he was doing, Silver saw he had another black arm to brand. He plied the iron, then again, and again. The yelps of his victims became mingled with the general hubbub, and after a while he scarcely noticed them. After all, he told himself, this was better than rotting in gaol.

By the time the branding was done, John Silver, whether he knew it or not, had lost part of his youthful innocence; a callous of indifference to human suffering had begun to form over his wounded sensibility. He had taken the first steps along a path that would lead him to brutality and murder.

But he had also acquired a nickname, for Feeney's gibe as he handed him the hot iron was gloatingly retold by his shipmates, and John Silver answered to 'Barbecue' for the rest of his days.

5

⋐ *Barbados Bound* ⋑

Three days after Feeney and his slaving party returned to the sweltering port of Anambu, the *Osprey* set sail for the West Indies. Brief though this respite was, it provided young Silver with more instruction in the ways of the Guinea coast and of the slavers that battened upon it.

Mongo Jack and Feeney first settled the matter of the price of the two hundred or so slaves who arrived from up-river, and were then packed into the factor's pens. Each man knew the other well enough by now, but they haggled as fiercely as if fighting for survival on a scrap of desert island. Feeney's crisp blasphemies mingled with Mongo Jack's high-pitched protestations of penury. But they agreed soon enough, after Mongo Jack's fat white palm had been greased with three hundred doubloons and twenty thousand choice Havana cigars.

The crew of the *Osprey* busied themselves with preparing the slaves for the voyage across the Atlantic. Having so recently flourished the branding iron, Silver now found himself wielding a razor to shave the slaves' heads prior to loading them aboard.

He first sought out George Thompson. 'Why do we have to do this, George?' he asked. 'It seems plain cruel to bare their pates under this scorching sun. Why, their skulls'll shrivel up as like as not. I don't hold with it.'

'Look'ee here, young Barbecue,' said Thompson. 'A dab hand at branding you may be, but your own brain's been steamed like a plum duff on this sweet shore, I see. We've no call to take lice and disease and what not aboard the *Osprey*. Captain Feeney's no fool, my lad, and you'll have enough of illness and filth when we set sail, as sure as you draw breath.'

So Silver buckled to, and kept his thoughts to himself. The slaves were brought alongside the *Osprey* in the ship's boats and then driven up the side. Some shivered and moaned with terror as they were hauled aboard, others rolled furtive eyes at the white man's 'great wooden canoe' in which they were now confined. Men were put in one section of the ship, women in another, and boys and girls in a third. Crammed together in mindless apprehension, these unfortunate beings now began their journey to the New World.

Silver always claimed, that, compared with other captains he had known, Desmond Feeney took great pains with his slaves. Not relishing the financial loss involved in wholesale slave deaths, Feeney allowed privileges that more brutal masters would have laughed to scorn.

The crew fed their captives twice a day on a diet of corn porridge flavoured with salt, pepper and palm oil. Three days a week the slaves were given boiled horse beans, which so delighted them that, in Silver's words, 'They threw their black arms about and screeched as if they'd caught a whiff of Michaelmas goose, stuffing and all.'

Although old hands like George Thompson grumbled at the work involved, and cast their minds back to more carefree days, Feeney also ordered that the slaves should be exercised in the fresh sea air once a day. Silver, in fact, found little to complain of at the outset of the voyage. 'You might be thinking, Jim,' he said, glancing slyly at me, 'that it was a cruelty to make the savages lie down on boards a'nights, but let me tell you, my son, they're short of feather beds on the Guinea coast, and you may lay to that.'

On one point only was Feeney lax, and this was the matter of crew discipline. As long as his men carried out their duties, he turned a blind eye to their swilling raw black rum. Worse still, he allowed the crew free access to

the negro women. By no means all of them satisfied their
lust in this fashion, but those that did caused anguish
enough among the poor female slaves who had little choice
but to submit to their lascivious advances.

Silver, though tempted by the physical beauty of many of
the slave women, was sickened by the debauchery that surrounded him and by the cruelty which so frequently accompanied it.

Finally, he made so bold as to voice his misgivings to the
first mate, Grierson.

'I don't hold with it, sir,' he said, as Grierson listened im-
passively. ' 'Tis surely bad enough these black wenches are
snatched from their homes, and packed below decks like
lumber, without tormenting them. They're only women
after all.'

'I'm not captain hereabouts,' said Grierson sourly. 'Captain Feeney gives the orders.'

'Yes, sir,' protested John, 'but rules is rules. Cap'n
Feeney he said, back on the Guinea coast, treat 'em fair.
Firm but fair, he said. Now that ain't happening, is it?'

'Before you're much older, boy,' said Grierson, 'you'll
learn when to keep your trap shut and let sleeping dogs lie.
I hope you're no troublemaker, no forecastle lawyer in the
making. Back to your duties, or you'll feel the rope's end!
I'll watch you, boy!'

So John Silver bit back his complaints, only too well
aware that the world was a crueller place than he, in his
callow way, might wish it to be.

But young John soon had other things to occupy his
mind, for when the *Osprey* was twenty-four days out from
the Guinea coast her slave decks were turned abruptly into
stinking hell-holes. Fortunately, it was not smallpox that
raged throughout the vessel, but the white flux. Silver put
the outbreak down to the stifling, airless conditions below
deck caused by the closing of the port-holes during a period
of rough weather. My own opinion, though necessarily

secondhand, is that some dietary unbalance was the most likely cause of the disorder.

But howsoever it arose, the white flux was horrible to behold. The slave decks were not at the best of times spotlessly clean, due to the negroes relieving themselves in conditions of gross overcrowding. Rats, too, infested the hold, and at night dropped their dirt onto the faces of the sleeping slaves. But when gripped by the flux, the negroes literally swamped their quarters with bloody vomit, mucus, and filthy discharge from their afflicted bodies.

Feeney and the stern Grierson had to force the crew below, to try to bring some order to the shambles. Silver's stomach revolted at the stench and chaos, and, overcome with the foetid atmosphere, he added his own vomit to that all around him. But boatswain and quartermaster, as well as captain and first mate, were unflinching in their resolve that all hands must help quell the contagion. So Silver and the others stumbled through the writhing, wailing mass of humanity and hauled onto the deck those they considered in sorest need of fresh air.

I daresay their choice did not always reflect the nicest diagnosis; still, it was better than failing to act. Several of those they carried aloft, as well as a score and a half of those left below, perished, wracked with delirium and pain. Their bodies were simply dropped overboard, and the sharks, which had swum hopefully behind the ship since she sailed, fought and snapped and turned the water red.

So after nearly three months at sea, the *Osprey* hove into Carlisle Bay, within sight of Bridgetown in the Barbados, with her slave cargo reduced by nearly a quarter. In addition to those carried off by the white flux, a few slaves had refused to eat and had pined away, one woman had died in childbirth, and two more, defiled by the crew, had cast themselves over the ship's side.

The shackles of the surviving slaves were struck off, and they were given a diet guaranteed to quickly fatten them up. Silver confessed both amusement and contempt for these manoeuvres.

'Why, that damned ship was turned into a beauty parlour as well as a hog-market, Jim,' he told me. 'We had to rub them slaves with oil to shine them up like new boots, and brush their woolly hair. I'll give my affydavy that Feeney would have had us clean their teeth and wipe their noses, if he'd dared!'

As it happened, the *Osprey* could have debouched a verminous, unkempt horde for all the slave-auctioneers and estate overseers on shore cared. Many planters believed that it was best to work slaves to death and then buy fresh stock, rather than preserve them into a useless old age. They therefore sent their agents scurrying to meet each new slaver as it docked.

As Silver helped to march his spruced-up slaves along the dusty streets of Bridgetown he was amazed at the throng that followed the procession. Estate overseers and agents in broad brimmed hats strove to pinch and prod the negroes even as they walked to market. Slaves already working for white masters called out at the newcomers, both mocking and encouraging them.

George Thompson laughed at Silver's incredulity. 'Why, this ain't nothing, Barbecue,' he said. 'Once I heard as how a hundred blacks jumped in the sea afore they could be landed. And why? Because some wag of a seasoned slave came aboard and promised them they was going to have their eyes put out, and then be cooked and eaten! Bless you, we've done better than that already.'

And, indeed, they had. After selling off the handful of sick and dying slaves for a few pounds, Feeney had no difficulty in getting a handsome price for the remainder. The agents rushed in to claim their purchases, sometimes fighting among themselves when mistakes occurred.

Silver and his mates were now paid half their wages, and turned loose upon the taverns and brothels of Bridgetown.

At first, Silver caroused with the rest, but within forty-eight hours had sobered up and formed a fair impression of his surroundings. The clear green waters of the Caribbean, the white coral reefs, and the exotic tropical fish and vegetation formed a far stronger impression upon his young imagination than the coast of West Africa had done. Already his boyhood in Bristol, and even the misfortunes of his trial and imprisonment, seemed far behind him. He had found a new world; threatening, hazardous and cruel it might be, but it was also stirring and, somehow, full of promise.

6
❦ Mutiny ❧

After selling his slaves and letting the crew of the *Osprey* brawl and drink their way through the taverns of Bridgetown, Desmond Feeney took on a full cargo of sugar and sailed for Bristol. The homeward trip completed the third side of that infamous triangle of trade that linked England, West Africa and the Caribbean. When they docked, young Silver skulked on the *Osprey,* not daring to show his face in the city of his birth. Nor did he try to communicate with his parents, save on the day of the ship's departure for the Guinea coast once more, when he sent a brief but cheerful enough note to the cobbler's shop in Sheep Street to signify that he was still alive following his escape from prison.

Then Silver sailed for a second time on the slaver, and heard for a second time Mongo Jack's self-pitying whine. Back on the Rio Orto the crew's slave-hunting activities were conducted much as before, except that the King of Oba treated them to the spectacle of a human sacrifice to the angry rain god. The juju man, with lion's claws and hideous mask, presented ten virgins, covered from top to toe in white clay, to the multitude of onlookers. Then, at a nod from the King, the poor girls' heads were struck from their bodies and their still trembling limbs hacked to pieces.

I have no doubt that John Silver's early contact with the savage customs of West Africa, and his experiences as a slave-trader, slowly, almost against his will, hardened his heart to the taking of human life. Why, I myself saw him strike down the worthy Tom on Kidd's Island with no more feeling than a man crushing an unpleasant cockroach.

Yet, even as he recalled the horrible sacrifices that he had witnessed so many years before, I could have sworn that his blue eyes were clouded with what might have passed for sadness. But then it was gone, and bluff Barbecue was restored, with his forthright utterances and his insistence that the weak should go hang!

This glimpse of a tenderness lurking behind his oaths and rough talk intrigued but did not altogether surprise me. After all, I had witnessed on board the *Hispaniola* how John Silver could mask designs of base treachery with an utterly convincing show of affability and good will. He was, in short, a many-sided man, his qualities difficult to pin down, his nature as varied as the coats of the chameleon.

When he landed for the second time at Bridgetown and saw the *Osprey's* surviving slaves marched to market, John Silver did not know that he was but a few months from a crisis which was to give him the chance to discover his powers of leadership.

The voyage back to England was unremarkable, save for one particular. This was nothing less than the appearance of Mrs Feeney a day before the ship sailed. Geraldine Feeney was the daughter of a Barbadian planter and had left her husband to ply his trade while she wintered with her family in a stout mansion inland. But now she wanted a home in the better part of Bristol, and a more settled way of life into the bargain.

Silver and his mates soon saw that their captain was no match for his wife. Mrs Feeney's terrible rages swept through the ship from stem to stern. Feeney would stop short while issuing orders, say, 'Ha-hum, gentlemen, that will do for now,' and slip below to answer some shrill summons. Once Mrs Feeney in her fury gathered up the white linen cloth from the captain's table and hurled it, crockery, knives, forks and all, into the sea!

It came as no surprise to the crew to leave Bristol for West Africa under a new master. The *Osprey's* owners put

Grierson in Feeney's place. At first, all went well. Grierson tightened up discipline and kept the men on their toes. Silver saw little wrong with this, though some of the hands complained that they were being hazed, and muttered dark threats behind Grierson's back.

Before the *Osprey* left Anambu with a fresh cargo of slaves, however, Grierson took on a new man. He was a pale youth with a Kentish accent, and a cold, sneering way about him. As it happened, he was less than a year older than Silver, who was by then eighteen years of age and so tall of stature that his mates called him 'Long John' as often as 'Barbecue'.

Silver was intrigued by the newcomer. He relished his surly confidence of manner and laughed at his cruel jests, though many were directed at Grierson and some at Silver himself. Little by little Gabriel Pew (for that was the new hand's name) gained young John's regard, just as his soft, sing-song voice came to exert a considerable influence over his crew-mates.

Silver's acquaintance with Gabby Pew might have ended with the latter slipping off into the Bristol dockland with a farewell wave of his damp hand, but for a misfortune which struck the *Osprey* in mid-Atlantic. Wrenched loose during a squall of foul weather, the mizzen yard crashed into Grierson as he stood alone on the poop deck. They carried him below to his quarters and laid him on his bunk. His forehead and scalp were terribly lacerated, as if he had been mauled by a ferocious animal, and for a time his eyes vanished behind mountainous bruises.

For three days Grierson moaned and shrieked in a state of semi-consciousness. Silver was one of those who tended him, and patched up his bleeding skull. Then suddenly the captain's feverish wanderings abated and, pulling his hat upon his head, he staggered back to his post. But the accident had wrought some strange alchemy in his brain, for where previously he had been punctilious he now became obsessed with detail, and the stern disciplinarian was transformed into a raving martinet.

Grierson seemed never to sleep. He peered into the ship's darkest corners, and haunted the whole crew with orders and interrogations. None escaped him. He made his men do double watch, routing them out of their hammocks at any hour of the day or night. The slave decks had to be washed and polished, and then swabbed down again.

Silver might be bent over some task when the captain's figure would loom between him and the sun.

'So, Mr Silver, sir!' Grierson would say in his flat voice. 'This is how Bristol vagabonds do their work, is it? Well, Mr Silver, my dear sir, these boards are covered in filth and grime! How dare you skrimshank, sir, how dare you? I know you, you whining ship's lawyer, sir!'

And with this, the captain would kick over John's bucket of water, and rave at him till he cleaned the deck once more. Even then, the demented man would return to find some minute flaw in the work and straightaway order the culprit onto half rations. None of the ordinary seamen escaped such treatment.

After four days of this lunacy, Grierson summoned all hands on deck and harangued them.

'So, my dear sirs,' he began, 'do not think I am fool enough to be blind to your plotting and skullduggery. I see it all, dear sirs, I see it all. I see you whisper and spit behind my back. My spies are out, I know your plans. But mutineers pay a heavy price for their folly, my dear sirs. You'll hang for it, I promise you that.'

An angry, puzzled murmur rippled through the men, and Grierson took a quick pace back and rested his right hand on his pistol butt. He was flanked by his first and second mate. Boatswain and quartermaster stood close by. None looked happy at Grierson's tirade, which now took a new and ominous turn.

His voice cracking with hysteria, the captain continued,

'Dear sirs, you are being corrupted by poisonous vermin aboard. Two young pups have sworn to cut me down, and send you all to Davy Jones. One is Gabriel Pew, a choice gutter-bred murderer if ever I saw one! The other is John Silver, Pew's confederate. His honest face is but a mask for vile treacheries, believe me, good sirs, believe me! But I watch you all, night and day. Get to your tasks, get to your tasks!'

The crew broke up, stunned and enraged. Within minutes the men off duty had congregated in the forecastle, posting look-outs to warn them if Grierson should approach.

Pew was the first to speak, and his words were packed with venom. 'Well,' he sneered, 'if we ain't heard a gentle mouthful from Cap'n Grierson, or maybe I should say Cap'n Fearsome! The bastard's mad. I've killed better men than him, and I'll strangle him in his berth afore he claps me in irons, I'll tell you that!'

'Yes, do it, Pew, by God,' another exclaimed. 'We've been hazed and overridden, we have. Let's pitch him overboard, and give the sharks the bellyache!'

These sentiments won general approval, and a violent assault might have been made on Grierson there and then, but for the intervention of John Silver.

'Mates!' he cried, standing like a young giant in the cramped forecastle, with one strong arm barring the door. 'Mates, hold hard a minute, and hear me out. You're men of spirit, you are, as anyone can see with half an eye. And a finer leader than Gabby Pew you couldn't wish for, and no mistake. But 'tain't so easy to kill off a boney fidey captain flying the King's colours. Rules is rules, order's orders!' He paused, surprised at his own eloquence.

'God dammee, Silver,' snarled Pew, 'you're a yellow swab, and you'll swing in execution dock in consequence, you will, and God rot your cowardly hide!'

'Ah, Gabby,' replied Silver mildly, fighting down his ris-

ing fury. 'You've a brisk way with words, and a brisker way
with a knife, I shouldn't wonder. But Grierson ain't the
only officer aboard this ship. We must kill them all, or nobble them all, and with your leave I'll try to nobble them.
Then it'll look legal, like.'

Pew's white face twitched with contempt as he listened.
But others, whether from fear of hanging or because they
recognized good sense, responded favourably to Silver's
words. He and the old hand George Thompson were
deputed to persuade the first and second mate, and the
boatswain and quartermaster, to help depose the unhappy
Grierson. .

The second mate was young and scared and needed little
prompting to agree to the plan. The boatswain, too,
assented after a token show of dismay. But the quartermaster, a stocky bull of a man who spoke sparingly but hit
often, held aloof. So, it seemed, would the first mate. Long
John battered at this officer's resolve, using a per-
suasiveness he had just begun to discover, but which was
smon to become his stock-in-trade.

Jenkins, the first mate, was pompous and fussy, and fearful of stepping out of line. 'It will never do, Silver,' he
protested. 'I've had no part in mutiny in thirty years at sea.'

'Right you are, sir,' said John, 'but maybe there's never
been the like of this here Grierson in thirty years neither. If
he breaks the rules, we must make amends.'

'But the risk, young man,' spluttered Jenkins. 'I've my
reputation and profession to think of. No, no, it will never
do.'

'Begging your pardon, sir,' said Silver relentlessly. 'How
will your reputation seem if this ship goes down in bloodshed and strife? And those poor lads out there, why bless
me if they ain't a rooting for you for their next captain. Just
lie low and let us do this Grierson down, and you'll be cock
o' the quarter deck before it's dark, and you may lay to
that.'

'But – but – you'll spill no blood, my man?' asked Jenkins, wavering.

'The only thing that'll spill will be the wine in the cups of the *Osprey*'s owners as they toast you for a brave gentleman, sir,' said Silver coaxingly. 'It's Captain Jenkins for me, by thunder, and a bolder firmer man I couldn't hope to see.'

And he had won. Within the hour Grierson and the quartermaster lay bruised and manacled aft. Jenkins took over the office of captain, puffed himself up, and barked out orders. But increasingly the real power in the ship lay elsewhere: it lay in the nimble tongue and upon the broad shoulders of John Silver, and in the sinister ambitions of Gabriel Pew.

7

❦ The Slave Rising ❧

As the *Osprey* ploughed towards the Caribbean through the great billows of the mid-Atlantic the newly exalted Jenkins wrestled with his conscience. Here he was, walking the quarterdeck as master, while the battered and deranged Grierson howled and sobbed in a small cabin below, with the quartermaster, Markham, lying sullen and dark-browed beside him.

How could he, Jenkins, properly justify this overturning of authority to the *Osprey's* owners? They might choose to believe that Grierson's broken head and demented deportment was the result of a murderous and cowardly assault made by bloodthirsty usurpers.

True, there would be the ship's hands and officers to back him up, and there lay his salvation. But there, too, lay his possible ruin. For what if the crew, to save their own skins, conspired to saddle him with the full responsibility for Grierson's overthrow? How could he gainsay them?

Tormented imaginings such as these began to haunt Jenkins's waking hours, and transformed the hours of darkness into a sweat-drenched hell. They turned his port wine sour in his mouth, his salt beef stuck in his dry gullet, and even his fine snuff clogged his nostrils.

In his desperation, Jenkins sought to keep the crew sweet and reasonable. He doubled their liquor ration, overlooked countless misdemeanours, talked rashly of a handsome share-out of profits, and smiled and nodded and smiled again.

'God, how that fool do smile at us,' sneered Pew to his fellow seamen in the forecastle. 'I reckon he'd smile hanging by his heels from the yardarm, and strike me lame if I wouldn't smile to see him there.'

'There'll be time and plenty for that, Gabby, when we're all tucked up neat and tidy in Carlisle Bay,' said Silver primly.

Pew's face reflected his contempt. 'Big-boned and long-legged you may be, John Silver,' he replied, 'but you've got the guts of a girl in petticoats, and no mistake.'

'Better than having the head of a lad not long rid of the wet-nurse, Gabby,' said Silver coolly.

'Your head ain't nothing to boast of, according to my lights,' replied Pew softly. 'Your skull's stuffed full of your dear mother's prayers and your father's high principles. You're no more cut out for brisk action than them niggers shackled down below. Give you a cutlass and you'd say grace afore using it on anybody's meat, God dammit.'

Silver paused, as if to catch his breath. He then cocked an amused eye at the half dozen men leaning forward eagerly, half-hoping for a scrap between himself and Pew. He was fast learning all the skills of a forecastle debater battling to trim the violent excesses of gutter-bred villains like Pew.

'Mates,' he said at last, slapping the palm of his hand upon his knee, 'them's fighting words from our friend Gabby over there, and maybe now you'll fancy pitching into Cap'n Jenkins, and good luck to you, my brave boys, says I.'

'But' – and here his voice assumed the sober and earnest tones of a quack-doctor about to reveal untold wonders to a gaggle of rustics – 'you'll have seen, as plain as a pikestaff, that right now we need this Jenkins like a dying man needs water.

'He'll navigate us back to Barbados, he will. He'll see us right with the owners to save his own bacon. He's our bond, in a manner of speaking, and our affydavy too. If you call that bible talk then you go right ahead and spit on it, though it would take a bolder man than me, and maybe even Gabby here, to spit on the Good Book.'

He saw with relief, from the faces of his audience, that these points had hit home; even Pew's expression was wavering. Anxious and perspiring, Silver was about to cap his arguments with further pious sentiments when the crack of a pistol sounded from the quarterdeck.

The men in the forecastle scrambled to their feet. From the deck came a pandemonium of sound: war-cries, curses, the hiss of swinging blades, bellowed orders, the thwack of clubs on bone and flesh, the moans and shrieks of the stricken.

Silver burst out of the forecastle with Pew and the others at his heels. There he saw that the slaves had broken out from their pens in the hold. They must have knocked down the guard at the after-gratings and then poured onto the deck. The sentry at the fore-hatch had been luckier or more alert: he was still holding back the mob at that point by sweeping the cook's axe round his head in great threatening circles.

In a flash Silver sized up the situation. On the quarterdeck stood Jenkins, the boatswain, the helmsman, and about a dozen others; they had the ship's arms chest open and were successfully confronting fifty or so howling negroes. About halfway along the starboard side of the deck, another knot of seamen armed with hand-spikes and knives was fending off a mere cluster of them.

The slaves, for all their fearsome shouts and cries, were ill-armed, carrying the staves of broken water casks and other odd pieces of wood they had managed to find in the hold. There was even a touch of farce in the affray: the ship's cook had been instructed previously to pour scalding water from his coppers upon any insurgents in the event of a slave uprising, but the mealtime had passed some hours before, and the terrified cook was now reduced to hurling ship's biscuits and the lukewarm remnants of stew at the heads of his foes.

Silver, seizing a length of rope and shouting to Pew and

the others to follow him, flung himself at the mêlée of slaves and seamen on the starboard side of the deck. In a trice he had wrapped the rope round the necks of two of the slaves and was twisting it like a tourniquet. As his victims struggled for breath, he hauled them to the gunwale and with one great heave of his broad back tossed them overboard. Scarcely had the shrieking slaves hit the water, before Silver grappled with two more, smashing their skulls together and pitching them, too, over the ship's side.

'Avast there, Silver,' Pew gasped as he struck out at a cowering slave with a hand-spike, 'that's a hundred golden pounds you've just dropped in Davy Jones's lap. Batter their woolly heads, says I – 'tis cheaper.'

And so saying he felled another victim with a thunderous blow upon the right temple. With that, the resistance amidships collapsed, the slaves lost heart, and the whining survivors were driven below decks with scant courtesy.

But even as Silver and Pew were launching their counter-attack, the struggle for the mastery of the quarterdeck took a perilous turn. Four slaves, more courageous or more agile than their fellows, had clambered up from the deck and fallen upon Jenkins and his companions.

Silver saw Jenkins's turkeycock face turn crimson as a pair of black hands closed round his throat. Another seaman reeled under the impact of a jagged-edged barrel stave.

Yet amid this murderous assault, one man upon the quarterdeck kept his head. This was the old hand George Thompson, who had prudently stayed to the rear of the fighting and had busied himself with the arms chest.

'I spy you, Barbecue,' Thompson shrieked as he saw Silver and Pew at the head of a dozen seamen bearing down on the quarterdeck. 'Here, make them beggars dance!'

And with a few deft flips of his arm the old man cast five pistols and three cutlasses at his comrades' feet.

Pew picked up a pistol with a quick scoop of his white,

cold hand, and snarled with joy.

'Damme, if it ain't loaded and primed, let's see the colour of them niggers' brains, lads.'

'Why, Gabby,' cut in Silver sharply, 'And there was you a-frettin over lost gold a moment back. Aim for their legs, says I, a blackamore who's dead ain't worth a gobful of warm spit, and one as limps a bit will still fetch a pretty penny, and you may lay to that.'

With that he let loose a brace of pistol balls at the milling slaves' bare feet. Other pistols exploded on either side of him. The negroes wavered, caught between crossfire. The battle for the quarterdeck swung decisively against the slaves, as those who defended it shot down and hurled back their assailants.

Within half an hour the slaves were back between decks, driven into the dark corners of the hold by revengeful seamen who cowed them with kicks and blows and threw freshly-heated scalding water into the faces of those who resisted most steadfastly.

The deck lay littered with bruised and broken men. The affray had lasted barely fifteen minutes, yet eleven negroes had been killed, five by Silver's own hands. Moreover, another ten had been felled with cutlasses, clubs and knives, and some seven or eight howled from wounds in their nether limbs.

Jenkins was carried to his cabin, barely conscious, with his nose flattened and his neck raw and swollen. Two others of the crew were concussed and senseless; another four nursed scarred forearms and battered shoulders. The second mate Harrison, a stooping stripling, with paltry reserves of self-confidence and resolution, lay in his cockpit clutching a wounded thigh and flinching whenever he heard footsteps approaching. The victorious men laughed and hooted as they took the *Osprey* in hand again, and shackled the subjugated slaves.

'Three cheers for Barbecue!' piped up a dark-browed

Suffolk man, Tom Brooks, who was old enough to be John Silver's father. 'He's the lad who did the trick. He drove the niggers back. He show'd us how!'

'Yes, Barbecue!' shouted other voices. 'We'd be dead as pork if you and Pew and t'others hadn't come a-running!'

'That's right enough. Did ye see the way he pitched four o'them blackamores straight over the ship's side?'

'John Silver for captain!' cried the Suffolk man.

There was some laughter at this, but also shouts of approval.

Silver stood amidships, uncertain how to react. He felt a rush of pride. Captain, eh? He'd make a better fist of it than Jenkins, he was sure of that. Could it be that these men trusted him, looked up to him even, and him so young?

He looked at the grinning faces. The fools. They were ready to cheer at the drop of a hat. To take jests at face value. How many of them gave a thought to the practical difficulties now facing the whole ship's company? They must be set to rights.

'So,' he demanded harshly, 'who's to navigate this ship now that Jenkins is more dead than alive, and Harrison has took to his bed? You, Tom Brooks? You, George Thompson? I tell you we'll be cast ashore on some heathenish isle to be ate by savages, we will. Your trouble is you can't look ahead. Leastways you can't look ahead and chew tobacco at the same time, I reckon.'

'Hold hard, Barbecue,' said Thompson. 'You're forgetting Captain Grierson down below. He's a first-rate seaman to be sure, though he pulled up his sheet anchor sharp-like awhile ago.'

Silver turned and made his way below decks. What was this? The door of Grierson's cramped cockpit had been wrenched open. He entered quickly. It was if he had stumbled into a slaughterhouse. The corpse of the quartermaster, Markham, lay in one corner, blood still seeping from his battered skull. A dead negro was sprawled across his legs. Over the edge of the bunk tumbled the broken body of Grierson; his eyes were gouged out, leaving sticky saucers of dark blood, and at the terrible gash across his throat flies were clustering.

'So Cap'n Fearsome'll do no more navigating. He's only fit to navigate us all to Davy Jones by the look on it!'

Startled, Silver swung round. There was Pew in the doorway, smiling a thin, satisfied smile.

'You, Gabby! Did you have a hand in this, then?'

'Not I, Barbecue! Though I can't say I ain't had a hankering for cutting Grierson's throat afore now.'

'But 'tis murder! We'll all swing now, I reckon.'

Pew stepped close to Silver. As always, his breath stank; like carrion, Silver thought, turning his head aside. Pew hissed, 'Use your eyes! There's a dead nigger a-tangled up with Markham. There's the answer as plain as a pikestaff! They burst in here after weapons and such like while they was a-rioting, and when they found out there wasn't no weapons, and being gentlemen of excitable dispositions an' all, they sets to and chops up our dear departed officers here.'

Silver's gaze flickered but he said calmly, 'I don't doubt that's the way of it, Gabby. But where's the witnesses to bear it out? I can feel the noose about my neck this very minute! If we don't all tell the same tale when we docks in Barbados, we're done for, like so much pork!'

'Not took with fright, John, surely? A man like you?'

'Just looking forrard, matey. Still, this won't do! 'Tis speckylation, that's all. Tidy up Grierson and Markham, Gabby, there's a lad. I'd best report this news to Cap'n Jenkins, if he's in a fit state to hear me.'

Silver left the bloody cockpit, and Pew, turning towards the corpses, kicked the dead Grierson hard in the face.

8

❧ *The Hurricane* ❧

The slaughtered negroes were pitched overboard with no more ceremony than a few curses over lost revenue. The corpses of Grierson and Markham, presumed to have been murdered by the rioting slaves, fared somewhat better; they were stitched into canvas shrouds and dropped over the taffrail. At George Thompson's insistence, Silver, being one of the few crew members – apart from the remaining officers – who could read, intoned some fragments from the Book of Common Prayer.

The Lord giveth and the Lord taketh away . . .
Ashes to ashes, dust to dust . . .

Pew spat into the waves as the bodies plunged into the sea and bobbed in the *Osprey's* wake in some weird semblance of a dance of death.

'Ashes to ashes, God damme and strike me blind,' he shouted into the wind. 'Crow's meat to shark's meat, more like, and good riddance and damnation to both of 'em, says I.'

With the corpses out of the way, a nice dilemma faced the survivors. Jenkins, it transpired, was too badly injured to navigate the ship. The only other surviving officer was the second mate, Harrison, who remained unnerved and incapacitated by the terrible events of the slave mutiny and the murder of Grierson and Markham. Who then was to command the *Osprey,* or at the very least ensure that it reached Barbados without foundering with all aboard?

The crew assembled to debate their plight. The enfeebled Harrison declined to take responsibility, while the men hooted and jeered and shook their fists in his face. At length it was decided on a show of hands that three men would work together to try to navigate the vessel. Harrison grudgingly agreed that he could take the vital noontide readings of the sun and set the *Osprey's* course. There were two seamen chosen to aid him. One was Gianni Riviera, a short-legged mariner from Genoa who had sailed in both the West and East India trade and had consequently picked up the rudiments of navigation. The other, naturally enough, was young John Silver whose quickness of mind and evident resolve during the slave rising had given such confidence to his fellows.

For a time all went well enough. The days passed, and the *Osprey* approached the Caribbean.

One morning, about seven days out from Barbados, the air grew heavy and warm, and the ship began to roll more sharply than before.

Suddenly the Genoese mariner, Riviera, standing near the helmsman, grasped the mizzen shrouds and leant over the side of the quarterdeck to eye the weather. Dark clouds were racing towards them from the west. He sniffed the wind that was rapidly increasing in force; it was stiflingly hot.

Quickly he turned to the stooping Harrison, who had just come up on deck and was desperately clutching his hat to his head.

' 'Urricane!' shouted Riviera to the uncomprehending Harrison. ' 'Urricane, Mr 'Arrison. We got to get ship 'ove to, and quick.'

Even as he spoke, the wind became a shrieking blast and began to rip the sail from the fore topsail yard. Shreds of canvas were torn off and whirled away. The waves assumed gigantic, terrifying proportions. The *Osprey's* crew, lacking proper orders, flung themselves haphazardly at the shrouds and struggled frantically to haul in the straining, tearing sails. They were only partly successful, for though they managed to clew up the more accessible canvas, the topgallants and topsails on both the main and mizzen masts were utterly destroyed.

To Silver's inexperienced eye, the great waves that now bore down upon the *Osprey* were monstrous portents of doom. Though they approached the battered vessel at an almost leisurely pace, they towered as high as the tallest house he had ever seen.

It seemed impossible that the *Osprey* could surmount any of the mountainous ridges. Yet the ship climbed the slope of each great wave, hung for an agonising moment at the crest, and then plunged headlong down into the trough, only to face the approach of another wave of equal magnitude. The vessel's decks were swept with waist-high surges, and the crew clung on to rails and masts and rigging as best they could. Below decks the battened-down negroes screamed with terror as they were hurled about in the darkness by the wild movements of the ship.

Silver clawed his way to the quarterdeck where he saw that Riviera had tied himself to the wheel and was trying to keep the *Osprey* head on to the waves. Behind Riviera crouched Harrison and three seamen. All were drenched to the skin and were squinting desperately into the hurricane, which had transformed Harrison's long straggly yellow hair into absurd streamers blowing out from his hatless head.

Timing each effort to coincide with the intervals between the great billows, Silver cut himself a length of bowline with his sheath knife. This done, he contrived to lash himself to a starboard section of the taffrail. Now, even though more than once his legs were lifted clean off the deck by a surge of water, he felt more secure. His security, though, would last only as long as the *Osprey* herself, and, judging by the wreckage of her rigging and the twisting and straining of her timbers, that could not be for many more hours. The ship must already have taken hundreds of gallons of sea-water in her hold, and this could only serve to speed her destruction by rendering her more clumsy and un-manageable in her dreadful encounter with this night-marish wind and these towering waves.

Silver gave himself up for lost. The rope binding him to the taffrail was cutting into his flesh, rubbing raw his lower chest, which now began to sting abominably from the salt water that swept the vessel continuously from bow to stern. Steadily, and with intelligence, Silver began to curse his fate: to curse his morose father for failing to reconcile him to the gentle craft of shoemaking; to curse his own restlessness that had led him to dabble in smuggling; to curse the misfortune of his arrest after the murder of the two customs men; to curse his ill-luck at sailing with a mad-man like the dead Grierson and an incompetent, puffed-up toad like Jenkins; to curse the act of divine malignancy that had guided the *Osprey* into the teeth of a raging hurricane.

Yet even as Silver braced himself unwillingly for death, the terrible force of the wind began to abate, and the raging-hot breath of the hurricane began to cool as well. Though the huge waves remained, the *Osprey*'s few remaining shreds of canvas had evidently helped keep her bows to the sea and thus avoid the danger of capsizing.

Darkness fell with the vessel's fate uncertain. But with the dawn the parched, exhausted seamen saw that they would probably ride out the tail of the hurricane.

As the sun rose higher in the sky the *Osprey*'s crew struggled to clear away the havoc. There was snapped rig-ging to repair, tattered sails to mend, splintered yards to be replaced. There was also the human cost to be reckoned. Despite their buffeting below decks, the majority of slaves had miraculously survived the tempest, though a fair few screamed with the pain of broken limbs and bloody cuts and bruises.

The crew members had also suffered. Two seamen had died while lashed to the foremast, their skulls shattered against the hard wood of the mast. Five others had simply been swept overboard. Among those missing was the second mate Harrison, who had lacked the resolve to tie himself securely to the ship's structure. The wounded Jenkins had saved his skin by wedging himself into a corner of the captain's cabin in the stern.

But as the *Osprey* limped towards Barbados and Jenkins recovered his strength, his thoughts repeatedly turned towards the unenviable task of explaining away the series of tumultuous events that had led to the vessel's present sorry plight. Somehow he had to justify the overthrow of Grierson, to explain his subsequent murder, and that of the quartermaster, Markham. He would have to account for the negro mutiny and the loss of valuable slaves during the affray. Then there were more dead slaves as a result of the hurricane, as well as seven crew members lost during those terrible hours. His management of the *Osprey* seemed little short of a recipe for disaster and financial ruin. So Jenkins vowed, nursing a broken jaw and his injured self-esteem, that he would somehow wriggle out of his responsibilities by a daring bluff, and by the time the *Osprey* struggled into Carlisle Bay his plans were formulated and his trap was sprung.

9

❦ *The Betrayal* ❧

'And so, my Lords,' Jenkins concluded, his voice rising to an undignified squeak as he sought to convince his audience, 'I was powerless to prevent the terrible events that I have described to you. Manacled as I was, overthrown, and rejected by all but a noble faction of the men, I was an unhappy witness of deeds of treachery and violence revolting to any Christian person!'

Rear Admiral Sir Richard Scarisbrook, President of the Court of Admiralty for the Island of Barbados and the Leeward and Windward Islands, shifted his gaze from the perspiring Jenkins to the dozen men standing in the dock before him.

'Prisoners at the bar,' he said, civilly enough, but with the hint of reprobation in his tone, 'how plead you to these charges brought against you by Mr Jenkins? Speak singly, if you please: guilty or not guilty? The clerk of the court will call your names.'

Scarisbrook, florid of visage and inclined to portliness, was flanked on either side by his fellow judges. On his right sat Sir Henry Willis, Secretary to the Crown Colony of Barbados, and Mr Henry Dodson, merchant of Bridgetown; on his left were Captain Fellowes of the Royal Navy, and Mr Michael Barnsley, representative of the Bristol joint-stock company that owned the *Osprey*.

The clerk to the court, black-robed and sweltering in the humid air of the oak-panelled room, rose to his feet. He read out the names from a scroll bearing the seal of their Lords of the Admiralty.

'Gabriel Pew?'

'Not guilty.' Then, under his breath, 'God damn you,

every man jack!'

'Giovanni Riviera?'

'No,' muttered Riviera.

'Enter that as a plea of Not Guilty,' interposed the President evenly.

'John Silver?'

'Not guilty, my lord.'

'George Thompson?'

The old man glowered at Scarisbrook. Five weeks of Bridgetown prison fare had reduced Thompson's weather-beaten face to a pallid mask, but within that mask his eyes blazed with hatred and contempt. Hatred for Jenkins for indicting him and the others for murder, mutiny and attempted piracy; contempt for the legal trap in which he found himself ensnared.

'George Thompson?' repeated the clerk.

'Answer, my man,' said Scarisbrook, still polite, but with an underlying threat in his voice.

Thompson leant forward, against the rail that separated the prisoners from the body of the court, and spat. The spittle splashed down the front of the clerk's black robes, causing him to recoil violently.

'Prisoner,' said the President amid the hubbub, 'You are obliged to answer the question as put to you, or the court will take steps to make you answer.'

'I'll not do it, sir,' croaked Thompson. 'There's been no truth heard in this court today. I'd rather go to my Maker afore I stoop so low. I'm an honest man, not like some I could mention.'

The President conferred with his fellow judges while the court was stirred with whispers and exclamations of surprise. At length, Scarisbrook spoke to the serjeant-at-arms, who clattered out of the court-room. Within ten minutes the serjeant-at-arms returned, accompanied by a mild-looking man who wore a great leather apron that reached from his chest to the tops of his stockings.

The President now spoke again to Thompson.

'Prisoner, if you will not plead to the charges brought against you, the executioner here will break your thumbs with whipcord.'

Thompson stood mute and pale in the dock, until he was seized by the executioner and the serjeant-at-arms and hauled before the judges' bench. Then, to the horror of his shipmates, the old man's thumbs were bound tightly around with two lengths of whipcord and slowly pulled until the bone first of one then the other snapped. Thompson cried out from the agony that he endured during this barbarous process, but still he would not plead.

At last, the President ordered the haggard but defiant old man to be taken away. The rest of the prisoners were charged, and to a man pleaded not guilty. The court was then adjourned until the next day.

Silver was sickened by the torture inflicted upon Thompson, and shaken and outraged by the accusations made against him and his shipmates by Jenkins – accusations which the court gave them no opportunity to rebuff. By its apparent partiality and evident brutality the law, backed up by the authority of the Crown, now seemed to him to be little more than a charade by which the wealthy and influential members of society ground down all those that allegedly opposed them.

The proceedings in court on the following day amply confirmed these views.

Scarisbrook calmly announced that George Thompson had been pressed to death during the night. The old man had been tied down in a filthy cell and a great weight of stone and iron had been heaped upon him. Still he refused to plead guilty or not guilty, so they had loaded more weight across his chest and belly, and denied him water. At last, a little before dawn, he had died.

Jenkins licked his fat lips uneasily at this news, but continued to play with zest the role of the wronged party. He

spelt out the alleged misdemeanours of the accused men; he
called witnesses from those of the crew whom he had made
privy to his plans; he huffed and puffed in virtuous outrage
at the imaginary wrongs he had suffered.

When Jenkins had been allowed his say and had been
questioned by the judges, the accused were given leave to
speak. Scarisbrook, recognising in John Silver a man of considerable intelligence, was more than half-inclined to give
credence to his robust rebuttals of Jenkins's charges. But
the others accused were, in the main, a sorry, tongue-tied
bunch, confused, ill at ease, and poor witnesses.

The court's verdict was predictable enough. Jenkins was
a gentleman of sorts, and he had witnesses who were
prepared to support his tale. Above all, the judges, as
representatives of the Crown, the Royal Navy, colonial and
commercial interests, had every reason to stamp out the
slightest hint of piracy and mutiny.

'Prisoners at the bar,' intoned Scarisbrook. 'You are
charged with entering into a wicked combination and con-
spiracy to murder your officers and superiors, in the per-
suance of which evil intent you did indeed foully murder
Captain Grierson, Mr Harrison, Mr Markham and diverse
others. You are also charged with entering into a con-
spiracy, in open contempt and violation of the laws of your
country, to assume the command of the vessel named the
Osprey and to use that vessel for acts of common piracy and
robbery against the goods and vessels of His Majesty's subjects and those of other trading nations.

'Therefore, each one of you being adjudged guilty, you
are sentenced to be carried back to the prison from whence
you came, and from thence to the place of execution,
without the gates of the aforesaid prison, and there to be
hanged by the neck until you are dead. After this you shall
each of you be taken down and your bodies hanged in
chains.'

Pew snarled as the sentence was pronounced; Riviera

and the others looked dumbfoundedly at the President of the Court. But Silver spoke out, young though he was, as bold as a lion.

'My lord,' said he, 'I have heard all that's been said in this court by you and Mr Jenkins and the rest, and I have but two things to say. The first is that it's a poor day for old England, and King George himself, God bless him, when innocent men such as we, only doing our duty, and you may lay to that, are hauled before gentlemen like yourself and found guilty on the words of them that's no better, nor one mite as honest, as we ourselves. If you call that justice, then damn your justice, says I, and long live King James over the water and may the niggers rise up and cut your throats and have your wives, and God rot your souls in hell!

'And the second thing, your honour, is this. You can't hang me because I can read like a scholar, I can. I know my rights, and I claim benefit of clergy, so make what you can of that, by thunder!'

There was a moment of complete silence, followed by hubbub. Panicstricken, Silver dredged through his memory. God! Was he mistaken after all? They'd clap him in the madhouse, like a shot. But no! He was right. He knew it. His father had spoken of it often enough. This privilege – benefit of clergy. For those who, like the clerks of old, could read. Such fortunates could claim the right to be sentenced by another court. A church court it was; long ago, at any rate. Church courts used to hand out lighter sentences to felons. Instead of death – whipping; or branding. Still possible to claim it. He was sure. He'd be made to read a passage from the bible. Was it the fifty-first psalm? Like a clergyman. That was it. Save himself from hanging.

The noise in the courtroom died down again.

'Hand the prisoner a copy of the bible,' said the seemingly unruffled Scarisbrook. 'Now, my man,' he continued, 'kindly read me Isaiah, chapter eleven.'

Silver paged through the book, cleared his throat and began, haltingly, 'And there shall come forth a rod out of the stem of Jesse, and a Branch shall grow out of his roots: and the spirit of the Lord shall rest upon him, the spirit of wisdom and understanding, the spirit of counsel and might, the spirit of knowledge and of the fear of the Lord.'

And he read on, his voice growing in confidence, until the President of the Court interrupted him and abruptly bade him stop.

'So, prisoner,' said Scarisbrook, 'you claim the ancient right of benefit of clergy, do you? A right that is still recognised in Barbados. Can any of you other rogues read, eh?'

The condemned men muttered and shuffled their feet, but not one of them could make out the written words of the English language with any certainty.

'Very well,' continued the President. 'You, John Silver, shall not hang. The court revokes its sentence, but we have no church court here where you might be tried. The law, however, demands some revenge for your vile plots and deeds, and I therefore sentence you to be taken from this court to a convenient place and there to be sold into lifelong slavery. May you prefer a slow death to a speedy one. The court will now end its sitting.'

Now trembling in the aftermath of his desperate attempt to save his neck, Silver was separated from his fellows and taken to a stifling cell to await humiliation in the slave market.

10

Sold into Slavery

The slave market at Bridgetown, John Silver told me, was little more than a sprawling yard containing pens into which the batches of negroes were herded. It was in close proximity to the harbour and was flanked by well-built houses fashioned out of stone. Even as he sat abjectly, a halter round his neck, leaning against a low wooden platform, Silver's keen gaze took in the fact that most of the houses had glazed, sashed windows. Some of the more recently constructed buildings had been raised three or four stories high, like the houses in Bristol he was accustomed to.

The older dwelling places, however, tended to be lower; the result, it was said, of prudent building in the aftermath of the Great Storm that had wrecked so much property during the middle years of Charles II's reign.

The main streets of Bridgetown were paved with cobbles and coral stones, and along them moved a leisurely stream of passers-by – vendors of a variety of goods from fresh fruit and fish to pickles and smoked meat, house-slaves bent on some errand or other, seamen on shore leave, merchants and tradesmen. Occasionally a planter would ride past on his thoroughbred, or a pony-cart would clatter by, driven by a slave, but carrying a bevy of prosperous ladies bedecked in finery brought from England or smuggled from France through the northern mainland colonies.

The day that Silver was taken to the slave market was evidently a slack one for business. No slaving vessels had docked recently, and the only trade in progress was the re-selling of a handful of house-slaves – cooks, porters, garden boys and the like. Despite this, a considerable crowd eventually gathered round young John who, as a white man about to be sold into slavery, excited a good deal of curiosity among the Bridgetown populace.

Even after the passage of half a century and more, Silver's face, as he recounted these events to me, reflected the profound humiliation he had suffered during those hours.

'Why, Jim,' he said, his eyes cold with rancour at the remembrance of these past wrongs, ' 'tis easy enough for a man to forgive and forget his punishments if so be they were fair and square, in a manner of speaking. But this court of lubbers in Barbados, they was another thing altogether. And for me to be sat there amid the slave pens with the grand gentlemen from the plantations a-puffing their baccy smoke in my face, and their daughters a-giggling, and even their blackamores smirking and rolling up their eyes at me – why, I'd rather have my leg took off again by the saw-bones, and me biting on the leather strap for the pain of it.

'To be sure, I well nigh blubbed like a babby, to be cast so low, and all for the lies of that ship's rat Jenkins. 'Twas then that I saw how I stood with the whole pack of them, with sea captains, fat merchants, company men and crown men alike. They had turned the law on me to break me, and, by the powers, I swore then and there to break their laws, in turn, across their skulls if howsoever I was given half a chance! I was out to feather my own nest from then onwards, and the devil take the hindmost!'

As far as I can remember, those were John Silver's precise words to me, and as I heard them I understood why he had eventually chosen to live outside the law, though he had not yet revealed to me the exact manner of his baptism into the brotherhood of piracy.

After this impassioned outburst, Silver continued with the narrative of his hours of degradation in the Bridgetown slave market.

It seems that the Barbadian planters and merchants that

sauntered round him were disinclined to purchase him, owing to his spurious reputation as a mutineer and cut-throat. It may be that they were also discouraged by the price that the crown authorities asked for him: £100 seemed an excessive sum when docile negroes could be bought at that time for as little as £20.

So Silver sat despairingly, propped against the platform, while he was appraised and scoffed at by free men and seasoned slaves alike.

At length, raising his head, he perceived that a tallish man with black hair and a foreign cut about his clothes was regarding him intently.

After a few minutes, the stranger turned and walked towards the auctioneer, who was dozing under a canopy with his broad-rimmed hat tilted over his eyes.

'Ah, Mr Dubois, sir,' said the auctioneer, stumbling to his feet. 'And what might I do for you this day?'

'That white man over there,' replied Dubois, speaking fluent English, though with an accent that at first Silver could not place, 'has he any brains?'

'Brains, Mr Dubois!' cried the auctioneer, 'This man, as you call him – his real name is Silver – is so sharp-witted he could cut down the sugar cane just by talking at it! He can read the bible as well as that born ranter John Wesley, so I've been told, and as for —'

'Yes, yes,' said Dubois, impatiently interrupting this catalogue of virtues. He turned and walked back towards Silver. 'Stand up, my man,' he said.

John pulled himself up to his full height.

'Yes,' said Dubois thoughtfully, as if to himself. 'You stand well. More than six foot tall. Broad shoulders, too, and a strong back,' he continued as he walked round John Silver's imposing frame. He peered again at his face. 'Good, clear eyes. Open your mouth. Wider! *Oui, excellent, vous avez les dents très fortes, je crois.* Good, Shut your mouth, man.'

'Now, see here,' he said briskly to the auctioneer, 'it

seems that I am the only one to want this man, eh? Is not that true? Well, even if that were not the case, he is a dangerous *félon,* criminal, is not that true? So, I will give you £50, and there's an end to it, and you get your commission. Do you agree?'

'Oh, come now, Mr Dubois,' protested the auctioneer. 'The crown sets double that on this man, and well you know the value of him once you have broken him in to your way of doing things. £80 say I, and not a penny less.'

As the two men haggled, John Silver stood with bowed head, his whole being suffused with shame at being bargained over like a young bullock at a cattle market.

At last he heard Dubois exclaim, 'Right! Done! £60 paid to you in silver coin of the realm. Good!'

The money was handed over. Dubois bound Silver's wrists with a thick cord, and then took him to his horse on the other side of the slave market. There Silver's halter was tied to Dubois' saddle.

Once this was done, Dubois turned to him. 'See here, man,' he said. 'You are now my slave. You work hard for me, eh? But I am not cruel. I give my slaves good food, good huts. If you work well you may be head man of my niggers, tell them what to do, eh? Very well, we go.'

And with that he mounted his horse, jerked its head round and made off, narrowly skirting a cart piled high with barrels of molasses and drawn by four oxen. Silver was naturally obliged to follow his new master at the end of his halter, and although Dubois walked his horse at a reasonable speed, it was all young John could do to keep pace without stumbling over the rough cobble stones. He soon learnt to walk with his feet lifted high to avoid tripping over. The sun blazed down, and the perspiration began to soak through his shirt.

As Silver made his sorry way through the streets of Bridgetown, he turned over in his mind the prospects that lay before him. Stretching limitlessly ahead was a lifetime of back-breaking labour amid the humid groves of sugar cane or in the torrid heat of the boiling house. It was always likely that he would be punished by his master for some real or imaginary misdemeanour, and he had heard hair-raising tales of slaves being flogged to death, or having their feet amputated, or their noses and ears clipped off. He could hope to avoid such torture by accepting his servile status, biding his time, and hoping eventually to escape or to secure his freedom by legitimate means – after all, there were freed black slaves in the British colonies in the West Indies and on the mainland.

As he trudged behind Dubois, who sat confidently on his fine horse, he toyed with the idea of escaping as soon as the track they were following took them away from the fringes of Bridgetown and into the wilder country beyond. Yet he soon put this idea firmly behind him: to begin with, his chances of escape were small, his wrists were bound and his neck encompassed with a halter; moreover, the punishments meted out to recaptured runaway slaves in- cluded death by slow burning, the victims of this barbarous fate having first been nailed to planks set upon the ground, and John Silver felt no compulsion to emulate the martyrs of antiquity in suffering such an exquisite and agonising death.

The path Dubois had chosen wound northwards, close to the western coast of the island. For seven miles or so they passed along a dusty track that bordered on estates of sugar cane, now nearly ready for cutting. Rough signs, set at in- tervals, gave notice of the families that owned the great es- tates, and Silver began to repeat their names, again and again, like some catechism of Barbadian nobility.

'Stoneham, Stoneham, may the Devil stone 'em.'

'Howard, coward, Howard's a damned coward.'

'Browne, Browne, God rot you, may you drown.'

'Reade, Reade, may your brats go in need.'

At length, Dubois turned aside from the track, tethered

his horse to the trunk of a young palm tree, and cast himself down upon the coarse grass. He unhitched his canvas saddle bag and took out some salted pork, a hunk of rough brown bread, and some fresh fruit. He also took out a leathern flask from which he drank long and noisily before turning his attention to his food.

Silver leant exhausted against the flank of the horse that was nuzzling the ground for mouthfuls of sweet, young grass-roots.

'Here, man,' said Dubois. 'Take this flask. Drink. There is some bread for you, too. When you have eaten that you may rest for a little. See, I will cut the bonds from your wrists. Sit down if you wish.'

And so saying he took out a clasp knife and severed the cord that had cut and chafed at Silver's wrists. Then he carelessly tossed his leathern flask and a piece of bread towards John, who had already slumped down. Silver gulped thirstily at the flask and chewed eagerly on the bread. Even though he was still tied to the horse's saddle and had to make small shifts of position as the animal, though tethered, sought for more food, the meal seemed to him to be fit for the table of the gods on Mount Olympus.

After some thirty minutes of rest, Dubois got to his feet once more, and remounted his horse. The sun was already stooping in the sky, and dusk was but a few hours away. They set off again, but Silver found the journey a good deal easier now that his wrists were not bound together. The pathway was still rough, however, and his feet were swollen and painful inside his boots.

At last, Dubois turned off the main track and led Silver past a sign that said simply 'Philippe Dubois', and then through acre upon acre of sugar cane plantations. The daylight was fading fast now, and by screwing up has eyes Silver could see some four hundred yards ahead a cluster of mean huts, and beyond them a solid two-storey mansion. Lights beckoned from the ground floor windows.

Dubois halted by one of the huts nearest to the house. He kicked open the door and pushed Silver inside, the halter still round his neck.

'You sleep here, man,' Dubois said. 'I shall not lock the door, but if you try to escape, my wolfhounds will tear your throat out. Tomorrow, you will work.' He slammed the door shut, and led his horse away.

Silver sat down upon the earth floor of the hut, leaning wearily against a wooden post that supported the low ceiling. In the gloom he could make out the shapes of a crude table and two stools; a sleeping mat and a blanket lay against the furthest wall. The stink of human urine and sweat permeated the miserable hovel.

In abject despair, Silver threw himself onto the sleeping mat and dragged the dirty blanket over him. His halter still trailed absurdly from his neck. As he fell into an exhausted sleep, he was dimly aware of a distant commotion, of girlish shrieks of joy, and of Dubois' voice calling out: 'Annette! Annette!'

11

❧ *The Plantation* ❧

At dawn Dubois came to Silver's cabin and threw open the door. He was attended by a wrinkled old negro, whose woolly hair was flecked with white.

'On your feet, man,' said Dubois briskly. 'This man here,' and he indicated the wrinkled negro, 'is Jean-Pierre, my head nigger. He will show you how things are on the plantation, how we work, when we rest. You understand?'

Silver hauled himself to his feet, and blinked at Jean-Pierre, who was regarding him slyly through narrowed eyes. He saw that the negro was wearing a blue cotton shirt and stained flannel trousers; in his right hand he carried a cart-whip.

'Yes, sir,' said Silver slowly, 'I understand well enough.'

'Excellent,' said Dubois. 'Right, now we have roll-call, *réveillé*, you will see,' and he turned and walked away from the hut.

As Silver followed behind Dubois and Jean-Pierre, the first rays of the tropical sun were beginning to pierce the chill mist that hung over the estate. The rank vapours were unpleasant to breathe, and Silver coughed violently. Groups of slaves began to troop after Dubois and Jean-Pierre.

As they approached the fields of sugar cane Jean-Pierre stopped until Silver caught up with him. He then spoke out of the corner of his mouth.

'What your name, *ami*? I know "Silver", but what your christian name, eh?'

'John,' replied Silver civilly enough, for he had already sized up the other as an unrelenting foe if once his ire was aroused.

'John!' crooned Jean-Pierre, 'Same name as me got, but me own name a Frenchy one, see, on account of me belonging once to the father of Monsieur Dubois when they all live in Martinique, way back. Anyhow, I call you "Johnny", so we no make mistake.'

'Well, John-Peer,' said Silver, 'That'll be fine by me, I reckon. But how come this Dubois, being a frog an' all, gets landed high and dry on an English isle like Barbados?'

'Why, Johnny,' replied Jean-Pierre, 'I tell you sure as eggs is eggs, though it's plenty long tale, but *mon Dieu,* here come Monsier Dubois right this minute, so the tale best wait.'

Dubois bore down on the two men even as Jean-Pierre spoke.

'See here, man,' he said to Silver. 'If you want to save your skin you have to learn to work like a nigger. Then, maybe, you will be allowed to help Jean-Pierre keep an eye on things. He's no chicken, is Jean-Pierre. One day he will just want to doze in the sun outside his cabin, or perhaps scratch his pig's back a little. In any case, he has served me well. I have no complaints. But maybe you will wish to step into his place, if so you best do as he says. Jean-Pierre, I hold you responsible for this man.'

With that he turned on his heel and strode off towards the plantation house.

By now the morning sun had dispelled the mist and was warming the slaves' damp clothes. They shook their stiff limbs and began to work in gangs at the task of cutting the sugar cane. Jean-Pierre handed Silver a bill-hook, saying coaxingly, 'You put your back into it, Johnny, and you be all fine with me. Me tell Monsieur Dubois you good man to help along o' me.'

Silver set to with a will. He had, after all, little choice in the matter.

So for two months and more, Silver's life followed the same monotonous pattern of dawn rising, unremitting toil, and periods of exhausted sleep.

Yet he soon adapted to his unenviable lot. He measured the expenditure of his energy as precisely as a physician administers his medicines; he began to till the plot of ground next to his hut, and planned what victuals he might grow there, for the slaves supplemented their inadequate diet with home-grown fruit and vegetables; through Jean-Pierre's good offices he acquired a decent straw-filled mattress, clean blankets and tolerable eating utensils. His labours, moreover, had the effect of strengthening his already imposing physique so that his muscles became iron-hard and his back able to bear almost any burden. Though his fellow-slaves were at first inclined to mock him, revelling in the fact that as a white man he had sunk even lower than they, the gibes soon stopped after he picked up two of his tormentors and shook them till they shrieked for mercy.

From Jean-Pierre he gradually learnt more of Dubois' origins. It seemed that Dubois' father had eventually become unacceptable to the French authorities in Martinique due to his anti-clerical views and his continuing flirtation with heretical doctrines – in fact, he had been suspected of Huguenot sympathies at the best, of devil worship at the worst. So old Dubois had sold up his property, quit Martinique, and settled in Barbados where his capital and his Protestant leanings were equally acceptable, and his French origins more or less forgivable. When his father died, Philippe Dubois had taken over the plantation and lived as a loyal subject of the British crown. He had never married, but had lived with one of his slave women, an ebony Venus from the Bay of Benin, according to Jean-Pierre. As a result of this liaison a daughter had been born, though the mother had died of a mysterious fever shortly after the birth. This girl, now sixteen years of age, lived as her father's lawful daughter, and had been given a homely education and a fond upbringing.

Annette Dubois was a girl of remarkable fire and beauty. Her coffee-coloured skin glowed with vitality, her brown eyes sparkled, her long dark hair shone blue-black over her shoulders. Flouncing about the plantation in her long dresses and petticoats, she seemed to John Silver to be a vision, a mirage, unobtainable but infinitely desirable. Certainly she seemed to be unaware of his existence, and he noticed that whenever by chance their eyes met she would quickly turn her head away or busy herself with something near at hand. Dubois doted on her, and she repaid him with a passionate devotion that was in turn playful, solemn and coquettish.

In any event, Silver told himself bitterly, there was no reason why such a rare and beauteous creature should be even aware of his existence. He still laboured as a field-hand, his clothes were in rags and tatters, his status servile.

Then, some nine weeks after he had been brought to the plantation, Dubois came to his cabin as he and Jean-Pierre were sharing their evening meal. Silver and the old negro got promptly to their feet. Dubois' gaze was searching, but his tone was not hostile.

'Well, Johnny,' he said, 'You have worked well. You now know what my slaves have to do. You know their tricks, their lies, well enough. So I will make you now my overseer, "chief driver", we say here. Jean-Pierre will help you.' Here Jean-Pierre grunted, sullenly, so Silver thought. 'You will still be my slave, naturally, but you will have better food, decent clothes. I will reward you well. Understand?'

'Yes, indeed, and thank you kindly, sir,' said John. 'Me and John-Peer here will make your plantation the most ship-shape and Bristol fashion in all Barbados, and you may lay to that.'

'Very well,' replied Dubois. 'But remember always that you are a convicted *félon*. Any trouble, and I will string you up, and the judges in Bridgetown will applaud me for it.'

He turned to leave. 'Ah, yes,' he said suddenly, pausing in his tracks. 'Last night I heard from my neighbour Richard Stoneham of the fate of your fellow criminals in Bridgetown. They all danced at a rope's end, it seems, some weeks back, and the sun has shrivelled their corpses by now. Except for one. He cut his way out of the prison, and murdered two of the guards. The militia have searched for him, and mastiffs have been sent to track him down, but, *hélas,* he has got clean away, it seems. Now what was his name? "Drew", I think, or "New" – some such name.'

'Pew,' broke in Silver, hardly able to restrain his excitement, 'Gabby Pew's the name, sir.'

Then, realising that such enthusiasm was likely to antagonise his master, he said with a show of indifference, 'And a viler cut-throat you couldn't hope to meet. May his freedom be short-lived, say I, and God protect His Majesty's subjects while he be at large.'

'Amen, to that,' said Dubois slowly, watching Silver's face intently. Then he walked away, past Jean-Pierre's two pigs that were rooting and scuffling under the trees, and was swallowed up in the purple gloom.

John Silver took to his duties as plantation overseer as does a duck to water. Dressed in Dubois' cast-off clothes, his tanned face half hidden under a large straw hat, strong leather boots upon his feet, a heavy-stocked whip tucked neatly into his belt, he was an imposing representative of authority – solid, yet alert and agile.

For the most part his duties were agreeable enough, and he was, for the moment, inclined to abide by the plantation's rules. He soon came to the conclusion that it was fruitless to terrorise the slaves, deny them victuals, or force them to work at a pace which they could not sustain. In any case, since he was not himself a free man, drawing wages, he had some sympathy with those who had no hope whatsoever of altering their lot and were condemned to a lifetime of servitude.

But he also believed that men, even slaves, could best be made to work if discipline was tempered with fairness and a little humour.

For their part the slaves gave Silver little trouble. Seeing that he was not disposed to play the tyrant, they had no inclination to take advantage of his good humour and occasional benevolence. At the same time, he could inspire them with blind terror when the occasion warranted it. His sheer physical size, his prodigious strength, positively demanded respect and obedience, as did his subtle and iron will, the tenacity of his purpose and the power of his reasoning.

Dubois congratulated himself on his good fortune in acquiring Silver. He even sought his advice on a variety of matters concerning the running of the plantation, and came to depend upon his shrewd judgement.

Jean-Pierre, on the other hand, plainly resented Silver's advancement, and, though nothing was said, John had the uneasy feeling that the old negro would rejoice at his downfall.

Jean-Pierre's chance came some two years after Silver had first been taken into slavery. It must be said, however, that John was in part responsible for springing his own trap. He was always reluctant to reveal too much of the episode, but the fact is that he came to form a passionate liaison with Annette Dubois. It matters little now who took the initiative. Silver had taken a negro woman called Charlotte as his mistress, and though he had begun to tire of her, Charlotte's position as maid to Annette may have helped to make the new liaison possible. At any rate one night a meeting was contrived and pledges were exchanged that were to bind the two together in a lengthy if unorthodox compact.

It was, of course, a situation that posed impossible

problems. Sooner or later their furtive meetings were bound to be discovered, no matter how skilfully they dissembled, and Silver, despite his passion for Annette, was constantly fearful of betrayal.

Silver's premonitions of disaster were dramatically fulfilled one morning in the cold, dank hours before dawn. Before he could be conscious of his fate, he was seized from his sleep by four stalwart negroes of the estate's heavy work gang. Even as he struggled against his captors, Silver was aware of Jean-Pierre's brooding and malevolent presence as he supervised the arrest.

Within minutes Silver had been hauled brutally to the estate's punishment hut, a squat, stone-built edifice where delinquent slaves were locked.

His hands bound fast behind his back, he was dragged into the presence of Dubois, whose eyes blazed with fury, and whose face was white and twisted with loathing.

'So, man,' Dubois screamed, 'You have seduced my daughter, have you? You have polluted my household, disgraced my family? Do not attempt to deny it! Jean-Pierre has seen it all. He has watched your secret meetings. Everything is known!'

'For pity's sake, Mr Dubois,' Silver cried, desperately seeking for the right words, 'You're way off course, and no mistake. Your daughter's as much a maiden now as the day she was born! Me seduce her, by thunder! She came a-running after me, and proud I am of it, she being such a beauty an' all!'

But before he could say more, Dubois stepped forward and slashed him across the face with his riding crop. A purple weal sprang up ol Silver's cheek, and the pain burnt into the back of his skull.

'How dare you speak to me in such a way?' Dubois shouted. 'You are a thief, a criminal and a liar!'

Then making a great effort to control his overwhelming sense of outrage, he said more calmly, but with venom in his voice, 'You have tried to take my daughter from me. The one creature that I love. You have failed, but in your failure you have sullied my daughter's purity. I have witnesses. Now that I have discovered your plot I shall be revenged upon you.'

He walked towards the stoutly barred window and looked out into the growing light of the day.

'Out there,' he said, almost wearily 'is my house. In the topmost room of the house is my daughter. She is, no doubt, still weeping from the stripes I have given her across her back and rump. Her door is locked, and an old house-nigger sits outside on guard.

'And you, man,' he said, retracing his steps to stare into Silver's face, 'will never see her again. Why? Because I am going to put you to death. We need no court of law out here. Hanging is too quick, and it is my belief that only niggers should be burnt alive. But in France, as you may have heard, we tie a man to a cartwheel and the executioner breaks his limbs one by one with a crowbar while the victim shrieks away his life. It is not an easy death. Think of it in the few hours that remain to you.'

'Jean-Pierre,' he said curtly, as he prepared to leave, 'Guard this man with your life, or you will be victim instead of executioner.'

As Dubois strode out of the room, Jean-Pierre bowed and cringed, and Silver, transfigured with fear, leant forward and vomited upon the floor.

12

❦ *The Raid* ❦

Jean-Pierre's sneering voice helped to rouse Silver from
his despair.

'Why, don't you make a pretty picture, Johnny, a-
crouchin' in your own spew down there? You reached too
high, you white bastard. You reckoned you could get Miss
Annette and lord it over all of us, huh? Well, you sure is
wrong. You done for, boy, you know that? And I be the one
who done you down. I see'd you with Miss Annette the first
time, in the store house. Then I watched you plenty other
times, so did Charlotte – she sure hates the both of you, you
and your fancy gal.'

And the old man spat upon the floor.

Silver felt a hot fury suffusing his body, dispelling, for the
moment, his misery.

'John-Peer,' he said grimly, 'If so be I get the chance, I'll
cut your throat from ear to ear and stuff your entrails in the
gash, so help me.'

'Heh, heh! Some likelihood of that, my boy,' replied
Jean-Pierre. 'This time tomorrow mornin' and you be half
dead upon that good old wheel already, and Miss Annette,
up there, she'll hear your screams the while!'

Silver turned away his head. How could he avoid so
horrible a death? By appealing to Dubois? Impossible; the
man was possessed by an insane desire to revenge supposed
wrongs, and Annette's influence over him had, for the time
being, completely vanished. Escape from the punishment
hut was out of the question; not only did Jean-Pierre sit
glowering over him, but two other negro guards were
posted outside. In any case, Silver knew how stoutly the
punishment hut was built: the heavy door was reinforced

with iron bands, and the bars across the window were as thick as a man's wrist. Could he, at the very least, wriggle free of his bonds and then overpower Jean-Pierre by the exercise of his superior strength? Cautiously he tested the cord that bound his hands together; then he wrenched with all his might; the fibres of the cord creaked, but they did not come apart.

He was doomed, Silver realised. This was to be the end of his earthly life. He had survived a variety of dangers aboard the *Osprey;* against the odds, he had saved his neck in the Bridgetown courtroom by remembering the ancient, much abused right of benefit of clergy; he had transformed his servile status upon Dubois' plantation into one of substantial power and authority.

Now all this was of no avail. He was doomed, and doomed to a death that would have been fitting for a victim in the Roman circus or for the assassin of a Bourbon king of France.

He felt icy cold, and a terrible fatigue overcame him. Why should he struggle to keep awake? He keeled over upon the dirty, straw-covered floor, and fell into a deep sleep.

Silver must have slept for twelve hours or more, for when he at last opened his eyes the daylight was fast fading. He could hear a strange commotion beyond the punishment hut, muffled cries and shouts which, he realised, must have been responsible for arousing him from his death-like sleep.

Jean-Pierre was clinging to the bars of the window, desperately trying to see what was happening outside. At last, he gave a sharp yelp of alarm, and, wrenching the door open, ran out, calling on the two negro guards to accompany him. Somewhere, far off, great trumpeting sounds came, urgent, panic-stricken sounds.

The alarm! But why the alarm? Silver's quick mind raced through the possibilities. A slave rebellion, as like as not urged on by the obeah men – the practitioners of black magic among the negroes; such risings were not uncommon and provoked planters and overseers, indeed the whole white population of the sugar islands, to countenance horrifying acts of retribution. Or could it be that Dubois' long-standing quarrel with the Reades, who owned one of the neighbouring plantation, had overflowed into violence? What was the quarrel about? Silver racked his brains for the answer. Ah yes, both parties claimed ownership of a small bay, Spikes' Cove, where their estates reached the sea, and which was essential for loading barrels of sugar and molasses onto coastal schooners.

What was that now? A pistol shot. And Dubois' wolf-hounds baying frantically. Women shrieking, and men shouting out. More shots, and then a long, harsh cackle of laughter, blood-chilling, careless and cruel.

Silver sat up. His hands were still tied behind his back, but by first kneeling, then pushing against the wall with his right shoulder, he was able to lurch to his feet. He stumbled towards the door, which Jean-Pierre had left open in his haste, and cautiously looked out. Through the gloom he could make out little except that terror and confusion had gripped the plantation. Small groups of slaves were confusedly running hither and thither; on the ground lay the bodies of several negroes. Lights flickered here and there – men carrying torches. Further off, flames crackled higher and higher: the slave cabins were on fire.

Silver pushed open the door of the punishment hut and stepped outside. Before he could draw breath, strong hands gripped him round the throat, forcing him back against the door with a clatter. Bloodshot eyes bored into his own; Silver's assailant was a man well nigh as tall as himself.

'Belay there, Job,' a hard voice called, some yards off. 'Let's see what fine fish you've caught there!'

A second man approached Silver. He was less tall, and wore a cocked hat, and a coat and breeches of good sea cloth. Though he carried a cutlass in his hand, he had an air almost of respectability. He peered closely at Silver, who caught the reek of rum mingled with sweat.

The man who had attacked Silver released his grip, and spoke slowly to the newcomer.

'I don't rightly know, Mr Bones,' he said, 'whether 'tis fish or fowl, for he's a white man, but all trussed up as you can see.'

'And thankful to fall in with gentlemen like yourselves,' said Silver rapidly, seizing his chance. 'That damned Frenchy, who's cock o' the walk hereabouts, has done me down and tried to break me. Now, you cut me loose and I'll lead you to his gold and silver, and I can't say fairer than that!'

The man called Bones rested the point of his cutlass on Silver's left cheek bone, just below the eye.

'Right you are, matey,' he said, and as he spoke Silver thought he could detect a Yankee accent. 'You lead us to this here gold, and we'll see you fine and dandy. But you try to trick us, and I'll skewer you on this blade!

'Cut him free, Job,' he said curtly. 'Now, show us this treasure trove you speak of, and quick about it!'

Rubbing his numb wrists, Silver led the two men towards Dubois' mansion. Making as rapid progress as he could, half running and half trotting, he saw that the estate was being plundered by a score of men, seafaring men to judge by their garb. Pirates! That was it. A pirate raid! They had doubtless landed at Spikes' Cove that afternoon, and had waited until the approach of dusk to attack. Now they were looting and burning, ruthlessly destroying all who opposed them. Silver had heard tales of gangs of buccaneers attacking coastal plantations, seeking victuals and treasure. Dubois' estate was now suffering such a fate, it seemed.

There was the mansion. Its great door was wide open, swinging gently on its hinges. All hell seemed to have broken loose inside: cries of terror mingled with terrible oaths and the crash of overturned furniture.

As the three men approached the door, a burly ruffian, with a red kerchief over his head, burst out of the house dragging behind him two shrieking negresses; one of them was Charlotte, Annette's maid. Silver hesitated at the threshold.

'Get in, you fool!' shouted Bones from behind him, and Silver felt the sharp point of a cutlass jabbed into the small of his back.

He plunged into the stone-paved hallway. Light poured from the door of the parlour on the right of the hall. Bones pushed him roughly into the room.

Silver blinked in the bright light. There was Dubois, seated on a high-backed wooden chair, his arms pinioned behind him. Three men crouched over him, shouting into his face and brandishing knives; further away, a fourth sat calmly on a well-upholstered couch.

Even as he took in the scene, Silver heard one of the three men surrounding Dubois snarl, 'If you be too proud to tell us where 'tis hid, we'll roast you slow over your own fire. We'll see how proud you are when you smells your own flesh a-burning!' And with that he slashed with his knife at Dubois' unprotected face.

The man on the upholstered couch stirred himself. 'Avast there, Mr Flint,' he said, in almost gentlemanly tones. 'You know full well I can't stomach the ill-usage of prisoners. A few cuts about the face, dear sir, well, there's nought to that. But slow burning, Mr Flint, I'll not stand for it, as I'm an Englishman.'

Flint turned his blotched, pock-marked face towards the calm-spoken man, and Silver could see at once that his features had been marred by some sort of burn – from gun-powder, as like as not.

'Why see here, cap'n,' Flint hissed, 'You'll be quick enough to spend the gold, I'll warrant. Now you let me prise it out o' this rare gentleman as I see fit! In any case, 'twill be good sport to see him smoulder!' And he threw back his head and laughed, the harsh, spine-chilling cackle that Silver had heard shortly before, when the raid began.

At this, Bones stepped forward, pulling Silver with him. He spoke quickly to Flint's adversary. 'Why, Captain England,' he said, 'Here's the key to our treasure chest, and no mistake. Job Anderson and me, we found him trussed up like a fowl for the pot, and him spitting hate against his master over there. He'll show us what's what!'

'That's right, Cap'n England sir,' said Silver eagerly. 'I know where the loot is hid. Now I don't want no share of it, but you best take me with you when you skedaddle from here, for my life ain't worth a pinch o' salt if I'm left behind.'

Captain England waved a courtly arm at John Silver, lace trailing from his cuff.

'We'll see about that when the time comes, my man,' he said. 'Show us the gold first.'

'Right you are, sir!' said Silver, and he turned and led them upstairs to the back room where he knew Dubois stored his valuables. Captain England, Bones, Anderson and two other buccaneers trod close behind his heels, but the man called Flint hesitated, and did not accompany them.

The men smashed open the concealed cupboard where Dubois kept his hard currency and jewels, and proceeded to stow the booty into bolster cases taken from beds in nearby rooms. Silver, watching them, thanked his stars that his position as overseer had enabled him to learn many of the secrets of Dubois' household.

Then he thought of Annette! Her father had locked her in one of the rooms at the back of the house, and no doubt she was out of her mind with terror. No one heeded him as he ran out onto the landing to search for the room where Annette was imprisoned.

He saw a door ajar, and burst in to find Annette crouching against the wall, weeping hysterically. A man was clawing at her, tearing at her dress, while she frantically tried to push him away.

As Silver entered the room, the man spun round, startled. It was Jean-Pierre! The old negro's face froze with fear as Silver leapt at him. John lifted him high above his head, as if he were no more than a rag doll, and with one great heave threw him right through the sash window. Jean-Pierre crashed among the bushes below, broken and screaming, and there Dubois' wolf-hounds, hungry for blood, found him and ripped him to pieces.

Silver lifted Annette into his arms; she felt light and warm, and suddenly he realised how much he loved her and how much she now depended upon him. As he made his way down the stairs, she sobbed slowly and quietly.

When he reached the hallway, Silver saw that the pirates were moving off, back to their ship. They were driving a number of negroes before them, and were laden with plunder. Silver followed blindly, while Annette hid her face upon his chest.

Before he took the downward path that led to Spikes' Cove, he turned to look behind him. Flames were already devouring the mansion, and, from an upper window, illuminated by the fire, a pathetic figure dangled from a rope. Dubois! Silver hastily shielded Annette from the horrible sight, but she seemed to have fainted away already.

The man called Bones passed them, his pockets jingling with coin, his cutlass sheathed. He noticed the direction of Silver's gaze and said, coolly enough, 'Why, that's Flint's handiwork, I'll be bound. He could never abide Frenchies, nor gentlemen, couldn't Flint.' And with that he disappeared, whistling, into the darkness.

Silver paused. With Dubois dead, Annette would inherit the plantation as like as not. They would be safe – free to marry at last! As her husband he would have authority, wealth, a position in society.

Annette mumbled and stirred in his arms, and, as if in

response, he suddenly saw reality. Wealth and authority, eh? The chances were he'd be accused of Dubois' murder! This time they'd hang him for sure. No, best for him and Annette to take a chance with the buccaneers. At the worst he could strike à few blows at established society, and at the best he might end up a pirate king, his pockets overflowing with doubloons! He could do it! Hadn't the lads on the old *Osprey* hollered for him to be captain?

His mind was made up. Bearing the unconscious Annette, he stumbled down towards the cove.

13

⟪ *Captain England* ⟫

I t was all Silver could do, bearing Annette in his arms, to keep up with the pirates as they straggled down to Spikes' Cove. Not that there was much difficulty in hearing their progress, for they chattered and shouted and sang as freely as if they were at Widdecombe Fair. But the path was narrow and sometimes precipitous, and when he occasionally lost the light of some guiding torch or other, John had to tread warily indeed.

At last he reached the beach of the small bay, and drew close to the buccaneers who were grouped at the water's edge. He saw that the men and their booty were waiting to be ferried to their ship which was standing out at sea. The vessel's boats were busy plying the still waters, while above them the stars shone sharply in the black sky.

Silver approached the man called Bones, who was squinting out to sea; next to him stood Flint, stroking the thin, dark moustache that adorned his upper lip.

'You'll be keeping your word, sir,' said Silver to Bones. 'About seeing me fine and dandy? Can we come aboard with you?'

Bones swung round to look at him, but before he could reply, Flint said mockingly, 'Why, is this the trussed fowl you picked out of the hen coop, Billy? And damme if he don't want to bring along a lump of extra freight an' all.'

He poked a blood-stained finger at the unconscious Annette. 'Now see here, mate,' he said viciously to Silver, 'Cap'n England, being a true buccaneer, don't hold with women aboard his vessels. They leads to quarrels and good sailormen a-breaking of each other's heads. So dump her on the shore, and maybe we can accommodate yourself, though you can stay and swing for all I care!'

'Well now, Flint,' said Billy Bones, 'I'd not heard that Captain England had stepped down to make way for you! The last I knew, you were only quartermaster. If things have changed I'll be obliged to you to tell me so, straight out!'

Flint's dark face clouded with fury, while Bones continued blithely enough, 'But if, as I fancy, you ain't captain yet, and I'm still first mate, I'll do the deciding, if you please.'

He then said to Silver, 'You come aboard with me, friend, and Captain England will decide what to do. You'd best bring your gal too, though Flint speaks the truth when he says they ain't welcome for long among gentlemen of fortune such as ourselves. However, we've already took a dozen bonny nigger gals onto the old *Cassandra,* so I reckon one brown-skinned lass won't make no difference.'

And so it was that half an hour later John Silver found himself upon the deck of the *Cassandra,* while all around him the buccaneers busied themselves with stowing away their plunder and preparing the vessel for her departure.

Silver was standing amidships, his arm round Annette, who had recovered consciousness in time to make an agile ascent of the ship's side, when Bones touched him on the shoulder and bade him follow him. He led Silver and Annette to a great cabin in the *Cassandra's* stern; there, seated at a badly scarred mahogany table, was Captain England, thrusting great pinches of snuff into his nostrils and scowling at a map. Silver suddenly felt vulnerable and ill at ease; at his side Annette drew in her breath in an anxious gasp.

At the sight of Annette, Captain England rose gallantly to his feet, begged her to be seated, and tut-tutted while Bones dragged forward a chair which, when new, might have graced a Governor's mansion anywhere in the Spanish Indies. Briefly, Bones explained the situation.

'Ah, yes,' said England, politely, 'a new recruit to my noble band is always welcome, Mr Silver. Particularly one so stalwart as yourself. But we don't generally carry ladies aboard the *Cassandra,* though I fancy we've a few black lasses stowed away for sport on this occasion. My officers, however, might take it amiss if I broke our regulations on your account.'

He paused, and shook out more snuff from a silver container.

At length he said, 'I presume that you're indeed anxious to join my crew, Mr Silver? If your principles don't allow it, I'll be glad to set you down as a maroon on some rocky islet, or hand you over to the King's justices at the first opportunity.'

Silver began to protest his enthusiasm for the captain's service.

England cut him short, saying, 'Of course, of course, welcome aboard. But this girl, now there's the problem.' He paused.

'Ah, of course, of course. You'll marry her right here and now, and later you can settle her in New Providence, where other gentlemen of fortune keep their wives and children. So that's settled. Good. Mr Bones, kindly step outside and bring Ezekiel Winthrop here this instant, if you please.'

Bones left the cabin. Silver was for once rendered speechless, but Annette raised her head and smiled at him. A smile of consent mingled with tears of remorse, it seemed to Silver. Well, it would have to do.

Captain England spoke again. 'You'll find preacher Winthrop a proper man of the cloth, my friends. That cloth may be a trifle threadbare by now, for poor Winthrop fell on hard times in Massachusetts – something to do with keeping his wife's sister as his concubine, if I recall. But no matter, he can spout the Good Book from dawn to dusk, if he has a mind to.'

At that moment Bones returned, accompanied by the

erring priest. Ezekiel Winthrop's eyes were red from rum; he wore a tunic of sombre hue, dirty orange breeches and well-worn seaboots; a flint-lock pistol was stuffed into his belt. When he saw Annette he leered and nodded at her.

'Here, Winthrop,' said England, 'hitch this loving pair together, and smart about it!'

'Why, praise God, Captain England!' cried Winthrop in a high-pitched nasal voice. 'My work is never done. However, the Good Lord in His wisdom seems to have clean forgot to provide me with the Book o' Common Prayer!'

Here he patted his pockets, and raised his eyes to the heavens in mock despair as if searching for the book in the rafters of the cabin.

'Belay there, Winthrop,' said Captain England brusquely, 'we've no time for sermons with the lads about to weigh anchor. One good book is much the same as another, I reckon, so make what you can of this!'

And opening a nearby cupboard door he drew out a small book and tossed it to Winthrop.

'Ah,' said Winthrop, blinking at the book. 'Master Bunyan. I have always declared there's nought more stirring than his *Pilgrim's Progress.*'

He thumbed through the pages and eventually said, 'Why, this seems fitting enough for those about to undertake matrimony's great journey. Stand up, my children!'

Then he hiccupped, and began to intone, with repeated glances at Annette's bosom.

'Whose Delectable Mountains are these? And whose be the sheep that feed upon them?

Shepherd: These mountains are Immanuel's Land, and they are within sight of his city; and the sheep also are his, and he laid down his life for them.

Christian: Is this the way to the Celestial City?

Shepherd: You are just in your way.

Christian: How far is it thither?

Shepherd: Too far for any but those that shall get thither
         indeed.'

Silver stood bemused, with Annette clutching his arm,
amid Winthrop's tipsy rendering of the Pilgrim's Progress
to the Delectable Mountains. Then, from the bows of the
ship, came the noise of the crew singing as they pushed on
the capstan's spars to raise the anchor. It was a wild sort of
song, punctuated with guffaws and drunken oaths:

Fifteen men on the dead man's chest –
Yo–ho–ho, and a bottle of rum.
Drink and the devil had done for the rest –
Yo–ho–ho, and a bottle of rum.

The cabin was filled with a whirling cacophony of sound,
composed of Winthrop's droning voice and the crew's
reckless sea shanty. Annette flinched, and Bones smiled
grimly.

Suddenly Captain England thumped his fist upon the
mahogany table. 'Enough, Winthrop!' he roared. 'You're
marrying them, not ordaining them for God's service! In
any case, I've my duties to attend to.'

He said, civilly enough, to Silver and Annette, 'I declare
you to be wed. It ain't precisely according to God's laws,
but you'll find it will do fine and dandy among the buccaneers of New Providence, where we're bound.'

He stood up. 'You're welcome to bed down in the
after-lazarette,' he said to Silver. 'And if I were you, I'd
keep her under lock and key till we reach the Bahamas.
There's plenty hereabouts that ain't shy of dipping into
another man's treacle, including our holy friend the pastor
over there.

'Winthrop,' he said to the fallen priest, 'get out! Mr
Bones, follow me.' And he left the cabin, anxious to sniff the
breeze and set the vessel's course.

And so it was that John Silver fell in with the Brethren of
the Coast, as the pirates of the Caribbean often called
themselves, and acquired a wife into the bargain. It came as

a distinct surprise to me to discover that his 'old negress', his 'old missis' to whom I had heard him casually refer aboard the *Hispaniola* was none other than Annette Dubois! But then, that was a good many years after the events I have just recounted; and, of course, Annette's blood was half negro on account of her mother.

Not that Silver would have cared twopence whether Annette's blood was mixed with mercury or boiled lead, for he loved her as honestly as he ever loved any living creature. Indeed, their dramatic flight from Dubois' estate and their abrupt coupling aboard the *Cassandra* created a bond between them that somehow survived all manner of subsequent stresses and misfortunes.

But Silver's main concern, as the *Cassandra* made her way north-westward towards the Bahamas, was to ingratiate himself with Captain England and his confederates. This was easy enough: John had an obliging way with him and was a first-rate seaman, while the captain seemed disposed to like him. He was also a fast learner. He quickly saw that Captain England's position rested upon his ability to lead his men to ample spoils. If he had failed to sniff out prizes, then the crew would have voted him down, and elevated another in his place. Worse still, if he had been suspected of any treachery, the buccaneers would have tipped him the black spot – after which he would have been best advised to look to his prayers!

Billy Bones was Captain England's first mate and sailing-master. Before he was drawn into piracy, Billy had skedaddled from his home in Connecticut and had shipped with a skipper plying an illegal trade between New England and the Spanish Indies. He had become a dab hand at navigation and chart-reading, but his good fortune ended when the British authorities seized his ship due north of Jamaica: he was sent to a penal settlement in Georgia for twenty years' hard labour, but managed to bribe his way out after six. He then found his way to New Providence where he met up with England; both men got on in fine style, perhaps due to their common maritime experience, for England had been mate of a sloop sailing out of Jamaica before he was taken by pirates and threw in his hand with them.

Next in England's hierarchy was Jethro Flint, who was quartermaster, responsible for crew discipline and the sharing-out of booty. Flint was the son of a Welsh dissenter, who had fled to Rhode Island to breathe freer air and had eventually moved to St Kitts in the Caribbean. Old Flint had perished during a French privateer's raid, but his son Jethro had got clean away and drifted into the company of buccaneers in the Leeward Isles. Flint was a cruel, cold, merciless man, who enjoyed torturing captives for the sport of it – something which Captain England could never tolerate, and which put the two men at loggerheads as often as not. He detested women, did Flint, and Silver swore he never saw him lay a finger on one, save in fury, in all the time he knew him; but his greatest hatred was reserved for the French, who had killed his father, and for the Spaniards – the dons – whom he associated with Papist plots and religious tyranny.

After the quartermaster there was the chief gunner, the boatswain, the coxswain, and the carpenter, as well as various armourers. Of Captain England's officers only the carpenter, a slow, tousled man called Tom Morgan, and Job Anderson, the boatswain, later served with Flint and then sailed aboard the *Hispaniola*. From the captain down to the armourers, these men were known as the 'Lords' and took a greater share of any spoils than the 'Commons', who were the ordinary seamen. Not that any great gulf of breeding separated the two groups, though the Lords tended to have greater seafaring skills than the Commons. But if the leadership of a pirate vessel faltered badly, then the Commons would try, as like as not, to overthrow the Lords.

Silver soon realised that such discipline as prevailed upon

the *Cassandra* depended upon continuing success, backed up by a strong arm and a quick tongue. During the long progress of the vessel to New Providence, he served as a foretopman, clambering expertly into the shrouds to attend to the sails and rigging. He became popular with his fellow Commoners, and also won praise from England and Bones for his diligence and hard work.

For Annette the voyage was a mixture of joy and misery. She clung happily to John whenever she could, but she took the news of her father's death as hard as only a passionate woman can. Though Silver prudently declined to spell out the details of Dubois' murder, Annette sensed that Flint was responsible and entertained a deep loathing for him in consequence. Since Flint regarded her as a veritable albatross, a portent of disaster for the ship, their antipathy was mutual and deep-seated. This hostility in turn put a barrier between Flint and Silver, of which the latter was more than uncomfortably aware.

It was, therefore, with some relief that John Silver saw the island of New Providence stand out upon the horizon, a green mound set in a sparkling sea, though tenanted, as he knew, with some of the bloodiest cut-throats on the Spanish Main. But, at the very least, he was approaching this hornet's nest as a free man.

14

{ To The Malabar Coast }

Captain England spoke plainly enough to the three-score men seated before him at the harbourside of New Providence, but Silver strained to hear every word.

'Brothers,' England was saying, 'I plan to take the *Cassandra* out of the Main for a while. The dons have put more warships into these waters of late, and Cartagena, Caracas and Havana bristle with guns. I don't care one jot for the dons, mark you, nor for the Frenchies, nor the Dutchmen neither, and King George's ships can go hang, say I, but that ain't a reason to risk us all dangling from some yardarm.'

Silver let his attention wander for a moment. He glanced at the buccaneers' faces as they listened to England's discourse. There was Billy Bones, nodding thoughtfully, as if in complete agreement; close to him was Anderson. A little further off Tom Morgan gazed vacantly at his boots, while to his left Flint's blotched, blue face seemed angry and contemptuous. As for the others, what a motley crew they were: Englishmen of all sorts, Scotch, Welsh, an Irishman or two, mulattos and quadroons, a renegade Spaniard, a couple of heavy Hollanders, a tall, pallid Finn, a disgraced Portuguese captain, some French privateers, a sprinkling of Yankees, and a fire-eating Baptist from Carolina.

Most appeared to be listening intently as England continued. 'Our last voyage, down to the Gulf of Paria, off Trinidad, was well nigh a disaster. The dons had two frigates lurking near Port of Spain, and we had to turn tail before we could make a killing. If we had not then raided Grenada and Barbados we should have had to return here empty-handed!'

There's a rum do for me, thought Silver; to have been brought up hating Spain and popery; and then to be saved from death because the dons sent two frigates to the Gulf of Paria! Why, God save His Most Catholic Majesty – this once, anyhow!

'So, my brethren,' England went on, 'I propose to sail for the East Indies, to the Coast of Malabar. There are rich pickings in Hindustan, so I've been told, for all the powers there are at daggers drawn, be they English, Portuguese or French, or even the Great Mogul himself. We can scoop up pearls and gold and spices as we please. We can raid Goa and Surat and Bombay. And if we burn our fingers, why, we can cruise off to Madagascar where gentlemen of fortune like ourselves do rule the roost!'

'Now, lads,' he said, lowering his voice a little, 'it ain't an adventure that'll tickle every man's fancy. There's some of you that won't take kindly to absenting yourselves from New Providence for maybe two years. It's up to you. You could be as rich as lords, or starving in some Portugoose's dungeon. Let's hear your voices!'

Flint spoke first, in his thin, hard voice. 'I'll not deny that you've a shrewd head on your shoulders, Cap'n England,' he said. 'But I see it this way. 'Tis odds on the government in London'll be pitching into the dons afore long. They be quarrelling something fearful over the dons stoppin' and searchin' English ships o' trade. Well, if there's a proper set to in the Main, we'll declare ourselves boney fidey privateers, and shout long live King George, an' that! In any event' – and here his thin lips were cruelly set – 'I ain't killed enough Spanish swabs for my likin' yet.'

Billy Bones was the next to speak. 'We all know Flint's little ways,' he said roughly, 'and he can suit himself. But I vote for Captain England. He's right, the heat is on in these waters and I don't hold with being boiled alive.'

A good many of the buccaneers shouted approval of these

sentiments. Flint, cold and withdrawn, shrugged his shoulders.

Silver's imagination was juggling with England's proposal. The Coast of Malabar, with its fabulous riches, its anarchy and opportunity, beckoned him like some oriental siren, distant, mysterious and seductive. But there was Annette to think of, and though there were other women-folk in the squalid shacks of New Providence to keep her company, would she forgive his leaving her for two years or more? Damn it, he thought, she'd forgive him soon enough if he came back laden with gold! Why, maybe they could quit New Providence and settle elsewhere, even return to England and live in style.

He stood up. 'Mates,' he cried. 'I'm for Cap'n England, and I'll tell you why. Because you're a fool, says you! No, because he makes good sense, says I. Things is getting tighter hereabouts, the dons are closing in, and our own Lords o' the Admiralty would like us dead and gone, and you may lay to that! So I'm for the Coast of Malabar, and damme if I won't bring back the Great Mogul's moustache pickled in a jar!'

Cheers and laughter greeted this jest, and Silver sat down well pleased with himself. Captain England then put his proposition to the vote, and close on two-score men raised their hands to say aye to the venture. Flint, it was clear, would not join them. Indeed, he began soon afterwards to canvass support for a series of raids upon the coast of Florida.

Two days later Captain England summoned his sup-porters aboard the *Cassandra,* there to sign articles, and also a round robin – which ensured that no man could be ac-cused, if things went wrong, of being the leader. Silver was one of the few who could properly write his name, and for the most part the pirates put their thumb-prints to the documents or laboriously scrawled their marks upon the smudged paper.

When this business was completed, Captain England spoke to them all, first snapping shut the lid of his snuff box and sneezing copiously.

'Now, men,' he said. 'We sail in four days' time, after we've got our victuals loaded and made sure the *Cassandra's* shipshape. You've all signed articles, but for those that don't read too well I'll sing out the main items: no women shall be brought aboard on this voyage; no playing of cards for money, neither; no duels to be fought, and no drinking of spirits below deck after midnight; the quartermaster will share out the plunder; all disputes shall be put before the Lords for arbitration.'

And so he continued, for well nigh fifty articles, until it seemed to Silver that there was little to choose between serving under the skull and crossbones or the Royal Navy's union jack! Not that England, or any other buccaneer, flaunted the black flag from his masthead; indeed the *Cassandra* carried the flags of all the chief maritime nations to run up as occasion arose – so that one day she could be masquerading under the red and gold of imperial Spain, and the next under the red, white and blue bars of the Dutch republic.

Silver saw that Captain England had a businesslike way of preparing for his enterprises, and respected him for it. For his part, England had apparently formed a favourable impression of John's seamanship and particularly of his understanding of a ship's rigging and tackle. As a consequence, he asked him to serve as boatswain aboard the *Cassandra*, and put this and other appointments before the crew for approval. Silver was voted in with scarcely a voice raised against him, an acclaim which both surprised and gratified him. Bones carried on as England's mate and sailing master. The new quartermaster, however, was the stocky old Portuguese captain, whom England reckoned would be handy should they wish to enter Goa or any of Portugal's trading stations along India's western coast. Job

Anderson came as chief armourer, Tom Morgan as carpenter, and one of the Hollanders was put in charge of the guns. The coxswain was a slight youth with lank black hair and such a mournful, hang-dog expression that he was known simply as 'Black Dog'.

Among the Commons was a number a men whom Silver privately marked down for careful watching on account of their potential as trouble-makers: one was a long man with yellow eyes named George Merry – an ill-fitting name for so dark-browed and scowling a ruffian; another was a violent, shambling Irishman called O'Brien who had been shipped out from Donegal to Barbados as a convict after being arrested for poaching after curfew.

Once the business of forming Captain England's crew was over, Silver hastened back to Annette. They were lodged in a small room at the rear of the long wooden building that served as a storehouse for the buccaneers of New Providence.

The keeper of the storehouse was a plump, alert woman of fifty named Margaret Bonny. Her man had left her thirteen years before on a voyage to raid the north east coast of Brazil; he had never returned, and Margaret Bonny now slept alone among the sacks of grain and dried horse beans, the keys of her office tied round her waist.

Silver pushed open the door of his room. It was late afternoon and the air inside was still so warm and sticky that it seemed possible to grasp it by the handful. The one small window, oblong and barred, was draped with a flannel petticoat secured by three nails to the rough timber frame. Rays of sunlight filtered through the flannel, but to Silver's eyes, accustomed to the violent and vivid colours outside, the room seemed very dark.

'Annette,' he said softly. Perhaps she was asleep, on the floor in the corner, lying on the straw-filled palliasse that served them for a marriage bed.

Yes, she was there. As his eyes grew used to the dim light

he could see her, face down upon the mattress, her long black hair falling diagonally across her shoulders and reaching the earthen floor, her blue cotton skirt pulled up above her calves.

Silver crossed the room in a couple of strides. He knelt down and gently stroked her hair; she was a rare woman, and no mistake; that neck, so smooth and brown beneath his finger tips.

'Annette,' he said again, louder than before. 'Annette, I'm all set to make our fortune. Wake up, my love, and hear my good tidings.'

To his surprise, Annette sat up before he had finished speaking. She had not been sleeping but crying, to judge from her eyes.

'I know your tidings, Johnny, all too well,' she said angrily. 'Margaret Bonny has told me. No one can keep secrets from her. You are leaving me. For the Indies, or some such place. You are sailing with Captain England, in four days' time. That is so, is it not? Do not dare to lie to me!'

'There's no lying hereabouts, my love,' said Silver. 'Captain England has made me his boatswain aboard the *Cassandra*. We're off to Malabar to scoop up pearls and spices.'

'Pearls and spices are no good to me! I want you here, to protect me and to love me. God knows what will become of me when you are gone – how shall I live? You fool!' she exclaimed, her voice rising towards hysteria, 'There will be other men perhaps, who will want to take me from you when you are gone. How shall I know that you will return? Margaret Bonny's man went away and never came back. Shall I end my days like Margaret, in this hovel?'

Startled by her vehemence, Silver stood up. 'Easy now. 'Tain't like that at all. If I don't sail with Captain England, 'tis odds on you *will* spend your days along o' me in this hovel. What sort of life is that?'

'A life with you, not without you!' interrupted Annette.

She seemed near to tears again, Silver thought. Before he could speak, she sprang to her feet and screamed at him, 'You took me from my home! You helped to kill my father! But for you I should be happy still, and well fed and clothed. You have made me a slut! I hate you!'

Suddenly beside himself with rage, Silver reached out, seized her by the shoulders, and shook her hard.

'You witch! You'd ruin everything. Coming uncalled for, like the devil at prayers, spittin' evil! Getting in my way!' He fought back an insane longing to smash her against the wall, like a rag doll, and then stamp on her body.

As he struggled for self-control, suddenly Annette was inside his arms. She was grasping him round the waist, the top of her head barely level with his chest. Kissing him through his damp shirt, and crying at the same time.

'How shall I live when you have gone? What shall I do? I am used to you now – I cannot be without you.'

Silver pushed her roughly from him. 'You'd better get used to one or two things more, then, Miss High'n Mighty! There ain't a man on this island as tells Long John what he may or mayn't do! As for women, well, they don't signify much among gentlemen o' fortune, and you may lay to that. You thank your stars I cares for you the way I do! Who finds you food and shelter? Me! Who talks to you, equal like, and no airs and graces? Me! And now you've the gall to scream at me for wanting to do proud by you, make you a lady o' leisure. I reckon you're the sort o' gal who'd take a handful o' gold from a man and then holler that one coin wasn't fresh minted!'

He paused, conscious that he had been shouting as loudly as if bellowing orders into a hurricane. The small room seemed crammed with the echoes of his voice.

Annette stared at him, mouth open; she had stopped crying.

Silver took a pace towards her, and said coldly and calmly, 'I thought you was smart. Smart as well as pretty.

Maybe you're only pretty after all, and if that's the way of it, then you may go hang, say I! But if you're a woman o' business after all, then you stay here and keep my nest warm till I comes back. If you can't do that, then, by thunder, you can peddle your carcass to Flint hisself – though what he'd do to it don't bear thinking on!'

At Flint's name, Annette's eyes dilated with fear; then she swiftly stooped and picking up a low wooden stool threw it hard at Silver's face.

Silver spun round to avoid the stool, but it caught him sharply above his right ear.

Hurt and infuriated, he lunged at Annette. She turned in terror, tripped, and sprawled onto the earthern floor. Silver swooped down her, entwined his fingers in her long hair and pulled her face round towards him. Suddenly he saw her for what she was, scarcely a grown woman, scared, humiliated and pitiful.

He bent his head to her face and kissed her lips and eyes. His rage slipped from him, ousted by his desire for her. He must be mad to think of leaving her, even for a day! How could he survive without the satin-smooth feel of her limbs, her soft rump, her breasts, her graceful shoulders – even her ridiculously short toes? What other woman could take her place? Now she was kissing him back. Digging her finger nails into his shoulders. Sobbing and laughing at the same time.

Silver picked her up and laid her gently on the straw mattress, pulling her skirt above her waist to reveal the brown flesh of her naked belly and thighs. He unbuckled his belt with his right hand and threw himself down beside her. The room that five minutes before had been cramped and squalid now became almost luxurious – languorous and aromatic.

Afterwards, as Annette nestled close to him, he told her, gently and kindly, of the arrangements he would make to keep her safe and happy until his return; how Margaret

Bonny would continue to lodge her and befriend her, how she would have a clear status in the piratical community as the wife of Captain England's boatswain.

For her part, Annette grudgingly came to terms with her unhappiness and fears – though Silver's powers of persuasion were strained to their limits in the process. At any rate they came to an understanding, early in their relationship, that allowed Long John the freedom to sail where fortune bade him. But it was no one-sided compact, for Silver felt bound to return to Annette whenever possible, and to live with her in between his buccaneering exploits as soberly as an alderman with his spouse. If the truth be known, it was a positive advantage for Silver to have Annette as a fixed star in his firmament, for she was to prove herself a shrewd manager of both his money and his property.

So it was, after reaching this painful agreement with his newly-wed wife, that John Silver began his career as a buccaneer. Four days after he had signed articles, he bade farewell to a tearful Annette and sailed from New Providence. The *Cassandra* made a brave picture as she set out to sea, her sails taut, the jolly roger flapping boldly overhead for once, the gold paint on her figurehead glinting in the sun. She was a snow, the largest of all two-masted vessels, and carried twenty-two guns. Captain England thought highly of her speed and seaworthiness, though Billy Bones had his doubts about her handiness in shoal water. She left New Providence with fifty men on board, which, though a great deal more than an innocent trading ship would have carried, was scarcely enough to man the gun-deck both port and starboard if by some misfortune she came to be attacked from both sides.

The *Cassandra's* voyage to the Malabar Coast was an eye-opener for Silver. After sailing across the Atlantic she approached the river Gambia on the west coast of Africa; there she took on fresh supplies in as orderly and law-abiding a fashion as an East Indiaman bound for Bombay.

But between the Gambia and Cape Corso on the Gold Coast, Captain England attacked every likely vessel of inferior strength. There were, to be sure, few pitched battles; mostly, the *Cassandra* fired a shot across the bows of her victims, having sailed close under a counterfeit flag, and then stripped them of all valuables.

In three months, England took eleven ships – vessels hailing from Brest and Rotterdam, Lisbon and Copenhagen, London and Cadiz. In the process, the *Cassandra* acquired a score of fresh recruits, for the crews of the captured ships were given the opportunity to throw in their lot with the pirates; those that refused were sent off in their shirt-tails aboard vessels picked clean as mutton bones.

After sailing boldly up to the fort of Cape Corso and then beating a prudent retreat from the guns of the Royal African Company, the *Cassandra* made off southwards. She followed the route marked out two and a half centuries before by Vasco da Gama and rounded Cape Agulhas, the southern tip of Africa, in heavy seas.

Provisions were running low and the men's tempers none too sweet by this time, but England was wary of resting on the Cape since the Dutch East India Company gave short shrift to pirates. So it was put to the vote, and passed, that they should make for Madagascar through the Mozambique Channel.

Silver had often heard of the pirate settlements on the island of Madagascar, where buccaneer chieftains lived like kings surrounded by slaves and concubines. The reality was something short of the fables he had been fed, for he found, disappointingly, that the pirate captains were not lodged in marble palaces, amid fountains and peacocks. All the same, the buccaneers had managed to carve out a handsome and useful sanctuary from whence they could strike at vessels trading in the Indian Ocean, or try their luck further afield in the Red Sea or the Persian Gulf.

In Madagascar the *Cassandra's* crew busied themselves

with careening the ship, collecting supplies, cutting wood, and taking on water. Then, leaving the security of Madagascar, and its liquor and whores too, Captain England set his course to the north-west, and, skirting the Seychelles, sailed for India. When he reached the Laccadive Isles, some two hundred miles from Calicut on the Malabar Coast, England dropped anchor off a fair-looking islet. Then he called his Lords to meet in council, so as to debate their next move. It was decided unanimously to make for the great spice-port of Calicut, to see what spoils, or what hazards, awaited them there.

15

❦ The Viceroy of the Indies ❧

From the sea, the ancient spice port of Calicut positively sparkled in the bright sunlight. As the *Cassandra* drew nearer, the crew could make out strange domes and minarets, and a number of great warehouses on the water-front. Flocks of birds whirled overhead, their tropical plumage dazzling to the eye, and a host of craft bobbed upon the waves – brigs and galleys, pinnaces and schooners, and the single-masted menchews that were much in evidence along the Malabar Coast.

Captain England peered eagerly through his telescope while Bones and the Portuguese quartermaster Gomes da Costa stood close beside him. Silver was in the main shrouds, relaying England's sailing instructions to the buc-caneers in the rigging and on deck. Below deck, the chief gunner, Van der Velde, crouched beside his men; the guns were run out, and the slow-matches smouldered ready to ignite them.

Suddenly England shut his telescope with a snap. He tapped Billy Bones smartly on the shoulder. 'Mr Bones,' he said, 'I'd be obliged if you'd look two points to starboard, beyond that Dutch galliot yonder, and tell me what you see.'

Bones squinted through his telescope. 'By the powers,' he said at last, his harsh voice pitched higher than usual with excitement. 'If that ain't rare! A troop of Moorish boats making out to sea. Pilgrims, I'll be bound.'

'Pilgrims!' said da Costa thickly. 'Is good tidings, pilgrims is. They off to Mecca. I see it before, up near islands of Diu. They sail for Red Sea; go to worship where prophet Mohammed born. Plenty rich.'

'Rich!' cried Captain England. 'Why, they'll be loaded down with treasures to lay in the holy places at Mecca! What's more, they'll needs carry a good sum of money to pay for their fare and lodgings throughout the journey.

'Lads!' he called to the crew, 'We're in luck! A few more hours and we'll be rolling in jewels and gold.'

A hubbub arose from the deck as the pirates digested this news, which was soon shouted down to the gunners below.

'Helmsman,' Captain England said quietly to the quadroon at the wheel, 'lay me alongside those Moorish boats and you'll have diamond pins to stick through your heathenish nose, and gold rings for your ears.'

As the *Cassandra* swung towards the pilgrims' vessels, Silver surveyed them closely through his eye-glass. They were strange boats, to be sure: a couple of caravels, a three-masted grab, a menchew, and four dhows. It seemed unlikely that they could keep tight together on the long voyage that faced them.

Now what was that? Way past the last dhow, which was already struggling to keep up. Surely Captain England had seen it too. Or was he mistaken? No, the line of pilgrim vessels must have obscured it from the sight of those on the quarterdeck.

His fears confirmed, Silver bellowed towards England, 'Cap'n, there's an armed brigantine a-tailing of them, and she's flying the union jack, by thunder!'

Why, of course, he thought quickly, he'd heard tell often enough of the bargain struck between the East India Company and the Great Mogul: in exchange for certain trading rights John Company had undertaken to protect Moslem pilgrims on their sea journey to Arabia; they had to be protected not only against European buccaneers but against Indian pirates – of whom the most fearsome was the legendary Angria.

Now Captain England was beckoning him to come at once to the quarterdeck. Other Lords were scrambling there too; Van der Velde climbed up through the hatches, followed by Job Anderson, and Tom Morgan and Black Dog were scurrying aft from the bows.

'Gentlemen,' said Captain England, 'Mr Silver's right, we've an awkward customer to deal with out there. That brigantine may carry more guns than us, and she'll be looking for trouble, I'll be bound.' He dug deep into his snuff box. 'Well, how say you, shall we turn about?'

'You've no worry, mynheer, sir,' said Van der Velde, 'my boys is ready. We blow them out of water!' And he flourished a brawny fist well nigh as big as a roundshot.

'My pudding-headed Dutch friend's right, Cap'n,' said Silver, jovially enough. ' 'Tis like as not those pot-bellied Company men'll be snoozing below decks, blown out with wine and dainties. We'll hoist the union jack and sidle alongside 'em and shiver their timbers with one broadside. 'Twill be as easy as taking eggs from a throstle, and you may lay to that.'

And so it was agreed. The *Cassandra* tagged behind the pilgrim flotilla, as innocent as a maid out for a stroll on the sabbath. The union jack fluttered from her masthead, and to any careless eye she looked quite devoid of menace. But aboard her, England's buccaneers were ready for action; they had eaten the rations issued to them in anticipation of a battle, and their weapons lay close to hand.

After an hour and a half, the *Cassandra* drew close enough to the brigantine to be hailed from her decks.

'Ahoy! What vessel are you?' came the shout across the water.

Captain England put his hands to either side of his mouth and called out, as bold as brass, 'The *Cassandra*, bound out of Madras with a cargo of silks. We're making for Bombay, and then home to London. Who are you?'

'The armed Indiaman *Mercury*, bound for Surat to pick up more pilgrims, and then across to the Gulf of Aden,' came the reply.

'You've a good breeze for such noble work,' yelled England. 'God keep us both from pirates hereabouts!'

Silver watched, fascinated, as the distance between the two vessels narrowed. Now the *Cassandra* was almost level with the *Mercury,* and he could see that a few of the company's men were waving cheerfully at them from the shrouds.

Suddenly England blew two shrill blasts upon a whistle, and at the signal the guns on the *Cassandra*'s starboard side fired a ragged broadside. Ragged or not, the vessel rocked with the recoil of the guns, while the men below decks let out a fierce cry of triumph and began to sponge out and reload the cannon for another volley.

Acrid smoke swirled round Silver, obscuring his view of the Indiaman. Now it was thinning.

'By God, we've shot away her mainmast!' shouted Bones.

There was the *Mercury,* her mainmast trailing absurdly over her port side, the square-rigged topsail dragging deep in the water.

Even as Silver took in the situation, he saw the ship yaw round and present her stern to the *Cassandra*. She was clearly unmanageable – perhaps for several hours, until her crew cut away the snapped-off mast and released her from the crippling impediment.

Two more – no, three – explosions came from the *Cassandra*'s gun deck. Van der Velde must have seen that some cannon aft still bore on the *Mercury*'s stern. One of the roundshot splashed into the sea beyond the vessel; another Silver lost sight of; but the third, by luck or good gun-setting, smashed into the timbers of the stern just above the water line.

Silver glanced at Captain England, who had been steadily stuffing his nostrils with snuff during the encounter; with a great sneeze, that was mingled with a cry of exultation, he cleared his overflowing nose.

'We've got her, lads! She's done for!' England cried. 'Damn me, if her rudder ain't been smashed off its pintles too. She's a danger to us no more. After those Moorish boats! We can take them at will now!'

The *Cassandra* crammed on every available inch of sail, and closed in on the pilgrim boats. One by one they surrendered, meek as lambs. Silver and Bones took the long boat and its crew to plunder them at leisure. Their occupants huddled away from the buccaneers as they ripped sea-chests apart and cut through sacks to discover their contents. Then, with rough hands, the pilgrims were stripped of their valuables, and cursed and kicked if they resisted.

After a few hours, the *Cassandra's* deck was heaped with booty – silver coin, precious religious ornaments, silks, tapestries, food and drink, any item that was at all desirable or useful.

Silver also hauled aboard the Moslem skipper of the three-masted grab, who knew a smattering of English. At first the skipper would give them no information of other shipping in the vicinity. Then, between them, Bones and Silver broke him down. Billy drew his cutlass and, while Captain England turned away his head in distaste, swore to cut off the skipper's toes, one at a time, unless he gave them good and fruitful tidings. John Silver, by way of contrast, appeared reasonable and kind, slapping the quaking Moslem on the back, and offering him pannikins of rum and titbits of salted pork – all of which the poor man refused in righteous religious indignation.

Finally, he gave in, and gabbled away in a wonderful brogue from which the buccaneers plucked out one choice piece of information. England banished his qualms at Bones's bullying of the Moslem and slapped his thigh for glee.

'Boys,' he said to the rest of the Lords, 'here's good fortune indeed! Three hundred miles north of here is Goa, held by the Portuguese and as bustling a port as I've set eyes on. This Moor has babbled on about the "Viceroy of the Indies". Now, it's my belief that he don't mean some Captain-General of the Portuguese hereabouts, but that a vessel of such a name is cruising in these waters – maybe leaving Goa for Sofala or Mozambique and then round the Cape for Lisbon.'

The Portuguese quartermaster Gomes da Costa butted in, speaking excitedly, his few words of English tripping over each other. 'This ship I know,' he said. 'Is called *Viceroy of the Indies*. It take money, things, from Goa to other colonies Portugal have in India.'

'A pay ship, by the powers,' exclaimed Silver. 'Packed to the scuppers with pieces of eight, doubloons and the like. 'Twill set us up as gentlemen of leisure, every man aboard.'

Da Costa struggled to speak again. 'It no easy,' he said. 'It big galleon, two decks of guns each side. Maybe sixty guns. We no shoot it to pieces. It shoot us to pieces, more like.'

'Why, Gomes,' said Bones harshly, 'we ain't dumb creatures for the slaughter. We'll fly the Portuguese flag, and you can speak the damned lingo and talk us aboard. Though what you'll say beats me.'

'Details, Mr Bones. Mere details,' said Captain England airily. 'We Lords will devise some deuced clever stratagem, I've no doubt. Meanwhile we put it to the men, and make full speed toward Goa. Agreed?'

The Lords agreed heartily enough, as did the crew when the proposal was duly put before them.

The *Cassandra* made her way to the north through pleasant seas, while the quartermaster divided up the booty from the pilgrim boats. In the share-out John Silver acquired some fine silks as well as a small sackful of gold coin and a number of trinkets. He also kept a bright green caged parrot that had been wrenched away from some unfortunate woman on one of the dhows. He showed a tender side to his character in the way he treated this bird, feeding it bits of sugar and tasty morsels, and talking to it as if it was a human being. The parrot could screech out a sentence or two from the Koran, but Silver soon taught it some good, strong English oaths to add to its vocabulary. This bird was, of course, the same 'Captain Flint' that sailed aboard the *Hispaniola* – though it got that name later, Silver simply calling it 'Mahommed' when first he took possession of it.

But the 'pieces of eight', for which the parrot was later to show such a passion, were stowed away aboard the *Viceroy of the Indies* somewhere to the north of the *Cassandra*. How could the pirates get their hands on them? Silver thought long and hard over this conundrum, until at last a plan formed in his mind. He made Captain England, da Costa, Bones and others of the Lords privy to his thinking. At first, England doubted the wisdom of John's scheme, but he argued his case as persuasively as he was able, and by the time the vessel drew near Goa they had reached agreement.

But where would they find the *Viceroy of the Indies?* Perhaps she was already far out in the Indian Ocean. Bones brandished his cutlass once more at the unfortunate Moslem skipper, who had been kept aboard as a possible interpreter, and the poor man rolled his eyes and squeaked out all he knew. The chances were, it seemed, that the ship had not quit Goa – the *Cassandra* might yet intercept her.

And so it proved, but only just. As the *Cassandra* dropped anchor off Goa, England and his men had no notion whether or not their prize had eluded them. At all events, they were ready: the red and green flag of Portugal flew from the masthead, and across the stern hung a fresh-painted nameboard bearing the proud legend *Magellan*.

For two days a variety of craft passed to and from the port. It was not until noon on the third day of the *Cassandra*'s vigil that the *Viceroy of the Indies* emerged from the bustle and stir of Goa. At once, Captain England weighed anchor and prepared for an encounter out at sea.

On came the Portuguese galleon, the gun ports on her two decks open wide, the full spread of her sails billowing beneath the blue skies.

'If once she gets away from us, we're done for,' said Captain England quietly. 'We'll not even be able to snap at her heels.'

'Belay such talk, cap'n,' said Silver. 'With Gomes here dressed in his fancy garb, and me beside him, you've nought to fear.'

Da Costa stood awkwardly upon the quarterdeck; he wore a heavy coat of purple cloth festooned with braid and insignia; a scarlet sash ran diagonally across his chest, and his thick legs were stuffed into white silk breeches and cotton stockings; square-toed black shoes pinched his feet. A long, dark cloak covered this finery from the view of the Portuguese galleon. Silver stood close to him, dressed in green breeches and an open-necked cream shirt; his hair was tied back like a gentleman, and he carried a pistol and a sword in his belt.

Closer and closer came the galleon as the *Cassandra* steered to meet her. At last she was in hailing distance. Silver nudged da Costa who bawled in Portuguese, 'Greetings, where are you bound?'

'To Daman!' came the reply. 'Then on to Diu, and our stations in the Persian Gulf.'

'May the Lord be praised,' shouted da Costa. 'We are the *Magellan,* bound out of Macao on the China coast. But we carry on board the Lieutenant-Governor of Macao and his secretary. They must be taken to our colony at Diu with all speed.'

'We know nothing of this,' came the reply from the *Viceroy of the Indies*. 'No orders have reached us to this effect.'

'As like as not. We heard that the caravel bearing the Governor-General's instructions was sunk by the Dutch off Malacca.'

'No such news has reached us. Our relations with the Dutch are cordial enough.'

'Enough of this,' roared da Costa. 'Let the Lieutenant-Governor explain in his own words. We'll send a boat to you straightaway.'

'As you wish. But remember we have two hundred and fifty men aboard, and we are on our guard.'

One of the *Cassandra's* boats was lowered into the water. Da Costa, who had thrown off his cloak and perched a three-cornered hat, frothy with lace, upon his head, sat stiffly at the prow, with Silver beside him. Six men, especially picked mulattos and quadroons, bent over the oars. The boat drew alongside the Portuguese galleon.

Da Costa clambered up the side, with Silver at his heels, and followed by one of the boat's crew, an ex-slave from Brazil who spoke fluent Portuguese.

As he stepped on to the deck da Costa was greeted by a ship's officer flanked by two rows of blue-jacketed troops.

'Welcome aboard, Your Excellency.' His tone sounded cordial to Silver, though perhaps reserved.

'May I present my credentials to your captain?' said da Costa, almost casually.

They were led into a heavy-beamed, ornate cabin, draped with Persian tapestries and encrusted with gilt.

A slim man of about forty years rose to greet them. His uniform was beautifully tailored, and he wore a powdered wig.

The officer who had escorted them hovered at the door.

'Greetings, Your Excellency,' said the captain. 'May I see proof that your mission is all you say it is?'

'Of course, captain,' da Costa replied. 'My secretary, Ferdinand Diaz, has the necessary papers.' He beckoned to Silver to approach the table where the Portuguese captain sat.

Silver bent over as if to clear a space on the table's surface. Then in one completely unexpected movement he seized the captain's throat with his left hand and pointed the muzzle of his pistol at his temple with the other.

Behind him there was a muffled cry of alarm as the Portuguese officer who had welcomed them aboard was felled by a huge blow from the Brazilian negro.

The captain's eyes stuck out from his head as John Silver's great ham of a hand gripped his throat; his wig was comically tilted over his right eye.

'Gomes,' said John. 'Tell this swab that unless he does as I say I'll blow out his brains and smear them over his grand tapestries!'

The captain croaked feebly in assent as da Costa translated this delicate message.

'Right you are,' said John. 'This is what you must do, *senhor* captain. Call in your first officer and order him to load your treasure chests onto the ship's boat alongside. Other boats will come from our ship to take what that one can't carry. When we've took what we want, you, *senhor*, will take a trip back with us to the *Cassandra* and, by the powers, you'll be smiling fit to bust the whole way, or I'll feed you to the sharks! But if you play our game, who knows, we may cut you in on a share of the gold.'

When the Portuguese captain heard this he flapped his hands despairingly.

'If so be,' Silver continued relentlessly, 'our powdered monkey here can't think too well on account of my pressing on his windpipe, I'll say this to help clear his head. Tell your officers that t'other ship, our ship, being a lighter craft, has got orders to deliver the pay-money, while the *Viceroy* here is ordered to Ormuz, at the mouth of the Gulf o' Persia, to squash Arab pirates thereabouts.'

Once this message had been translated the captain seemed relieved, almost grateful. Silver released his grip on him and sat down at his side, his cocked pistol resting on the captain's kidneys, below the level of the table.

Between them, da Costa and the Brazilian hauled the unconscious Portuguese officer behind a rich red curtain, and then sent word to the ship's first officer.

While waiting for the arrival of the first officer, Silver, though outwardly calm, sweated at the prospect of failure. But one mistake, and he and his two companions would be the victims of Portuguese justice which, according to rumour, was none too gentle.

In the event, his fears were not realised. The Portuguese first officer, a red-faced, stout, elderly man, heard his captain through, merely raising his eyebrows from time to time, and then clattered off to carry out his orders.

The buccaneers could hardly believe their eyes as the *Cassandra*'s long-boat and her two smaller ship's boats plied back and forth carrying chests and casks full of silver and gold coin. Silver was sensible enough to leave one fifth part of the treasure still aboard the *Viceroy of the Indies,* as a token of good faith, so to speak.

As the long-boat drew alongside the *Cassandra* for the last time, bearing da Costa, Silver and the Portuguese captain, Captain England leant triumphantly over the side, and the buccaneers about him waved and hurrahed.

Within minutes the *Cassandra* was pulling away from her still unknowing victim, dipping her false flag in courtly farewell.

An hour later they were clean away, with a good head wind, and the sea miles between them and the *Viceroy of the Indies* steadily lengthening.

16

❦ *Return to New Providence* ❦

Bones looked up from the bags of coin heaped on the floor of Captain England's cabin, and laughed short and sharp.

'I reckon we've scooped up near enough one hundred and twenty thousand pounds-worth of gold and silver,' he said. 'Add to that our pickings from the pilgrim boats, and from those vessels we caught off the west coast of Africa, and it's more like one hundred and forty thousand we've got aboard. Do you figure it out likewise, Gomes?'

'Yes. Is right. Same as my tally anyhow,' replied da Costa, flashing his gold-filled teeth in a rare smile.

John Silver made a rapid calculation. As a Lord he could claim one and a half the share of an ordinary deck hand. Why, close on three thousand pounds would be his! The size of the sum stunned him. It was an unbelievable amount, enough to set him up for life in the grandest style – even to buy him a seat in Parliament if he had a mind.

'Gentlemen,' England was saying, in that refined tone he adopted from time to time, 'we've done middling well. But we can do better. I propose we strike off north-westwards to harry shipping passing through the Gulf of Aden.'

Silver stirred uncomfortably. 'There's no call for more plunder,' he said. 'We're rolling in riches, every man jack. I'm for making for home, leisurely like. Maybe we can make a killing or two on the way. If not, we've still got our sea-chests packed with valuables.'

'I'm with John here,' said Bones quickly. 'Let's get back to the Main, and spend what we've taken. Set the old *Cassandra* up with new guns maybe, take it easy for a while.'

'No!' said England vehemently. 'You're plain wrong.

You can't see further than your feet. We can sail home with
threefold our present haul if you'll only heed me. Van der
Velde, I know, thinks likewise.'

' 'Tis best the lads make up their minds on this, Cap'n,'
Silver said tactfully. 'This is how it should be done, or I'm
much mistook.'

The congress that followed was raucous, yet serious
enough and well-argued too, after a fashion. The upshot
was that England found only six men to back his cause,
among them the chief gunner Van der Velde. It was clear
that all authority had slipped from England's grasp, and
there was no option but to depose him straightaway. Silver
and Bones took him the bad tidings.

Bones spoke first, his Yankee accent harder than ever,
perhaps from a sense of the occasion.

'The men have voted you out of office, Captain England,
and they've chosen me in your place. You'll oblige us all by
accepting this here decision.'

England shrugged an elegant shoulder, but his long
fingers tapped nervously on his snuff box.

Silver spoke next. 'We ain't hard men, cap'n,' he said.
'There's no call for blood-letting. Let's say this is our
"Glorious Revolution", same as when Dutch William
pitched that papist swab King James off the throne back in
'88.'

'What do you propose to do, then?' asked England wearily.

'We're sailing for Madagasky,' said Bones. 'Before we
gets there we'll drop you and your confederates off at
Mauritius. If that don't suit, you can choose between
keel-hauling and a walk off the end of a plank.'

'You'll be given food and firearms,' cut in Silver, 'and
damme if the lads ain't agreed you shall have a copy of the
Good Book, which I calls handsome. You'll be safe and
sound there, which is more'n we'll be on the long haul back
to Providence.'

'It seems I have a rare bargain indeed,' said England, with the merest irony in his voice. 'Well, so be it.'

'There's just one item John's forgot to mention,' said Bones. 'For the safekeeping of you, that Dutch gunner, and the few toads that think like you, you'll be locked in your cabin until such time as we reach Mauritius. We don't want any joker a-cutting of your throat, now do we?'

And so Captain England was cast down, without any of the violence which often occurred when buccaneers fell out. Two weeks later the *Cassandra* marooned him and his allies, together with the unfortunate Portuguese skipper, on the island of Mauritius, some seven hundred miles due west of Madagascar. It was a civil enough occasion, with little emotion shown by either side except for the Dutch gunner Van der Velde, who shook his fist and cursed loud enough to deafen God and all His angels as the boat pulled away from the shore and towards the *Cassandra*.

Since French East Indiamen used Mauritius as a watering station, it was likely, Silver told himself, that Captain England would be picked up by one of them. It was therefore something of a surprise to him to learn a couple of years later that England and his fellow maroons had fashioned a boat out of staves and odd scraps of wood and had managed to reach Madagascar. There they subsisted on the charity of their fellow buccaneers, who, after all, had no grudge to bear against them.

The *Cassandra,* naturally enough, made better time to Madagascar than Captain England. There the crew took on fresh supplies, and lived like kings for a while. They were the envy of their brethren upon the island, and the latter did all they could to part them, by fair means or foul, from their wealth. Some of the pirates lost their entire fortunes on one throw of dice, others frittered money away on women and drink, and three at least were murdered for their gold.

John Silver learnt a hard lesson on Madagascar, for

within a month he had scarcely twelve hundred pounds left. Gambling for money, you might think, ill became his natural sagacity, for though he was prepared to gamble with fate – having taken a searching look at the odds – gaming was decidedly more chancy. But gamble he did, as if he had to burn some fever out of his bones. Once the fit had passed, however, he cut his losses and kept his purse tight shut.

At last the *Cassandra* quit Madagascar, lighter of treasure but heaver with supplies, and marketable commodities like coral and ambergris. She was also packed to the scuppers with men, for the buccaneers of Madagascar had clamoured to be taken on board so lucky and prosperous a vessel. Among those recruited was a new chief gunner to replace the marooned Dutchman; the newcomer was blue-chinned, broad-backed, and the possessor of a wonderfully large pair of ears; his name was Israel Hands, and though his brain did not work as quickly as it might, he was a patient and expert gunner, who could be relied upon to make every shot tell.

Bones being captain after England's overthrow, da Costa was made up to mate and John Silver took over as quartermaster – an office well suited to his many-sided character.

Seven months later the *Cassandra* reached New Providence once more, amid scenes of wild excitement and rejoicing. There Silver was reunited with Annette and, to his surprise, handed a two year old son to dandle!

He stared long and hard at this prodigy. 'He ain't a deal like me, Annette, my love,' he concluded.

'Nonsense!' said Annette firmly. 'He's got your fair hair, Johnny, and he has your knowing way about him. Anyhow, I am the one to say whose son he is.'

She had become more resolute in his absence, Silver noted with mild surprise. Maybe having a child had given her a new sense of purpose.

As Silver himself slowly became used to fatherhood, he

found he also had to take account of Annette's insistence that since he had returned with well over a thousand pounds in coin he should take her to a more respectable habitation than New Providence.

'No doubt,' she said, 'you will be off on your travels before many months have passed. But that is no comfort to me or your son. We cannot stay here for ever. The other women disgust me, and, who knows, the settlement could be wiped out at any moment!'

Now John Silver could put the fear of God into any man living at one moment and talk the birds out of the trees at the next, but his wife became more than a match for him when she set her mind to it. In any case, he soon reckoned that it was better that Annette should sit tight upon his money than mope and fret upon New Providence. So they upped and left the island on a schooner bound on more or less lawful trade with Jamaica. There John settled Annette and young John at Montego Bay, where he bought the lease on a small tavern, the Porto Bello, and deposited nine hundred pounds with the Royal Bank of Jamaica.

For three years or so John lived at Montego Bay, puffed his tobacco, ate well, and sired another son, Philippe – named after Annette's dead father.

But such a life was insufficient for him. He began to seek out seafaring company in other taverns near the harbour, to hear tales of treasure lost and found and of less fortunate acquaintances strung up at Execution Dock.

It was, in short, not surprising that Silver should have drifted back into piracy. It was but a small step from thinking like a buccaneer to once more becoming one.

He was seated quietly in the Porto Bello inn one evening, enjoying the wild conversation of those around him, when he felt a claw-like grip on his shoulder and heard a sneering voice say, 'Well, if it ain't Long John, though you've put on a stone or two since we sailed aboard the old *Osprey*.'

Silver leapt to his feet. 'Pew!' he cried. 'Gabby Pew, by thunder!'

'The same,' said Pew, his eyes sharp as needles. 'And well set up an' all, since you was hauled off from Bridgetown gaol a while back.'

'I heard tell you wriggled out of prison pretty briskly yourself, Gabby,' said Silver.

'Ah well,' said Pew, 'I ain't never been one to stop at sheddin' a drop of some swab's blood. But that ain't here nor there.'

He settled himself down by Silver and said coaxingly, 'I'm doin' well enough, John, But how about yourself? I heard how you'd hauled up your anchor at New Providence after you and Billy Bones come back from the Indies three or four year ago.'

Quickly, as if he had insufficient time to express himself, Silver said, 'And a smarter thing I never done afore, or since. Why, I hadn't been away more'n a six month, and bless me if the whole place ain't gone up in smoke like a bonfire come Guy Fawkes day!'

'Well, we heard news o' that, John. 'Tain't a pretty tale.'

'The Royal Navy, Gabby. A squadron on 'em. Uninvited, you might say. They sank th'old *Cassandra* out in the bay, while she was at anchor with scarcely a man aboard. Then they burnt down every shack and building ashore. Them brethren as weren't killed or captured, took off into the bush. Billy Bones was one o' them, it seems, though where he is now beats me.'

'Let me tell you, John. I've heard more'n you it seems, though 'twill make you green with envy I reckon. The navy men quit New Providence within three weeks. They fancied they'd smoked out the hornet's nest right enough. Well, next thing, who should come a-breezin' back with a hold full o' loot, but our friend Flint. After a while Billy and th'others come a-skulking out o' the woods. Ragged they was, and near to starving. They runs to Flint like beggar children to some rich benefactor!'

'Flint ain't no particular friend of mine,' said Silver.

'Well, he has a cruel streak about him, that's for sure,' replied Pew. 'But he's a devilish talent for huntin' down dago gold, has Flint. Be that as it may, he comes ashore and he says to Billy Bones, Israel Hands, Anderson, and a good number of those that had berthed aboard the *Cassandra,* "Mates, I'll let you throw in your lots with me. You won't be sorry." And glad they was to do it. I joined up four months later, when the *Walrus* put in to St Kitts. We've had a rare old time since, John, though once or twice I thought we'd end up with the noose around our necks.'

'But this is nought but talk, Gabby,' said Silver coolly. 'I've heard bits and bobs of this afore. So now I know that Billy and the others is with Flint. What's that to me?'

'Only this,' said Pew. 'Flint's ship, the *Walrus,* is lyin' in the bay, and Flint hisself is dead drunk hereabouts, I'll be bound. Now, we badly wants a quartermaster aboard. The last one got the wrong side o' Flint and ended up below hatches with his belly ripped out. But more than that, we needs a steady hand like yours, for Flint's too partial to the rum, and poor Bill's goin' the same way, I reckon. I'm bosun aboard the *Walrus,* and I'll speak up for you. Join us, John, there's brave times ahead!'

For a minute Silver wavered, weighing the odds. Flint bore him no love, he knew that. Then he decided. Within the hour he had braved Annette's fury, dug out a brace of pistols, and thrown a pouch of coin into his hastily packed sea-chest. Soon he was helping Pew and a couple of others to row a boat out into the bay, where, invisible in the darkness, lay the *Walrus.*

17

❦ *With Captain Flint* ❧

The *Walrus* was a fine vessel, right enough. Silver saw that even as he climbed aboard. Daybreak confirmed his opinion. She had been stripped of excess superstructure, and could be expected to outsail all but the fastest craft on the Main. Before Flint laid hands on her, she had been a Spanish frigate, prowling the Straits of Florida, north of Havana. Flint had boarded her when half her crew were below decks dying of fever. After hanging the other half from the yardarms, he had decided to keep her, having smoked out the fever and scrubbed her decks with raw spirits. She carried thirty-eight guns, and had one hundred and three-score men aboard.

Shortly after Silver reached the *Walrus,* Flint was hauled up the side dead drunk, his face a ghastly mottled blue and grey. Billy Bones was with him, sweat standing out on his sun-burnt forehead; he, too, was the worse for drink, but he still recognized Silver and clasped him warmly, though a trifle clumsily; then he staggered aft to sleep off the rum.

By noon next day, Flint had sobered up sufficiently to bawl for more rum and to cuff his dumb servant Darby McGraw for not anticipating his wishes. Then he squinted with some distaste at Silver, and cursed him for a fool for joining up with Captain England before the *Cassandra* set sail for India. But Bones and Pew took Silver's part, reminding Flint of the high reputation John had won upon that voyage.

So, with a bad grace, Flint agreed to Silver serving as quartermaster. No doubt John helped this decision by tossing a handful of gold pieces into Flint's lap as, so he said, an investment and a token of esteem.

They were a fine set of villains, were Flint's men. Flint himself was a coldblooded butcher, with a good nose for a prize when sober. Billy Bones had become more ruthless after Flint had rescued him from the ruins of New Providence; now made up to mate and sailing master, he was as apt to cut a man down as wish him good day. Pew's cruelty had found full expression in Flint's service. Israel Hands, Job Anderson, Black Dog, Tom Morgan and the rest were bound together in a grisly compact of treachery, spilt blood and tainted money. There was a runaway surgeon, too, a dainty Yankee, fresh out of Harvard, and at first sight as delicate as a girl. Among the deck hands, Silver noticed, with some regret, George Merry and O'Brien, and also an uncertain, timorous, ex-farm labourer from Devon named Ben Gunn.

John Silver was in his early thirties when he joined Flint's crew aboard the *Walrus*, though in speech and bearing he seemed somewhat older. Certainly authority came easily to him, and, though he rarely needed to raise his voice in anger, men jumped to do his bidding. This was never more true than when he served with Flint. Perhaps the reason for his power over men as rough and ready as Flint's lay in his unfathomable personality. You never knew where you were with Long John, and thus strove to keep on the right side of him; whereas Flint's morose and sadistic qualities were predictable, though violent and intermittent, and Pew's sly cruelty was a constant factor of which to take account. Flint himself was wary of Silver; perhaps, deep down, afraid. Bones indeed became both jealous and wary of John during the years they spent together on the *Walrus,* and this no doubt accounted for his subsequent determination to keep the map of Kidd's Island, and himself, out of Silver's clutches.

Not that these dark undercurrents marred the early successes of the *Walrus*. John Silver joined her at a propitious time, during the early years of the War of the

Austrian Succession, when Britain was fighting Spain and France wherever the interests of these powers overlapped. The Spanish Main, of course, was one area of conflict, and there was much to play for – trade, both legal and contraband, the privilege of supplying slaves to the sugar islands, the possibility of snatching cargoes of precious metals, the profitability of sacking coastal settlements.

Flint, naturally enough, leapt at the chance of harming Spanish power, 'doing down the damned papist dagoes' as he put it. So, bold as bold, he sailed the *Walrus* into Kingston harbour and demanded a commission to operate as a privateer.

It was an awkward moment when Flint, accompanied by Bones and Silver, was ushered into the council room at Government House.

His Excellency the Governor, General Sir Richard Courtenay, red-faced and apoplectic, sat at a great polished table impatiently drumming his fingers on the shimmering surface. A keen-faced secretary sat on one side, while on the other a naval commodore was writing some dispatches in a bold, meticulous hand.

The Governor spoke first, barely attempting to disguise his contempt.

'Well, ah, Mr Flintstock?'

'Flint, Your Excellency,' whispered the secretary. 'Flint.'

'Quite so,' said the Governor irritably. 'Well, sir, you want a privateering commission, do ye, Mr Flintstock?'

Flint, whose dark face had worn a scowl of peculiar intensity ever since he had set foot in the grounds of Government House, took a step forward, his cutlass jangling at his heels.

Silver said quickly, stifling the oath that was bubbling in Flint's throat, 'That's about it, sir. We wants to sail under the good old union jack and do our country proud.'

'It is my view,' said the Governor, his blue eyes bulging, 'that I would do our country proud by having the three of you court-martialled and shot within the hour. But that's by the by. Times are changed and we have instructions from London to cut our cloth accordingly.'

'Now see here,' exclaimed Bones angrily, 'we ain't no beggars crawling for favours. We've enough powder and shot aboard to sink all the vessels out there in the harbour and to shoot the feathers off your damned hat into the bargain.'

'What my friend Mr Bones is trying to say, sir,' interposed Silver coolly, 'is that you'll find us fine fighters and a strength to your highness's elbow.'

The Governor looked long and hard at John. Suddenly he said, 'What's your name, sir?'

'Silver, sir; John Silver.'

'Silver, eh? Silver-named and silver-tongued, eh, sir, eh? Well, Mr Silver, I have but two things to say to you and to your friends here. The first is that I'd rather do business with a pack of wolves than with you. The second is that I don't, alas, have the choice. With the Spaniards and the French at my throat in these waters I need every vessel I can lay hands upon. But let me tell you this. If you and your fellow sea-robbers step out of line just once I'll have you crushed like cockroaches – and good riddance!'

As the Governor's words echoed round the dark-panelled room Silver said, 'Thank you kindly, sir. Them's uplifting sentiments, and I can't say fairer than that.'

Flint spoke next, his few words slurred and at the same time menacing.

'Well, God damn you, do we get it or not?'

'The privateering commission, Your Excellency,' prompted the secretary.

There was a slience while the Governor once more drummed noisily upon the table. The naval commodore, Silver noticed, had stopped writing and was minutely regarding the three of them as if he wished to commit every detail of their appearance to memory. For the first time since he had entered the room, Silver grew uncomfortable under this close scrutiny.

Mercifully the Governor broke the silence by saying dismissively, 'Report back tomorrow morning at ten o'clock. Commodore Mason here will tell you your duties.'

Outside the sun burnt down relentlessly. Flint wiped the sweat from his face with a dirty green kerchief.

'Grog,' he said. 'I wants a pannikin or two, mates, and no mistake.'

'Why, cap'n,' said Silver, 'don't tell me that His Royal Excellency Governor Turkey-cock has put the shakes on such a man as you. Now if it's just the thirst that troubles you, that's easy settled. Come here, boy!'

He beckoned to a water seller who stood among the crowd of street vendors that crowded round the gates of Government House. The boy approached, his wooden buckets dangling from the yoke across his shoulders.

'Fine spring water, gen'lemen. One penny a cup.'

'A penny a cup,' said Billy Bones. 'I ain't a-paying that, 'tis daylight robbery. Come here, boy! Spring water indeed! Dredged out o' Kingston harbour more like!'

He made to grab the urchin, but Silver said quickly, 'Easy, Billy! We're boney fidey privateers now, or near enough. We've no call to play at piracy upon the high roads of Jamaica instead. Here, boy!' He flipped a coin at the water seller's feet. 'Three cups for me and my mates, and there's a bit extra for you, too.'

The boy's white teeth flashed as he smiled up at John. Bones and Silver drank thirstily enough, but Flint took one mouthful of water and spat it straight into the dust.

'Rat's bile,' he said fiercely. 'Grog, that's what I want, not this muck!'

Well, Flint had his way, and within an hour or two was bawling out 'Fifteen Men on a Dead Man's Chest' in a dockside tavern and cursing those customers unfortunate enough to be sitting near him.

Silver drew on his pipe and looked meaningfully at Bones, who was deep in drink himself.

'Billy,' he said quietly, 'this won't do. Flint gets soused in rum too easy. Why, back there in Government House he could scarce tack two words together, and now he's roaring threats at all and sundry. The navy officers won't take kindly to working with such as him, and you may lay to that!'

Bones's face clouded for a moment as he searched for the right words. At length he said, 'You're right, John, but only up to a point. Get Flint to sea and he'll snap out of this fit and buckle down to business as right as rain. 'Tis kicking his heels on shore that'll be the ruin of him.'

'Maybe,' replied Silver. 'But I've seen him drink something terrible at sea an' all. Some of us have got to keep our heads, Billy, for when the going gets tricky. Now, I can do it, but can you do it? Bless me if you ain't a-going the same way as Flint, swilling rum and hollering when you should be speaking low, like.'

'Don't you go a-preachin' at me, Bishop Barbecue! Maybe you're the odd one out for sittin' here all prim and sober whilst Flint and me celebrate our good luck. Don't you care for good luck then?'

'Good luck mostly comes when you makes it come, Billy. I've learnt that the hard way, I reckon. As for rum, there's none as likes a tot more than me, but I'm not one to let it get topside of me, to fuddle my senses.'

'Well, ain't you just the paramour of virtue, John Silver!'

' "Paragon", Billy. The word is "paragon", and you know as well as me that I've a keen enough nose for gold and suchlike. I'll dip my hand into anyone's purse, but I wants to be sober enough to choose the right sort o' purse and to get away with my takings into the bargain.'

The two men stopped talking. Flint, who had drawn his cutlass, was tossing lemons into the air and slicing them in half with vicious sweeps of his arm.

Silver nodded at Bones. Billy went up to Flint and took

him by his right arm, the sleeve of which was soaked with lemon juice. John closed in on his left side and, despite his garbled oaths and protestations, they dragged him out of the tavern towards the quayside where the ship's boat was tied. Half an hour later they were aboard the *Walrus*.

18

⧚ The Privateer ⧛

By noon the next day Flint had recovered sufficiently to tell the crew his plans.

'Mateys,' he cried. ' 'Ere 'tis, our warranty for privateering in these waters.'

He unrolled the parchment, and squinting at the words began to read: 'Given hunder my 'and the third day of May in the year o' grace seventeen hundred and forty-five this commission for the vessel known as the *Walrus* to act as privateer 'gainst the shipping of France and Spain . . .'

He paused, the perspiration trickling down his nose, and said, 'But that's enough of this 'ere high-flown stuff.' He rolled up the document. 'Boys! We be all set fair now. We can strike at will throughout the Main. We can snaffle Frenchy shipping, all legal like. We can plunder dago settlements and leave them a-smouldering, and the Royal Navy'll cheer us to th'echo!'

He waited while his audience absorbed this information.

'What's this then?' George Merry called out in his quarrelsome way. 'You been hobnobbing with admirals and dukes and earls, cap'n? Yesterday we was the black sheep of the Main, today we're little white lambs, it seems. How come the change?'

'Hold your tongue, Merry!' Flint roared back. 'Or I'll clip an inch or two off it!' He drew himself up. 'Any as likes, can scan this 'ere document, but you'll see it's as I says. Yesterday I put it plain to the Governor of Jamaica. "You'd best have us on your side," I says. "So let's have the commission for privateering, and quick about it," says I. Mr Silver and Mr Bones was attendin' me,' he added modestly. 'They can bear me out.'

God give me patience, Silver thought, standing two paces to the right of Flint. But he said, affably enough, 'The cap'n has told you true. We can sail under British colours, and no one, not even the Peers in Parliament, nor the King hisself, can bring us to book so long as we limit ourselves to pitching into the dons and Frenchies.'

'Where's the proof, by God?' It was the Irishman O'Brien, Merry's companion, shouting up at him.

The proof. Silver had spent an hour and a half earlier that morning with Commodore Mason while the latter had issued instructions, told him the limitations of the *Walrus*'s privateering commission, and had, in general, subjected him to a searching cross-examination of his and Flint's motives. Mason was a cold, precise man; as an ally, Silver thought, he would not easily forgive failure, but as a foe he would be an unrelenting adversary. How could all this be explained to the assembled buccaneers? It was proof, of a sort.

Flint was speaking once more, though to tell the truth it was more like snarling. 'I'll have no more yelping from dogs like you, Merry, nor from dumb oxen like O'Brien over there. We have our instructions right enough. Plans is being drawed up with the Royal Navy – plans as'll very like make our fortunes.'

'What plans?' Another shout from among the buccaneers.

'Plans,' replied Flint savagely, 'of the hutmost himportance.' He hesitated. Then, reluctantly, 'Long John here has been a-parleying with the navy men, he'll let you know what plans.'

As Silver made to address the assembled buccaneers, Flint hissed venomously, 'Just you keep it short. These ain't the hustings for Parliament, nor for cap'n neither!'

Silver said equably, as if he had heard nothing, 'Lads, it's proud I am to sail under such a man as the cap'n here! Why, you wouldn't credit the plans that's a-hatching in his brain. Plans to make us rich men every one. I marvel how he does it!'

His broad face lit up with an expression of heart-warming affection. His bearing instantly, subtly, indicated the respect, love even, that an aspiring curate might feel for a distinguished episcopal patron.

Many of the buccaneers thronging the deck smiled too. Ben Gunn laughed for pure joy, and the goodwill spread like a contagion until even George Merry's yellow eyes twinkled briefly.

'The plan the capn's drawed up on this occasion,' Silver said, 'and bless me if the navy men don't fall in with it too, is to sail for New Orleans and to stir up trouble for the French in them waters. There'll be a squadron from the Royal Navy too. If we can keep the Frenchies locked up in their colony of Louisiana, then there's less chance they'll be much help to the dons in defending Havana and the like.'

'There'll be good pickings in the Gulf of Mexico, I reckon,' Billy Bones chipped in, 'and I don't fancy the waters'll be teeming with French frigates. They'll be hard put to scrape up enough ships to defend France itself, and their holdings in Hindustan an' all. Then there's Quebec and the St Lawrence, not to mention their islands in the Main, Guadeloupe and the rest. Why, we'll have a clean sweep, as like as not!'

'Well, that's the long and short of it,' interrupted Flint. 'I'm not the man to lead you on some wild goose chase. But it's up to you, you stinking lubbers. Is it aye or nay?'

'Aye!' came the roar from the deck, as the buccaneers shook their fists and stamped their feet.

Silver regarded them thoughtfully as they slapped each other on the back and dispersed to their duties. Why, they were little better than sheep. Already they fancied their pouches stuffed with gold louis and freshly minted doubloons. Did they give a thought to the hazards that lay ahead – shoal water, and enemy roundshot, and shattered limbs? No, not they, and thank God, too, or they would never man the guns and clamour to board enemy vessels.

'Buckle to, quartermaster!' It was Flint's voice grating in his ear. 'I want this ship spick and span before sundown or you'll be back among the rabble, you will, and no mistake! You ain't got no standin' commission from God for quartermaster, and you may lay to that.'

So the *Walrus* weighed anchor and sailed for the Yucatan Channel and the Gulf of Mexico. The voyage was uneventful save for a brush with a Spanish sloop off Cape Catoche, where the Yucatan peninsula pushes north-east towards Cuba. But the sloop was little inclined to tackle the *Walrus* and beat a prudent retreat towards the mainland of New Spain.

Back at Government House in Kingston, Commodore Mason had told Silver where the *Walrus* was to rendezvous with the British men o'war. The spot was one hundred and fifty miles south-east of New Orleans, ideally suited for intercepting enemy shipping making for the Straits of Florida or the Yucatan Channel.

At last the topsails of the British ships were sighted. Soon the lookouts in the *Walrus*'s rigging were shouting out the details. 'Two men o'war, an' a three-masted sloop!'

As the *Walrus* drew nearer to the warships, Flint summoned the Lords to his cabin and, casting a baleful eye upon the assembled company, reminded them of their duty.

'So here we are, 'bout to parley with the navy men. If any of you scum fancies stepping over and a-plottin' with these 'ere captains and commodores I'll blow his brains out! We're in this for our hown sakes, to fill our purses, not to bring glory to their lordships in Admiralty House.'

'Don't fret so, cap'n,' said Israel Hands. 'No man ever had such a crew as this. Loyal and that!' He flapped his arm lamely, uncertain how to continue.

Flint sneered, 'I don't doubt it, friend Hands, not for a minute! But just so as none of us feels we're being put upon,

I don't propose to let any one of you know more than the rest. So, like I say, when John Silver here goes off to hobnob with the navy men, from now on Black Dog'll go too and stick to him like his shadow.'

Silver nodded his great head sympathetically. 'Them's words of wisdom, cap'n,' he remarked. 'And, fair do's, Pew here, he'll be your shadow on like occasions, so as me and the lads feels safe and sound about you and your intentions.'

Flint opened his mouth to reply but thought better of it; instead he shot Silver a poisonous look. Job Anderson shifted uneasily, and Billy Bones smiled to himself.

'Cap'n!' It was George Merry sticking his head round the door. 'There's flags a-flying from the seventy gunner. A signal, like!'

'I'll read it off,' said Bones, rising quickly to his feet and reaching for his eye-glass.

Within five minutes he was back. 'It's from the *Berwick*. Cap'n Hawke. He sends his compliments and wishes to issue further instructions. He wants to talk to our officers.'

'I'm not leaving this ship,' said Flint vehemently. 'Not while she's afloat on the open sea, I won't. This is a mission for Barbecue and Black Dog or I'm mistook. So quick about it!'

An hour later Silver was clambering up the side of the *Berwick*, Black Dog at his heels, while the *Walrus*'s yawl with three buccaneers resting on their oars bobbed beneath them.

As Silver stepped onto the *Berwick*'s deck his keen eye feasted on the vessel's neatness and good order. Brass railings flashed in the sunlight, the deck boards were newly scrubbed, the seamen's clothes looked clean and fresh.

Now there was a flurry before him. Stamping and saluting. A young man, barely twenty years of age, with a long nose and a small chin that seemed to disappear into his white neckcloth.

'Welcome aboard, sir. Lieutenant Alexander Townsend at your service.'

Silver grasped the young man's hand. 'John Silver, quartermaster,' he said briefly. Black Dog stood timorously behind him, as if avoiding an introduction.

'Captain Hawke will be delighted to meet you in fifteen minutes,' said Townsend. 'I would take you to my cabin before then, but it's a stinking hole beneath the lower gun deck. Not fit for a dog, but then I ain't a dog, just lieutenant-at-arms and so can expect no better.'

He looked curiously at Silver. John nodded by way of reply. A lieutenant-at-arms, he knew, was likely to be the most junior officer aboard, save for the midshipmen. Odd how young men from wealthy families, titled families maybe, were content to inhabit stuffy kennels in the service of their country. Why, aboard the *Walrus* even the carpenter, Tom Morgan, would never put up with such conditions.

Townsend was speaking again, patting the great trunk of the main mast where it thrust up from the deck.

'Upon my word, Mr Silver, we need all the assistance we can get at this time. This mast here looks solid enough, eh? Damme if it ain't got the dry-rot, or so our first lieutenant claims, and I don't doubt his word.'

Silver peered at the mast. Several holes had been drilled into its massive circumference. He blew into one, expelling a small cloud of ill-smelling dust.

'It's the damned climate, d'ye see?' Townsend sounded apologetic.

The climate? Silver knew the perils of the climate right enough. But there was more to it than that. The Admiralty was notoriously tight-fisted. Rather than take officers off half-pay, and put ships to sea, it let good vessels rot at their moorings along the Thames. The *Berwick*, like as not, had been lying idle for years before the present hostilities. No self-respecting buccaneer would so shamefully neglect his ship. This took a bit of the gilt off the navy's gingerbread, and no mistake.

Now Townsend was leading them aft, still talking, though Silver could not catch half of what he said.

At last they reached the door of the captain's cabin. A red-jacketed marine stood bolt upright at their approach, then bent to open the door and let them through.

Captain Hawke sat opposite the door, behind a neat, smooth table. On the wall above his head there was a garish portrait of the King, recently painted by the look of it.

'Mr Silver, sir, representing Captain Flint of the *Walrus*,' said Townsend.

Hawke nodded. He was a well-built man, of some forty years, Silver estimated. Beneath his powdered wig, his face was remarkable for its dark eyes and eyebrows, and its firm mouth, though round his jowls there were signs of impending flabbiness.

'My compliments, Mr Silver,' said Hawke. 'And to Mr —' He gestured towards Black Dog, peering round Silver's shoulder.

'Black Dog, sir,' said John, suddenly conscious of the ridiculous sound of the name.

'Well, Mr Silver,' said Hawke. 'Sit ye down. Take a seat yourself, Mr Dog. You, too, Mr Townsend. We'd best start, Mr Silver, by your showing me your vessel's privateering commission. Thank 'ee. Let's see here. Issued in Kingston, Jamaica, etcetera, etcetera. Yes, that will do, I don't doubt.'

He pushed a map towards Silver, stabbing his forefinger towards the spot marking New Orleans.

'We have orders from their Lordships to prevent French shipping, and indeed those of other nations, from using New Orleans. In fact, to blockade the whole coast of Louisiana.'

He paused, as if debating whether to commit an indiscretion, Silver thought.

At last Hawke said, awkwardly, 'But there's more to it than disrupting French shipping in these waters. We had news in Antigua, before sailing here, that there's some plan to raise a Jacobite rebellion in Scotland. Stab England in the back, d'ye see?'

Townsend said, 'But surely, sir, those Highland savages would be cut to pieces before they reached Edinburgh? There's no danger there, sir, that I can see.'

Hawke's dark eyebrows contracted, and he said irritably, 'Thankfully, Mr Townsend, there are those that can see further than you. Supposing the French land troops on the west coast of Scotland, or raid Cornwall, or Kent? What if French men-o'-war win control of the Channel, even for a few days? There are plenty of Jacobites in England, let alone Scotland, waiting for a chance to destroy the house of Hanover. Why, sir, all hell could be let loose!'

He looked at Silver. 'Any French ship that slips out of the Gulf of Mexico or out of the Caribbean may be on its way to support this Stuart uprising in Scotland. Therefore, Mr Silver, no French ship *will* escape us. Think of the prize money, Mr Silver! Think of the plunder. Tell your captain that. Tell him, too, that your ship will sail with me, north--nor'-west, by nightfall. Those are his orders, Mr Silver. D'ye have anything to say? No? Well, then, I bid you good day. We'll soon see what stuff you and your fellow privateers are made of. Good day, sir. Thank'ee kindly, Mr Dog.'

Soon Silver was back aboard the *Walrus* and the crew were bustling to set sail, with the *Berwick* and Captain Hawke, for New Orleans.

19

The Scotchmen From Louisiana

Flint, as you may imagine, was beside himself with joy at the prospect of harrying the French colony of Louisiana. For a few hours he even refrained from cuffing the ears of poor, dumb Darby McGraw. For his part, John Silver was sure that twice Flint actually smiled at him – which made a change from scowling, at any rate, even though the smiles were fleeting, lop-sided leers as much as anything.

Not that Flint could see good in any situation for long. He was soon cursing at the indignity of trailing along behind the *Berwick,* and speculating that Captain Hawke meant to betray them to the Admiralty Court as soon as he had accomplished his mission. And where, Flint wanted to know, were the other two naval vessels bound for? They had struck off eastwards at nightfall. Very likely they had been ordered to wait until the *Walrus* was loaded down with booty, and then to close in and seize her. A fine way to end, dangling from a man-o'-war's yardarm.

But for all these morose imaginings, Flint's enthusiasm had been fired. His nose was already sniffing out plunder and prizes, and he drove on the crew with a fierce, exalted frenzy that was so close to religious fervour that John Silver dubbed him 'Friar Flint' behind his back.

As the *Berwick* and the *Walrus* drew nearer to where the great flat spur of the Mississippi delta jutted out into the Gulf of Mexico, several sail were sighted. Mostly they were small craft engaged in local trade, and since Flint refused point blank to pursue them, they flitted away unharmed.

Angry messages fluttered from the *Berwick's* masthead. 'Deeply regret your failure to capture enemy vessels,' Bones read through his eyeglass.

'Let Master 'Awke chase 'em for hisself,' said Flint. 'I'm after bigger game, and you may lay to that.'

Bigger game appeared within the hour, skirting Breton Island.

'A Dutchman,' came the cry. 'Heavy laden, by the looks of it!'

'That's our prize, right enough,' said Silver, upon the quarterdeck. 'A Dutch fly-boat, five hundred tons burden, I'll be bound, and so broad-bottomed she must needs go slow, like!'

'Never!' said Flint abruptly. 'I won't do it! Them Hollanders are Protestants to a man. I'll not lay a finger on 'em!' He glared at his peers.

Pew said, in an oily voice, 'Well, that may be true, cap'n, but here they be a-trading with papist Frenchmen and cocking a snook at us into the bargain.'

'Loot is loot,' said Bones heavily. 'I don't distinguish between papist silver and protestant silver, not so long as it weighs the same.'

Flint drew his pistol from his belt and blew gently down the barrel. 'No,' he said. 'I won't do it.' Not a man spoke, but Silver deliberately turned his back on Flint and gazed intently out to sea.

So the *Walrus* hung back while the *Berwick* closed in on the Dutchman, fired a shot across its bows, and took it easy as winking. Hawke put a prize crew aboard and stowed the Hollanders below decks on their own ship.

For fifteen days no more vessels emerged from the delta's northern passes. Word must have got back to New Orleans that British warships were prowling the waters beyond Breton Sound.

Impatient of this inactivity, the *Walrus* struck off southwards hoping to intercept shipping using the other passes where the Mississippi flowed sluggishly into the sea. There were no pickings here either. Tempers flared among the buccaneers and Flint finally lopped off the hand of a belligerent youth from Maryland, for 'hinsubordination and a-giving of the evil eye', as he put it; he then kicked his unfortunate victim senseless and stood over him while his life-blood gushed from the severed arteries in his wrist.

Thus purged, temporarily at least, the *Walrus* made off to the north-east to rejoin the *Berwick* in her vigil off Breton Sound.

Almost directly, a French frigate emerged from the delta. She was a nimble craft, flying speedily before the wind, and clearly counting on her speed to make her escape.

Both the *Berwick* and the *Walrus* swung round in pursuit, their sails soon filled with the same strong breeze.

'Pray God we get to her before Hawke,' said Silver quietly to Bones. 'He's twice the guns we have. He'll blast her to bits with one broadside.'

A high-pitched voice came from behind his right shoulder. Flint seemed to have materialised out of thin air, as he did so often, as if to intercept a private conversation.

'When you've been at sea as long as I have, Sir Barbecue, you'll yap a good deal less and do a good deal more. As for you, sailing master Bones, get for'ard and make sure we add an extra knot or two to our speed. Be off, the pair of you, or I'll split you both from top to tail like two herrings!'

As John made to follow Billy Bones, Flint said sharply, 'You, being quartermaster an' all, is now elected, unanimous-like, by me, to lead the boarding party against this 'ere French swab. I hopes as how your cutlass is sharp enough.'

Silver opened his mouth to reply, but Flint cut him short. 'Don't you bleat to me about *if* we catches 'em. The *Walrus* is made for chases like this. As for your friend 'Awke, we'll leave him standing, gasping in our wake, the stuck-up lubber! Horganise the boarding party as you will, but leave me three-score men aboard. Get away now, and tell Israel to hold his fire until I tells him.'

As he passed among the buccaneers milling about the main deck, Silver had to admit that Flint's words had not been idle ones. Under Bones's directions the *Walrus* had crammed on more square-footage of sail than hitherto, and was positively leaping forward through the water. The *Berwick*, on the other hand, was visibly falling behind. There was no doubt, then, that the *Walrus* could outstrip her for speed.

But now what had happened to the *Berwick?* She had slewed off course, her sails flapping wildly as the helmsman tried to claw back into position.

It was Pew's keen eyes that were the first to interpret the *Berwick*'s difficulties correctly. 'God damme, if her main mast ain't listing over towards the port side. It's only the rigging as is holding it up!'

Silver snatched Pew's telescope. It was true. The main mast now leant absurdly towards the port bow. Dozens of seamen were desperately hauling in the sails to prevent the *Berwick* from suffering worse disablement. Dry rot! That was it. The rotten core of the main mast had given way at last. Hawke would have to heave to and set his men to work to rig a jury mast. Then, with luck, he could make a safe progress to the logwood settlements along the Honduras coast and fit a new main mast.

Flint was screaming at the buccaneers, his blotched face twisted and triumphant.

'We've got the Frenchy to ourselves now, lads! The *Walrus* can run down any craft on the seven seas. We'll have her by nightfall!'

Slowly the *Walrus* closed the gap. The ten miles between the two ships became eight, then five, then two. It was mid afternoon, under a blazing sky, when Silver said to Flint, 'Permission to let the crew feed, cap'n? They'll fight better with full bellies and a pannikin of rum.' Flint nodded sourly, and Silver turned away to supervise the issuing of provisions.

An hour later, with the distance between the two vessels still shortening, Flint called the Lords to him and said, 'I'm not counting on any fancy gunnery, though no doubt, contrary to rumour, Israel 'ere could 'it a barn door at twenty paces, so long as he was inside the barn, that is.'

He paused briefly, giving Israel Hands the opportunity to digest the insult, but seeing him merely shake his head and smile encouragingly, continued, 'I don't fancy no broadsides a-smashing into this good old ship. I wants to enjoy my doubloons and sovereigns when I gets 'em. I'll not end up as a peg-legged old cripple, and you may lay to that! So we'll cut across the Frenchy's bows and board him brisk, like.'

Within half an hour Billy Bones was swinging the *Walrus* across the path of the fleeing frigate. As their guns bore both vessels exchanged fire. Because of the speed and angle of her approach the *Walrus* suffered only trifling damage: two gaping holes were torn in her fore sail, one fortunate shot severed her starboard main bow lines before whistling overboard, and another dismounted a gun sited beneath the main shrouds, killing two buccaneers and maiming a third into the bargain.

Clinging to the fore shrouds, Silver could see the flash of musketry from the decks of the French frigate, which bore the illustrious name *Colbert.* The musket balls whined through the *Walrus*'s rigging, and here and there struck a member of the boarding party waiting patiently for the moment of impact.

Straining his eyes to make out more details aboard the *Colbert,* Silver suddenly realised that among the blue and white uniforms of the French sailors and marines there were a number of men wearing an outlandish garb of brightly coloured bonnets on their heads, and what appeared to be blankets slung round their waists.

'Look'ee there, John, she's swinging away from us!' Pew was screeching into the wind and pointing with his cutlass.

Silver forgot the strange-bonnetted men, and watched as the French helmsman turned the *Colbert* hard to starboard, hoping to avoid the impending collision. But it was not enough: Billy Bones reacted immediately by pulling the *Walrus* in the wake of her quarry. As she surged to starboard the wind spilled out of the *Colbert*'s sails, and, like a falcon swooping onto a hovering dove, the *Walrus*'s bowsprit smashed square into her stern.

Amid the flying splinters and the crackle of musketry the buccaneers leapt and clambered onto the *Colbert*'s quarterdeck. Among the first to set foot aboard was John Silver, kicking his way through a small forest of swords and hand-spikes, and howling like a devil fresh from hell. Slashing with his cutlass, John cut a swathe through the Frenchmen on the quarterdeck. Out of the corner of his eye he saw Pew crouching over a dying opponent, and, a little further off, Job Anderson was tossing a struggling figure overboard.

Unable to fire their cannon to any effect, the French gunners were now pouring up from below deck. But there were not many Frenchmen all told, and Silver calculated swiftly that there were barely fifty in sight. More numerous were the bonnetted men who seemed to be grouping resolutely under the foremast. Silver suddenly realised that they were wearing plaid skirts of a sort.

'Scotch, by the powers!' It was Black Dog, peeping round a nearby barrel. 'Scotchmen. I seed 'em before, in Aberdeen.'

Before Silver could absorb this startling piece of information a tall, cursing French marine loomed before him and levelled his musket at point black range. As John bent to avoid the shot his foot slipped in a puddle of blood and he fell heavily upon the planks of the quarterdeck. Glancing up he saw with dismay that the marine's musket muzzle had followed him as he fell and was now a bare yard from his chest.

The man pulled the trigger. There was a click. Then nothing. Damp powder, thank God!

The marine collapsed, shrieking and clutching his knees. Black Dog, who always preferred fighting below the belt, had abandoned his barrel and had slashed with telling effect at the Frenchman's legs.

Silver scrambled to his feet. The battle had swept past him, down onto the maindeck. The quarterdeck had been cleared of the enemy. Now a score and a half of the French were being driven aft by the buccaneers with Gabriel Pew at their head, yelping in triumph. Job Anderson had seized a French musket and was using it as a club, beating down his foes with the blood-stained butt.

Even as John ran to join the fighting, the French wavered and broke. Some scampered below decks pursued by gleeful packs of buccaneers, while others ran to join the Scotchmen around the foremast.

Silver made his way towards the bows of the ship. On the main deck the tumult had died down, while below the last Frenchmen were, from the sound of it, being successfully hunted down.

What was this? More Scotchmen issuing up from below decks, plaids bright under the sun, their weapons in their hands. Why were they continuing to group together under the foremast instead of helping the Frenchmen resist the buccaneers?

The *Walrus*, trailing her shattered bowsprit, had now swung round until she lay side by side with the *Colbert*. Flint had ordered the two vessels to be lashed together, and they now drifted before the wind, bruised and blood-stained but apparently companionable.

Here came Flint now, hauling himself onto the *Colbert*'s deck, his thin lips almost betraying a smile as he surveyed his prize.

He thrust his way through the ring of buccaneers that surrounded the Scotchmen and the surviving French. Silver came up to him and said, 'Cap'n, I can't make head nor tail of this. One thing's certain, these Scotties don't seem over keen to fight us. Maybe we should parley with them. Find out what's what.'

Flint grunted. Taking this to signify agreement, John called out to the Scotchmen to send representatives aft to parley. As an afterthought he bade a bedraggled French officer accompany them.

It was an odd confrontation upon the blood-smeared quarterdeck. One of the two Scotch leaders spoke first. He was elderly, dignified and spoke as if well-rehearsed.

'I am Alistair Macdonald, chieftain of the Macdonalds of the colony of New Caledonia which lies under the protection of the French authorities of Louisiana, some four hundred miles up the Mississippi river. We are returning, some of us, to aid Prince Charles Edward in his bid to overthrow the Hanoverian upstart and to restore the house of Stuart.'

'Papist swabs!' It was Flint, hissing out the words. 'I'll see you all to Davy Jones first.'

Macdonald said, 'We have no quarrel with you. Unless I am mistaken, you are as much enemies of the English King as we are.'

'We're boney fide privateers, not pirates, see!' Flint said starkly. 'We sail under the union jack. You tell me why we shouldn't cut your throats and drop you overboard like offal.'

'Because we are not offal, but well-armed fighting men,' replied Macdonald calmly. 'You would pay a terrible price in overcoming us.'

There was a pause while Flint scowled at Macdonald and his companion, and the French officer looked anxiously from one to the other. Gabriel Pew appeared at Silver's side and whispered into his ear. John suddenly said, 'Well, it matters little to me who sits on the throne of England. Why, I'd have a republic as soon as a king any day. Damn all kings, say I!

'Damn all *Catholic* Kings!' said Flint vehemently.

'Look'ee here,' said Silver, 'we'll make a bargain with you. The gold and silver coin you've stowed below decks – now don't deny it, my friend Pew here has seen it – shall be our reward for letting you sail on, for England or Scotland or wherever you pleases! Your liberty and your arms is a fair exchange for your French-minted coin, and I can't say fairer than that. Cap'n Flint here will say the same, by thunder.'

Flint opened his mouth to protest, but Silver said quickly to Macdonald, 'The cap'n, bless him, agrees, d'ye see?' He turned and whispered something to Flint, who promptly closed his mouth.

'What do you say, chieftain Macdonald?' Silver insisted.

Macdonald pondered his reply for a moment and then, as if reading from a prepared address, said, 'We Scots, faithful subjects of the Catholic King over the water, accept your terms. We have not left our homes and families in New Caledonia, and our hard-won independence there, in order to be trapped like rats in the Gulf of Mexico.'

'Right!' said Flint, shaking his fist in Macdonald's face. 'We'll give you half an hour to cough up the blunt! And then off you go, matey, and may you all end up hung, draw'd and quartered, every mother's son! This French swab, too!'

He spat with deliberate care at the French officer's boots, and left the quarterdeck, bawling for Darby McGraw.

As the Scotchmen left to supervise the transfer of their treasure to the *Walrus*, Anderson said, 'Why d'ye let these heathen go then, Barbecue?'

'Job,' said Silver, 'you're a slow learner, and was as a lad, I shouldn't wonder. This way we've got their coin without losing another man, and I for one shouldn't have fancied a set-to with old straight-talking Macdonald and his lads. And another thing. Suppose they gets to England and helps this Charles Stuart stir up a sight o' trouble there. Why, that can only be for our own good!'

Anderson said, 'We're more'n three thousand miles from England, John. How will all that rebellion and such like help us, then?'

Silver put his arm kindly round Anderson's solid shoulder. 'Well, Job, if the lords in Parliament, not to mention their Lordships of the Admiralty, are in a great turmoil at home, how much thought d'ye reckon they'll give to clamping down on gentlemen o' fortune such as us?'

'Precious little.'

'Precious little, my old son, is right! Now set to, you lubber, let's strip this Frenchy ship of every penny we can lay our hands on, and then show her a clean pair of heels.'

Before long the *Walrus* was quitting the scene of her triumphant encounter with the *Colbert*. At the cost of eight dead and twenty-four wounded, the buccaneers had seized gold and silver coin worth, in Billy Bones's estimation, one hundred and ten thousand pounds.

As the *Walrus* headed south-east in friendly seas, the crew rejoiced at their good fortune. Black Dog sang a set of ballads in a mournful tenor, and Ben Gunn danced an ungainly minuet with Israel Hands.

Flint, who had been one of the last to leave the *Colbert,* with Darby McGraw clutching at the back of his belt, was soon pickled in rum. Silver sat next to him, drinking steadily but contriving to keep his wits about him. 'Well, cap'n,' he remarked, raising his tumbler of French brandy, 'here's to a good day's work. We've treasure in the hold, and have sent the Scotchmen off to stir up more trouble for King George. A good day's work, by the powers!'

For reply Flint choked into his glass and then said, still spluttering, 'They'll never get there, them damned Scotch papists! Darby and me, we poisoned the drinking water afore we quit the *Colbert,* and I told Darby to cut a few holes in the ship's bottom to make sure. He covered them with bales and that. They'll never know till it's too late.

Poisoned and drownded, by thunder!' He laughed in his shrill, cackling way.

Silver looked at Billy Bones and shrugged. After all, they had the treasure from the *Colbert* safely stowed below hatches. They had slipped away from Captain Hawke. The whole of the Spanish Main lay before them, littered with potential prizes, Flint, moreover, seemed happy, after his fashion. There was prime sport ahead. He was sure of it.

20

❁{ *Flint's Design on the Plate Treasure* }❁

F or three years after the taking of the *Colbert* Flint's men
struck almost at will throughout the Caribbean and the
Gulf of Mexico. The *Walrus* became a byword for terror in
those waters. It was said that the very name of Flint caused
Spanish grandees to blanch, and destroyed the peace of
mind of many a French merchant. The buccaneers not only
played havoc with enemy shipping passing through the
Straits of Florida or the Yucatan Channel, but also chanced
their luck further afield. Thus the *Walrus* left a trail of
smouldering ruins along the isthmus of Panama, raided
French settlements in the colony of St Domingue, and took
and sacked the port of Altagracia just opposite Maracaibo
in Venezuela.

Flint's men were bonny fighters and privateering brought
them wealth in plenty, though most of them let it dribble
through their fingers like fine sand. But if the *Walrus*'s
progress was vastly profitable, her wake bubbled with
blood. By some perverse reasoning Flint, though at war under the union jack, steadfastly refused to take prisoners.
Recruits to the *Walrus*'s company were a different matter,
and necessary in view of the losses that steadily ac-
cumulated, but for the rest there was no mercy. When a
boarded ship had been plundered, and its crew carefully
robbed, Flint had them tossed overboard – the wounded
and sick together with the hale and hearty. He would have
treated women in the same fashion, but Silver and Bones
drew the line at that, and instead female prisoners were
dumped, weeping and wailing, upon a convenient cay or
some deserted shore and left to the mercies of wild beasts or
local savages.

When peace came at last in 1748, Flint ignored the news for eight months. Even after that he carried on much as before, though he knew that if he overstepped the mark in British waters the Royal Navy's men-o'-war would be on his tail like a greyhound chasing a rabbit. Not that Flint saw himself as a rabbit. As the years passed he became still more determined to prey like some savage, grizzled wolf upon the Spanish Indies. He rejected out of hand John Silver's proposal that they should try their luck at protecting, for a handsome consideration, vessels trading illegally between the British mainland colonies and those of Spain, France and the Netherlands. When he was sober he spent hours brooding over plans which were for the most part over-ambitious and sometimes downright suicidal.

Early in the year of grace 1754, however, he called his Lords into the *Walrus*'s cabin and harangued them.

'Mates,' he said, taking a pull of rum, 'I've had enough of playin' games with the dons. 'Afore I die I wants to crack 'em hard.'

'You ain't got much time for that, the way you quaff the rum,' said Silver sweetly. 'You'll soon be below hatches, and you may lay to that.'

Flint glowered at him. 'Get to hell, Barbecue!' He continued, thickly, 'But there's one dream o' mine you lads'll be pleased to share.'

'Just so long as we ain't asked to share your nightmares, cap'n,' said Long John primly.

'The Spanish plate fleet,' muttered Flint. 'I means to have it, or go hang!'

The cabin buzzed with excitement. This, the annual treasure fleet of the Spanish Indies, was the greatest prize of all. Two centuries before, Sir John Hawkins had caught the laden mule trains on the isthmus of Panama, and in more recent times Captain Morgan had marched on Panama town itself.

Billy Bones whistled. 'Them's high stakes, captain,' he

remarked, cheerfully enough. 'But if we're caught the dons will toast us alive, as like as not.'

'I ain't planning to dangle from some dago's gibbet yet awhile!' exclaimed Silver. 'The plate ships are packed tight around with frigates, three-deckers and all manner of craft. Why, they'd sink us in five minutes flat!'

'Now, Barbecue,' said Flint savagely, 'you ain't the only one with brains in your skull. We all know as how the plate fleet gets together off the isthmus. But the silver don't come from there. Most of it's brought up from Peru. But some comes down from Mexico and is shipped from Vera Cruz – so that's where we'll strike, at Vera Cruz. They mostly only has one treasure ship there, and maybe three a-guarding her.'

'Three to one is still long odds, cap'n,' said Pew, his caution battling with his avarice.

'But we can do it, by the powers!' cried Silver. 'Why, Vera Cruz ain't much of a place, not like Cartagena and the rest. We'll sail in, under the red and gold ensign, and snaffle the treasure afore they can say snap!'

'I don't fancy getting shut up in Vera Cruz if things go wrong,' said Israel Hands. 'The dons'll stretch us on the rack if so be we fail.'

A steady silence greeted this sobering observation.

'I have it!' It was Silver crashing his great fist upon Flint's table. 'A fire ship! We'll loose a fire ship on 'em, all blazing with tar, and cut out the treasure ship while the dagoes holler blue murder!'

'It worked for Drake,' said Bones gravely. 'Let's pray it'll work for us as well.'

'It's not the prayin' as'll do the trick,' said Flint harshly. 'It's the plannin' and the horganizin', as well you know.'

He looked round the cabin. 'Mates, we've got two months to do it, accordin' to my reckonin'. I wants the ship careened and scraped so clean she'll fly through the water! I wants the best powder and shot. I wants your blades sharp as razors. Let's shake hands on it. The men'll back us, I know. Boys, it'll be a rare go, will this! As for me, well, I tells you here and now, I'm cuttin' down on the grog. Darby! Hide the rum, or I'll pare off your ears!'

He stood up. 'Get to it, mates! Let's be off to Vera Cruz. By God, that dago King in Madrid'll squirm when he gets to hear of this!'

And so, with her captain in high spirits, the *Walrus* passed beyond the Dry Tortugas and headed westwards towards the coast of New Spain.

As the *Walrus* approached Vera Cruz, flying the flag of imperial Spain, her men were on tenterhooks – edgy and eager at the same time. Among those who stayed cool was Long John Silver, drawing steadily on his pipe and always ready with a cheery word and an encouraging slap in the back for the more faint-hearted of the buccaneers.

The look-out had scarcely shouted that he spied the great seaward bastion of the fortifications guarding Vera Cruz than things began to go wrong.

The thump of distant gunfire could be heard, floating over the water from the harbour.

Israel Hands turned first his huge right ear, then his left, towards the far off, menacing sound. After a couple of minutes of intense concentration he spoke to Flint.

'That's no fancy cannon practice, cap'n. 'Tain't regular enough for that. There's a scrap goin' on, and there's more'n three ships at it. Drivin' towards the harbour mouth, or I'm a Dutchman!'

Flint's mottled face turned plum-coloured with rage. 'God damn you, Hands!' he cursed. 'We've been beat to the gold!'

'Steady on there, cap'n,' said Long John. ' 'Tain't Israel a-firing of them guns. Maybe we'll be quick enough to pick up some of the pieces if we keeps our heads.'

Suddenly the look-out screeched, 'There's some ships breaking out o' the harbour! One o' them's ahead of

t'others. There's two Spanish gunboats there, a-pounding
of a schooner!'

Soon all could see that there were five vessels involved.
Two Spanish warships had closed in upon a schooner and
were steadily shooting it to pieces. Further ahead a brig was
racing under full sail to elude a sleek Spanish frigate.

It took Flint no time at all to make up his mind.

'Helmsman!' he cried. 'Steer me small to that dago
frigate. I'll save that brig even if Satan hisself is her
skipper.'

The *Walrus* tacked rapidly through the water. The
Spanish frigate seemed neither to notice nor to care as she
approached, probably believing that she was a friendly
vessel.

The fleeing brig passed across the *Walrus*'s bow barely
half a sea mile to starboard. Deftly the helmsman swung
the ship round as if to pursue the brig, and by so doing
brought her to within two cables' distance of the Spanish
warship.

Israel Hands crouched over his port-side guns, sighting
and elevating them, ready for the moment when they would
bear on the Spaniard.

Then the two ships were side by side, and abruptly,
without any warning, the *Walrus* poured her broadside fire
into the unsuspecting frigate.

The air was filled with bitter-tasting smoke and whirling
splinters as the Spaniard took the broadside at almost point
blank range.

Peering eagerly at the frigate, the pirates could see guns
dismounted below decks and a great hole torn in her side
amidships. Cries of dismay, and the shrieks of the wounded, mingled with the splutter of musket fire from the
damaged vessel. A trail of smoke seeped up through the
Spaniard's gun ports, growing thicker and flowing faster
with every second.

'She's afire!' screamed Pew, his white hands raised in

triumph. 'She's turning aside, by thunder!'

Other voices joined Pew's, shouting in triumph, and the crippled frigate suddenly began to drift away from the *Walrus,* her captain, no doubt, preferring to douse her fire rather than pursue his quarry. Soon she was left stranded, way behind.

Flint pressed on behind the brig, which eventually hove to, showing its guns like the bared teeth of a defiant tigress. But the *Walrus* hauled down the Spanish flag and put the skull and crossbones in its place, whereupon the brig promptly displayed the white ensign of Bourbon France but with a crude black wolf's head daubed over the golden fleur de lys.

'A Frenchy buccaneer it seems,' said Billy Bones.

'French or dago, they're all damned papist devils, every one,' snarled Flint.

'Begging your pardon, cap'n,' said Silver with unexpected politeness, 'let's not be over hasty. There's plenty of French Protestants afloat in these waters, and, as we've see'd, this vessel don't seem to have much love for the Spaniards of Vera Cruz. 'Tis my view we best talk to old Black Wolf over there, and see what's what. I've a fair few words of French learnt from my missis, as you know, so with your leave I'll step aboard the brig and parley with 'em.'

Within the hour, Silver was back on board the *Walrus* accompanied by the French captain, a gaudy dandy with peacock feathers in his hat, and a dazzling sky-blue coat over a jewelled sword-belt.

John soon let Flint and the assembled Lords know the lie of the land. The Frenchman had tried, with another pirate vessel, to snatch the treasure ship out of Vera Cruz. But things had gone wrong, the Spaniards being less sleepy than usual, and he had been forced to flee. He showered Flint with thanks and compliments for rescuing him and his men, and bowed deep over his plumed hat. Quite soon, however, Flint tired of this flowery speechifying, and, pulling a feather from the Frenchman's hat, snapped it into two pieces.

They then got down to business, and the upshot of the talk was this: the French buccaneer swore that he knew where the rest of the plate fleet was to be assembled; the place, he said, was a small, ill-defended port called Santa Lena. By his reckoning, the main esaort vessels would not have arrived yet, and if he and Flint were to swoop now on Santa Lena the chances were they would pick up ten times the loot they had both failed to garner at Vera Cruz.

This, then, according to John Silver, was the genesis of Flint's famous raid upon the plate fleet. It was not exactly the 'fishing up of the wrecked plate ships' that Long John had craftily referred to aboard the *Hispaniola;* more like a 'plucking out of the wretched plate ships' from Santa Lena. Be that as it may, it was certainly the occasion when John's parrot learnt to screech 'pieces of eight', and it led, by a circuitous and blood-stained route, to the burying of the bar silver and gold upon Kidd's Island.

21

❴ *The March on Santa Lena* ❵

F lint saw the impending assault on Santa Lena as the crowning glory of his lawless and violent life. As he said himself, he would have turned down a dukedom just to have this chance of snatching the dons' treasure from under their dirty noses. He repeated this and similar sentiments time and again, as the *Walrus* sailed towards the Venezuelan coast accompanied by the French buccaneers in their craft the *Jean Calvin*.

The two ships avoided any other sail that appeared over the horizon. Flint's mind was on higher things, and, for once in his life, he was prepared to flee from any potentially hostile vessel rather than put the descent on Santa Lena at risk.

The French captain had a freehand drawing of the portion of the south-east coast of Venezuela that contained Santa Lena. It looked a miserable place at first sight.

Flint was beside himself with joy as he pored over the chart. 'Mates,' he cried. 'It'll be like taking sweetmeats from a babby!' He was alone in his cabin with Silver and Bones.

Billy Bones said roughly, 'That's how you'd like to see it, cap'n. But look again. Our map of this here coast shows one or two items that's missing from our French friend's sketch. Item one, this spit of land here that sticks out in the bay. It's got a fortification on it, or I'm a Dutchman.'

'Pah!' said Flint. 'The dons'll be dozing over their guns. Very like we can sneak right past 'em!

'Very like we can't, an' all,' replied Silver dryly. 'And even if we could, d'you reckon they'd stay a-dozing while we grabs the treasure? Then, I suppose, we sails back towards the harbour mouth, under them guns, and the dagoes tip their hats and say, "Thank'ee kindly and bon voyage"?'

Flint scowled at this. His scowl intensified as Billy Bones said, 'Item two. Where's the treasure hid? For all we knows it could be in the fortification here. Or in this stockade to the south of the town. Or here, in this grand house that the Frenchy's drawing shows. Or, on the other hand, it could be packed in the vaults of this here church, next to the grand house.'

'God damn you, Bones,' said Flint sharply. 'You'll send us all to the grave with your damn' moaning and snivelling. You could give Black Dog lessons in looking mournful, and no mistake!'

'Better to be straight-faced now than shot down by the dons,' said Silver. 'I never fancied drying in Execution Dock, and I don't fancy rotting at Santa Lena neither.'

'There's one thing above all as I can't stomach about you, Sir Barbecue,' said Flint maliciously. 'And that's the way you preaches. There's times when I curse that fool Cap'n England for letting you quit Barbados aboard the old *Cassandra*.'

Silver said gravely, 'Thank'ee, cap'n. You was always one for speaking your mind, straight out. I'm proud to be quartermaster under a man as plain-spoken as you, and you may lay to that.'

Then, turning to Bones, he remarked, 'Billy, the cap'n here has set me to rights. He's a shining beacon for us all, I reckon.'

As Billy Bones stirred uncomfortably, Silver continued, 'I'd like to put this humble plan before you, Cap'n Flint, for your valued opinion. Of course, 'tain't much of a plan compared with those you're no doubt hatching at this very minute, but I'd be glad if you would hear me out.'

Flint snarled and bared his yellow teeth at Silver, who said, blandly enough, 'Very grateful for your permission,

cap'n.' He gestured towards the two maps upon the table.
'If we adds these two maps together, we gets a pretty sharp
picture of our situation, and I says we can't just sail past
them fortifications as if we was wraiths, invisible to the
human eye.'

'Coward!' said Flint scathingly.

Silver continued, as if he were stone deaf, 'So we makes a
landing behind the fortifications and takes 'em at dawn.
Then we snaffles the treasure ships in the harbour!'

'What about the town itself, John?' said Bones.

'As soon as we've spiked them dago guns, Billy, we'll take
that grand house. That's where we'll find more treasure
hid, or the key to it, I'll be bound.'

'Supposing there's Spanish warships in the harbour,'
persisted Bones. 'We'll never get the loot out, and aboard
th'old *Walrus*.'

'Right you are, my boy! And that's where our
Frenchman friend comes in. He takes the *Jean Calvin* right
up close to the harbour mouth as if he's a-going to force an
entrance, bold as can be. Well, he'll draw any warships out,
won't he? As long as he turns tail quick enough, he'll get
clean away. But he'll have draw'd off any warships, like I
said, and then we can bring the *Walrus* round to the front
door, in a manner of speaking, and load her up!'

Bones nodded his approval of these proposals, and Flint
said grudgingly, 'It's a hare-brained scheme right enough,
but we'd best put it to the men, and to that French swab
that's tagging along with us.'

Within twenty-four hours John Silver's strategy for the
attack on Santa Lena had been fully accepted aboard both
the *Walrus* and the *Jean Calvin*.

It only remained to put the plan to the test. Three days
later, as the sun set, the *Jean Calvin,* flying the Spanish ensign, sailed up to the spit guarding Santa Lena's harbour
mouth and loosed off a broadside at the fort. Before the
Spanish gunners could recover from their shock the *Jean*

Calvin sheered away, a cannon in her stern continuing to lob roundshot into the fortifications.

Well, as you may imagine, all hell was let loose in Santa Lena. The dons were convinced that a raid from the sea was about to be launched, and kept eyeglasses trained in that direction. A Spanish warship emerged from the harbour within forty minutes – which was good going for the dons. But she was a clumsy two-decker with a towering poop deck and, to judge by the way her skipper handled her, either she had her hold packed with lead ingots or he was dead drunk, one or the other.

Believe it or not, that leaden-footed man-o'-war was the only escort ship the dons had at Santa Lena, and it was a sign of over-confidence or stupidity, maybe both, that she was ever allowed to quit the harbour. At any rate, the darkness soon closed in upon her, and for half the night the *Jean Calvin* danced before her like a will o' the wisp, luring her further and further from her duty. The French skipper knew those waters as well as the approaches to La Rochelle itself, and he soon doubled back towards the coast and into shoal water. He had his men taking soundings as regular as clockwork, and wriggled like an eel along the narrow channels. The Spanish warship was foolish enough to follow him, and a little after midnight she ran aground with a great grinding and splintering of her timbers.

What was the *Walrus* doing in the meantime? She had kept out to sea, and had then crept round to anchor close to the shore some ten miles south-east of Santa Lena. The coast there was wild and deserted, with a good deal of forest, and a range of small hills blocking any prying telescopes from the fortifications at Santa Lena. There was a stream that flowed from the hills down towards the town, and Flint soon decided that the pirates should use this as their guide-line towards their quarry.

Billy Bones was left aboard the *Walrus* with strict instructions to bring her round to Santa Lena at dawn on the next day but one, by which time Flint reckoned he would have stormed the fortifications. For his part, Flint was so determined to lead his men in their assault that he bade the *Walrus* adieu with only a half dozen remorseful looks over his shoulder as the ship's boats pulled towards the shore.

One hundred and forty buccaneers were landed upon that savage coast, leaving little more than two score to man the *Walrus*. The assault party made their way through the nearby hills, never straying far from the stream. Where the hills levelled down towards the open, marshy land that lay before Santa Lena, Flint called a halt. It was about nine o'clock in the morning, and already the sun was blistering down and the brushwood ringing with the cries of wild creatures.

Flint said to Silver, who was mopping the sweat from his face with a crimson kerchief, 'We'll have to lay up till dusk, then move off again and carry the fort at dawn.'

Silver brushed his breeches, stained and ripped from the night march, and said, 'Fair's fair, cap'n. The lads will need sleep afore the attack. They'd best sleep at noon, and we can rouse 'em again at nightfall. But between now and noon I don't propose to let 'em idle. There's plenty of timber hereabouts and we shall need ladders to scale the fort. With your permission I'll set the lads to work.'

He bawled instructions at the buccaneers as they lay exhausted among the trees and brushwood.

'Tom Morgan! Wake up! You're the carpenter. Get hold of three-score men and cut wood for scaling ladders. Make sure you binds the cross struts tight. We don't want George Merry's dainty foot a-slipping as he hurls hisself over the dagoes' walls. Black Dog, you help Tom Morgan there.

'Job Anderson! You're a steady enough lubber. Post look-outs on all sides. If any of 'em dozes, march 'em over Cap'n Flint or me smart like!'

He laid his hand on Pew's arm and said more gently to his friend, 'Gabby, you're a fine one for tracking things

down. Pick out a dozen men who know how to tread light
and talk soft and hunt down some food. But I don't want no
firearms blazing away. Do the work with traps and knives.'

Pew laughed and tightened his long fingers round the
throat of some imaginary prey.

Israel Hands was meanwhile explaining something or
other to Flint, who was nodding morosely as he listened. At
last Flint shrieked, 'Get to it then, and if it don't work I'll
settle the score with you man to man, by thunder!

By now the pirates were bustling about their duties,
though it was no great pleasure for them, you may be sure.
The sun was rising higher in the sky, and insects from the
marshes in front of them bit and stung as if they were under
a special commission from the King of Spain himself. Job
Anderson, patrolling four hundred yards off, trod un-
knowingly upon a vicious, hissing snake. But Job was no
lightweight and the snake expired under his heavy boot.

A little before noon Pew and his fellow huntsmen returned, carrying five dead goats, two piglets in a sack, and
several bundles of squawking hens. They had stumbled
upon a shack in a clearing, apparently owned by an old,
lone Indian woman. They trussed up the woman and
dragged her into the undergrowth, where they reckoned she
would not be discovered for days. It was then a simple
matter to carry off all the livestock from her wretched plot,
and a basket of fresh fruit into the bargain.

So Flint's men were able to eat their fill under the
post-meridian sun, and then, with look-outs still posted,
they lay down in the shade and slept or talked.

Silver slept like a baby for four hours. When he awoke the
fierce heat of day was abating. He looked across at Flint
and saw him sitting, red-eyed and irritable, against the
trunk of a tree. Israel Hands was nearby, lashing swathes of
canvas around an object the size of a pork barrel.

Flint saw that Silver was awake and beckoned him
across. It was clear to Silver as he approached that Flint

had not slept a wink that day, for his plum-coloured face was drawn with anxiety and fatigue.

'Well, Barbecue,' Flint said. 'I wants this here raid to put my name in them 'istory books, if it's the last thing I does. If it fails I'll cut your heart out, so listen! When it's dusk we moves off. I wants the lads split into two parties, equal like. I'll lead one to swoop on that grand house, Government House I'll wager, near the harbour. There'll be treasure there, I'll be bound; or them as I can coax into telling me where the treasure's hid. Seeing as how I've no one more suitable to delegate to, you'd best take the other party and storm the fort. Then we links up, and Billy Bones brings round th'old *Walrus* to pick up the loot.'

'There's the French swab too,' added Silver.

'There's the French swab too,' mimicked Flint, sneering. He went on: 'Speaking of swabs, you take Israel along o' you. And your pet, comrade Pew, and his creature, Black Dog. I'll have Anderson and Morgan, they ain't so good at speechifying and they does what I tells 'em straight off. Any queries, John Silver?'

John said, 'What's that Israel's wrapping up in swaddling clothes? He's treating it like it was a present for the Viceroy of New Castile.'

'And so it is, in a manner of speaking,' replied Flint. ' 'Tis an hexplosive device to blast a hole in the dons' fortifications and make your path straight.'

He rose unsteadily to his feet. 'Well, quartermaster, I wants us stepping out in half an hour. See to it.'

Soon the buccaneers were moving off, following the stream as the darkness closed around them. It was a hard slog all right, even though a full moon shone upon them. The marshy land around the stream was treacherous, and once the two men staggering under the weight of Israel's mine were nearly swallowed up in the mud.

Flint marched at the head of the column, cursing the conditions under foot, and striking any who trod on his heels with the flat blade of his cutlass.

If any man deserved praise for keeping those mud-spattered files together it was Long John Silver. Never before had his gifts of leadership been so much in evidence and so sorely needed. He worked like a man possessed – as indeed he was possessed, by lust for the treasure lying at Santa Lena. But that was not the only reason for his ceaseless activity. The truth is that Silver had come to regard the grand design on the plate treasure as his very own. The deeper he became embroiled in the project, the more he planned, exhorted, and pushed the buccaneers on, the firmer became his conviction that the lion's share of the booty was his by rights. He was a single-minded man in pursuit of any prize, was Long John, and the prize now dangling before him was indeed a stupendous one, the stuff that dreams are made of, and more than ample repayment for his past sufferings and humiliation.

So it was small wonder that he strove to the limits of his strength to ensure the success of the bid to seize the plate treasure. If any man in the straggling columns faltered, John appeared at his side with a jest or a word of encouragement. At one point George Merry and a runaway slave called Jacob Washington came to blows, but Silver was on them in a trice, shaking them by the scruffs of their necks and then booting them back into line. With Pew's help he kept the files on the right track, avoiding the more treacherous pieces of marshland, and pushing the buccaneers step by step towards Santa Lena.

At last they could see in the distance, lit by moonlight, a couple of tumbledown huts, and beyond them the dark shapes of a scattering of more substantial houses.

Flint called a halt. As the men gathered round him he hissed, 'That there dung-heap is Santa Lena. The half of you what's detailed to come along o' me is to 'ave the himportant task of taking Government House, beyond those shacks an' near the harbour. Mr Silver is to lead th'other half agin the fort, When you takes it, you hoists the signal from the flag pole to let me and Billy Bones and that French swab out there know all's well.

'The signal,' he continued, 'is to be the jolly roger what Black Dog's got wrapped around 'is midriff, so long as the fool don't get it ripped off him in the attack. But there ain't much chance of that, I reckon; he'll be skulking in the shadows when the rest o' you goes over the walls!'

Black Dog squirmed at this, and slunk to the outer edge of the circle of buccaneers.

'Anderson! Morgan! O'Brien!' he went on. 'You're coming with me and my party.' He looked round him with evident distaste. 'There ain't half a dozen real fighters among you, but I'll see you don't turn tail, you lubbers!'

Then to Silver, 'As soon as we see the sun's first light, we attacks. Together like. I'm moving off. You get your scum into position now.' With that, he turned and led his men off westwards.

Silver looked wryly at the remaining buccaneers. Then, throwing out his arms in a gesture of fatherly goodwill, he said, 'Lads, it's proud I am to march along o'you. Why, I never see'd a finer set o' men. Bless me if th'old Dook o' Marlborough wouldn't count hisself lucky to lead you agin that fortress over there!'

As his audience stirred, warmed and encouraged by his words, he continued, 'Not that the fortress seems much of a thing to me. I'll warrant there ain't a stone in it, just logs o' wood and a few nails. Why, we could tear it apart with our bare hands!'

'But' – and here his voice grew softer and more confidential – 'Israel has been and rigged up a devilish device that would lay the walls o' Cartagena in ruins, let alone that plaything over there! Boys, we'll catch the dons in their nightshirts, and no mistake. You'll be rich, every man, and I can't say fairer than that.'

'Over there,' he gestured towards the north-west, 'lies the

spit of land where the fort is sityated. We'll make for it now. As soon as the dawn comes up, we'll walk straight into it, and you may lay to that. I'll lead one storming party and Gabby Pew th'other. I wants a dozen men to accompany Israel and help blast down the walls and nobble them dago guns. Right! Let's move off, stealthy-like. You'll have something to tell your grandchildren after this day's work, I'll be bound!'

With this he began to lead his men towards the Spanish fortification while, to the east, the dark sky began almost imperceptibly to lighten.

22

❴ *The Attack* ❵

F lint's party was the first to attack. The buccaneers led
by Silver were a good five hundred yards from the fortifications when they heard the fitful explosions of muskets
and a devilish hullabaloo from the direction of Government
House.

Silver cursed softly to Pew. 'Goddamme if that pig-
headed swab ain't jumped the gun. 'Tain't properly first
light yet. Trust Flint to act as if we don't count for aught!'

Then, signalling to his men, he led them in a headlong
dash for the fort. Luckily the going was good – mostly firm
sandy soil, bound together with a top covering of grass and
reeds and with hardly a stone to impede progress.

The pirates fanned out as they raced towards the fortifications, with Israel and his encumbered helpers making
slow progress at the rear. Silver had guessed that the
Spaniards would have posted sentries along the north and
west sides of the fortifications to keep a look-out on the
seaward approaches. He was proved right even as his
storming party approached the southern wall and Pew's
the eastern. The Spanish commander had clearly not
anticipated a landward attack, and it was not until the
buccaneers were a mere one hundred yards from the walls
that the first enemy musket flashed in the murky light.

Doubtless the commotion from Government House had
alerted the sentries. Even so the pirates were under the fortress's walls before more than half a dozen shots had been
fired at them – only one of which struck home, killing a
young ruffian from Norwich in mid-stride.

Gasping for breath, Silver saw that the exterior of the fort
was constructed of tree trunks and rough-sawn planks. It

was hardly a forbidding edifice – nor was there any sort of moat as far as he could see.

From the east wall he could hear Pew's men crashing their scaling ladders against the timbers and whooping as they clambered up. Above his head, orders were being shouted in Spanish. Twenty paces to his left he saw Ben Gunn stepping out from the foot of the wall to gape at the fortification. The fool! He ordered him back with an angry flick of his hand.

It was getting lighter with every minute. Thank God! Here was Israel, his thick hair drenched with sweat, helping to haul his mine under the wall. It still looked remarkably like a swaddled pork-barrel to Silver – and probably that is exactly what it was. Israel was unrolling a fuse, maybe six foot in length. He shouted across, 'Barbecue! I'm lighting it now. Get 'em away, and lying down, quick!'

The buccaneers had barely time to fling themselves down further along the walls when Israel's mine exploded. It was like a volcano erupting. God knows what he had packed into it. Silver always swore that there must have been a gallon of Flint's favourite rum inside that pork-barrel, primed with a brace of his favourite oaths into the bargain! At any rate, it worked. While sand and fragments of splintered timber rained about his ears, Silver was on his feet, leading his men towards the site of the explosion. Israel Hands staggered towards him through the swirling smoke and dust, his face black as a chimney sweep's, blood trickling from a gash above his right eye.

'I near didn't make it, John,' Israel croaked. 'That fuse it burnt quicker'n I cares to think on.' He waved a fist towards the fort. 'But there you are, you could drive the London post-coach through that hole, I reckon!'

Leaving Hands to fend for himself, Silver ran towards the wall. Where the mine had exploded the fort's timbers formed a broken and charred frame round a breach some eight feet high by eleven across.

Silver darted through the gap, a pistol in his left hand, his cutlass glinting in his right.

Where were the Spaniards? He stumbled. Here was one, at any rate, a corpse swathed in a charred uniform, blasted, like the wall, by Israel's mine. Other bodies lay a few yards off, blown from the ramparts as like as not.

The buccaneers were surging round him. Some distance away Pew's men were struggling to win control of the eastern ramparts. There were the Spaniards right enough! A score of them at last, intent on holding the wall. Among them ran an officer, bellowing orders, his wig tilted comically over his left eye. Muskets exploded among the Spanish ranks, and Silver saw two of Pew's men topple from the wall. More shots, and a pirate fell screaming at the feet of the Spanish officer.

Silver made for the officer. Suddenly a tattered figure barred his path: a Spanish soldier, swaying from the shock of the recent blast, but sufficiently recovered to raise his musket butt to strike Silver down. John parried the blow with a sharp upward movement of his left arm. As his forearm smashed painfully against the man's musket, the hammer on his flintlock pistol slipped; there was an abrupt explosion and the Spaniard fell to the ground, clutching his throat, blood seeping through his fingers.

Thrusting the spent pistol into his belt, Silver paused for a moment to look about him. The rising sun had by now fully illuminated the interior of the fortification. It was a simple construction: heavy timber walls with a high parapet running their full length, and to the northern, seaward side, a wooden look-out tower from which flew the flag of imperial Spain. The dons' guns, he saw, were trained on the harbour and out to sea; that was only to be expected, after all, but it certainly gave the buccaneers a free hand inside the fortifications.

Here was Black Dog plucking at his sleeve. 'John, I can't

see no more than thirty dagoes hereabouts. But that there officer is worth another score, the way he's a-ranting and urging 'em on.'

Silver leapt forward, avoiding the dying soldier whom he had shot but seconds previously. As if warned by some familiar spirit, the Spanish officer swung round to face him, raising the fine point of his sword to fend off the attack. As his cutlass whistled through the air to crash against his opponent's firm Toledo blade, Long John plucked his pistol from his belt and hurled it at the Spaniard's head. The man flinched and threw up his left hand to protect his face, but even as he did so Silver's cutlass slid down past his sword arm and chopped into the base of his neck. Already off balance, the officer stumbled backwards, still grasping his sword. Long John was on him in a flash, leaning forwards as he slashed once more at his foe's throat. The Spaniard gave a dull groan and fell, almost gracefully, upon his left side.

After this the Spanish garrison gave up the ghost. Soon they were a disorderly rabble scurrying hither and thither for refuge. Pew was able to lead his men, whooping in triumph, over the eastern walls, and within half an hour the fortification was in the hands of the buccaneers.

With Black Dog at his heels, Long John kicked open the door of the watch-tower. Inside, a couple of Spanish soldiers fell to their knees, holding up their hands and gabbling for mercy.

An open wooden staircase led to the top of the tower. There was no one to defend it, and within minutes Black Dog had hauled down the Spanish ensign and hoisted the jolly roger in its place.

'That should bring Billy a-scampering in,' Silver said.

'And the Frenchy too, if he's hereabouts,' said Black Dog, squinting with pleasure at the skull and cross-bones fluttering over his head.

Silver turned his eye-glass towards the harbour. There

were the ships that were to carry the plate treasure across the Atlantic. Seven of them, lying like fat sows at the quayside. Men were clambering over some of them, and their gangplanks were thronged with moving figures.

Pew suddenly appeared at Silver's side, his pale face smeared with grime and blood. He was still gasping for breath, but he said, as best he could, 'We done it, then, matey! It warn't so bad. Not when you chopped down that swab of an officer. I passed him just now. He was still a–groaning, so I finished him off. Merciful like.'

'Turn your eye yonder, Gabby,' said Silver, simply. He handed Pew the telescope. 'Damme if they ain't trying to cast off them treasure ships and quit the harbour. We'll lose it all. What's Flint a-doing, the devil take him! I can't see no sign of him.'

He turned to Black Dog. 'Get Israel here, double quick, even if you has to carry him like a babby!'

Within a moment or two Israel hauled himself up the staircase and leant heavily against the parapet.

'Israel,' said Silver, 'you're just the man to save this here sityation! Heaven-sent you was, goddamme! Scatter them dago lubbers at the harbour down there. Blast 'em with their own guns! And do it now, or you can kiss that treasure goodbye. Why, we've lost enough likely lads already, a-taking this fort, without letting that loot slip through our fingers.'

Hands nodded. He seemed scarcely recovered from the shock of the exploding mine. But he was a rare one, was Israel, and as dedicated a master-gunner as you could hope to meet. Soon he was dancing along the ramparts, sighting the dons' cannon, and yelling orders as clear as a bell.

His first shot screamed through the rigging of the nearest transport ship and the second smashed into the quay, sending enough stone splinters flying to cut down a dozen men. Roundshot after roundshot crashed among the treasure ships.

After ten minutes of this bombardment Silver roared, 'Enough, Israel! I never asked you to sink 'em! I wants my pieces of eight in my purse, not amid the slime on the harbour bottom!'

As Hands called a halt to the cannonade, Pew screeched: 'Barbecue! The *Walrus* is bearing down on the harbour-mouth. Billy's see'd the signal! And there's the Frenchy, tagging a mile or two to the stern.'

Silver said quietly, 'That's it. We've got 'em now. They'll never get away.' Then, more loudly, 'Gabby, I'm taking half the lads to see what's what with Flint down at Government House. You stay here in charge o' the fort. Keep Israel on his toes behind them guns. Do what you like with the prisoners here, so long as they don't trouble us no more. And, Gabby, keep a good watch to seaward! We don't want any dago escort ships a-creeping up on us. They're due any day now, I should reckon.'

Soon Silver was leading his men past the quayside. They met no resistance: Israel's bombardment had scattered and demoralised the Spaniards in the vicinity of the treasure ships. It took all of Long John's self-discipline to pass by those ships and head for Government House instead.

Government House was a stone-built, three-storey building barely half a mile from the harbour, set back from the dirt track which was Santa Lena's main road. As the buccaneers approached it through palm trees and bushes of purple and pink oleanders, Silver saw with relief that Flint had seized it after all. Job Anderson and half a dozen pirates were standing guard on the steps of the house.

Silver bounded up the steps and grasped Anderson's broad hand in greeting. 'Job, my old son, so you've done it! Does Flint know where all the treasure's hid?'

Anderson said, ' 'Twas easy enough, John. The grandee and his folks were all a-bed when we took the house. I just booted the front door open and in we went. There was a couple o' servants in the kitchen that started screamin' till

Flint knocked 'em both on the head. One was a right pretty gal an' all.'

'Where's Flint now, Job?'

'He's upstairs a-trying to coax the key to the strongroom out o' the grandee and his missus. He's trussed 'em up in their own bedroom like. He'll have spilt a drop o' blood by now, I shouldn't wonder.'

'I shouldn't wonder neither. Now, Job, I've a task for you, my boy. Take these lubbers what's come with me, and head back for the treasure ships. Clear the dons off them transports and put a gang of our lads aboard each one. If the dons don't like it, cut 'em down! Billy Bones'll be sailing into the harbour within the half-hour, with our French friend not far behind. Tell Billy to start loading the stuff aboard the *Walrus* and the *Jean Calvin*. Tell him to count it, too, in particular all as goes into the Frenchy's hold. Can you remember all that, Job?'

Anderson began to repeat it stolidly: 'Now, Job, I've got a task for you, my boy. Take these lubbers what's come with me —'

'Avast there, Job! You'll do. Be off with you. I'll be down with the cap'n in a brace of shakes, and you may lay to that!'

As Anderson led the buccaneers in the direction of the quayside, Silver entered Government House and, passing quickly through the hall, began to ascend the wide sweep of stairs. There was little doubt that the house had been in Flint's hands for some time: tapestries had been ripped off the walls, shattered porcelain littered the stairs, and a great dark oil painting of His Most Catholic Majesty Philip V had been crudely scarred by a cutlass blade.

From an upstairs room came shouts and muffled screams, and, suddenly, Flint's rare, harsh, cackling laugh, reminding Silver uncannily of the taking of Dubois' mansion in Barbados so many years before.

As he entered the bedroom Silver saw Flint's hands closing round the throat of a woman of some thirty years of age. Flint shook her head violently from side to side, and the woman's dark hair fell this way and that across her face. She wore, Silver noticed, a blue nightgown, part of which had been ripped open near her neck.

Next to the young woman was a gold-encrusted four-poster bed. An elderly man, his pointed beard flecked with grey hairs, was lashed to one of the posts. He, too, wore a nightgown. At his feet lay the body of a middle-aged woman; his wife, Silver thought.

Flint stopped shaking the head of the dark-haired woman and hissed, 'Where's the key to the storehouse, you bitch? I'll lop off your fingers one by one, I will. I'll burn your cheeks with a slow-match, by thunder! Speak up, you papist whore!'

The woman sobbed, and turned her head aside. Silver saw she had large, dark eyes, and a thin, well-shaped nose.

Half a dozen buccaneers stood near Flint. Among them was Tom Morgan, chewing thoughtfully on some tobacco, and looking no more disturbed than a spectator at a cock fight.

Suddenly Flint thrust the woman roughly from him. He laughed again, the same harsh cackle as before, but containing, so it seemed to Silver, a note of panic.

As he approached Flint, Silver said blandly, 'You having a spot o' trouble, cap'n?'

Flint said viciously, 'So you got here at last, quartermaster. I thought you was too yaller to risk your skin near Government House! Well, now you're here, make these Spanish swine cough up the keys to the storehouse what's next to this mansion. Goddamme, if it ain't built strong enough to withstand a month's siege, and we've no gunpowder here to knock it down!'

'We can get enough gunpowder here within the hour to blow up all of Santa Lena,' said Silver calmly. 'But that

don't signify. 'Twould be easier to winkle the keys out o'
these prisoners here.'

'Easy!' cried Flint. 'I'd sooner squeeze blood out of a
stone! Why, I'll throttle the pair of 'em with me bare hands,
just like th'old cow on the floor there. Why won't they
speak, eh? Tell me that?'

'Well, it can't be on account o' your use o' the language,
cap'n. I never know'd a man talk sweeter, and you may lay
to that.'

Flint glanced quickly at Silver through his narrow eyes,
but John continued blithely enough. ' 'Course it might be
as how they don't speak English at all, being Spanish born
and bred. Now I know you've never let a word o' that papist
lingo defile your tongue, you having religious principles an'
all. But I can bring out a particle or two of their speech,
heathenish though it be to all right-thinking Englishmen.'

'Jabber away, Sir Barbecue,' said Flint scornfully. 'I'll
take me pick o' their belongings meantime. If you ain't
made 'em squeak in 'alf an 'our, I'll slice 'em up, like this!'
And he slashed fiercely at the bedpost, cutting a deep notch
a bare inch above the Spanish gentleman's head. The man
shuddered in a nervous spasm, and then went limp.
Fainted, poor old devil, thought Silver. Flint turned and
stamped out of the room, bellowing at Tom Morgan and
the rest to follow him.

Silver found himself alone with the young woman. She
was sitting on the edge of the bed. The look that she now
gave him was a mixture of defiance and despair, he noticed.
For the first time since the attack on Santa Lena had begun
he was conscious of feelings other than blood-lust and
aggression. This woman had not chosen to be an obstacle
between Flint's buccaneers and part of the treasure.
Possibly she was a daughter or daughter-in-law of the
bearded man lashed to the bedpost; the dead woman on the
floor was very probably her mother. What had such an ob-
viously well-bred young woman done to provoke this

slaughter and brutality? Did she deserve her present humiliation, or the prospect of sudden death?

Moving towards her, Silver said slowly, struggling for the Spanish words, 'I am sorry if you are hurt, miss.'

She looked up at him. For a moment she seemed about to reply. Then she turned her head away sharply, and pressed her lips close together as if to prevent any words issuing from them.

Silver said ponderously, not sure if his meaning was clear. 'My name is John. I will protect you. But we must know where the keys are. The keys to the . . .' He paused. What the devil was storehouse in Spanish? He suddenly recalled the word that had been used on Dubois' plantation years before. '*Dépôt*,' he said. The woman shook her head. That could either mean that she did not understand French or that she would not reveal the whereabouts of the keys.

He tried again, mixing Spanish and French words together. 'If you do not tell the captain he will kill you. Soon. First he will kill your father, as he has killed your mother, then you. Soon.'

She shuddered. So that *was* her father slumped against the bed-post.

'I will keep you safe. You and your father. But only if you give me the keys.'

The woman raised her eyes to his. They were as beautiful as Annette's, and no mistake.

She said, without emotion. 'No, you are English brigands. Soon our warships will come to Santa Lena, and then you will be destroyed.'

Silver said gently, 'Your warships are far away. It is our warships that control Santa Lena now. We have captured the fort, and, even as I speak, my men are loading your treasure onto our ships.'

'Are you the captain then? Are they *your* men?'

God, Silver thought, how do you explain quartermaster in broken Spanish and rusty French? He said, 'I am one of the captains, and maybe the only one that cares whether you live or die.' A half-truth that, but possibly effective all the same.

There was a silence. From the ground floor came the sound of breaking glass. Flint was ransacking the house as thoroughly as if it were were his first raid and there were no captured treasure ships lying in the harbour.

The woman suddenly said, 'If I tell you where to find the keys, how do I know you will protect us? Perhaps you are a murderer too, but one who speaks softly when he has the need.'

Silver smiled at her. 'That is true. But at least I talk of protecting you, not just of killing you.' He waited for a moment, and then said carefully, 'Soon the other captain will return. The one with the dark face. He will bring other men with him. You *must* hurry!'

What was this? The woman was clutching his hand, pressing into his palm with her smooth fingers. 'Do you give me your word, captain? Your word of honour that you will save us?'

'Yes, miss, I give you my word, so help me.'

'The keys are here. See!'

She rose and moved swiftly to the bedpost to which her father was tied. Standing on tiptoes she pressed one of the gilded knobs, high up, above his head. There was a click and a little door, nine inches by four, swung open.

Silver went to her side, towering over her. He fished in the cavity with his right hand. The keys, by thunder! He pulled them out. Six of them, on a ring; the storehouse keys must be among them.

Boots crashing on the stairs, and Flint's voice cursing and sneering. Silver took the young woman by the hand. Nodding towards her unconscious father he said, 'We best leave him. Come back and get him later. Now you come with me. Quick.'

As they stepped onto the landing they came face to face

with Flint, reeling against the balustrade, and evidently the worse for drink. He leered when he saw Silver and the young woman. 'My, ain't you a pretty picture. The two lovebirds about to quit the nest!'

He leant over the balustrade and shrieked, 'Morgan! Dirk! Come here, you swabs, and see Barbecue and his lovely bride Donna Maria Pigswill!'

Now, thought Silver; I could do it now! Pitch him over the balustrade, and say it was the drink. Set up as captain in his place, and take his share of the treasure into the bargain.

But Flint swung back to face him, and he merely said, somewhat reproachfully, 'Why, cap'n, been quenching that terrible thirst of yours again?'

Before Flint had time to reply, Morgan and Dirk Campbell and a pack of buccaneers clattered up the stairway.

Silver said, seizing the initiative, 'Lads, I've got 'em; the keys! And this young lady's still got all her fingers and toes, and not a scar on her face. The storehouse is ours to open as we pleases. Go to it!'

Flint snarled, 'Steady on, quartermaster!' He snatched the keys out of Silver's hand. 'I'll be the one to cast my eye over the storehouse. You get off and make sure them treasure ships is picked clean. Take Donna Maria Pigswill with you, she might get her throat cut if she tarries hereabouts.'

The Spanish woman said with dignity, 'Donna Isabella Fabiola Anna Mendez-Lalaguna.' She had somehow understood Flint's insult, it seemed.

Flint said succinctly, 'Go to hell!' He made off down the stairs, narrowly avoiding a headlong tumble towards the end of the last flight.

Silver turned to Donna Isabella and said in his awkward, formal Spanish, 'Go and dress, please, miss. Then return to this place as soon as you can.'

Within ten minutes the woman was back, properly dressed, and accompanied by her father whom she had revived and cut loose. Silver said, 'I will set you free. Both of you. But not here, it is too dangerous. For the moment you will be my prisoners.'

The woman nodded and smiled. Silver felt touched, both by her quick understanding and by her evident trust in him. He made haste to tie her wrists behind her back, and then trussed her father in similar fashion. Then, beckoning them to follow him, he led them out of Government House.

As he made towards the harbour Silver overtook Tom Morgan and a gang of buccaneers dragging an assortment of sacks and chests behind them.

'Ahoy there, Tom! Flint's managed to turn the key in the storehouse lock, I see. What you got there, my lad?'

Morgan halted and raised his dim brown eyes to Silver. The sweat was pouring down his face. 'Don't you go mockin' the cap'n, John Silver. He's a nose for loot, he has. We've cleaned out the storehouse good and proper. This 'ere,' he gestured clumsily about him, 'is the most of it. Precious jewels, topazes, emeralds and the like, set into brooches and bangles for the main part. But some is loose. There's some minted coin an' all, in that sack there.'

'Well done, Tom Morgan, you was always a sharp one when it come to business. Mind you stow it away good and safe. Well, press on my, lad, I'm just escorting these swabs of prisoners to the *Walrus*. They may come in right useful as hostages before we sets sail.'

Morgan nodded, though without real comprehension, Silver thought. Then, stooping, he shouldered a chest bound with three iron bands and trudged off towards the harbour.

There were no Spanish troops in sight. The approaches to the harbour were deserted, save for the occasional cluster of buccaneers scurrying back with items of plunder. A sharp exclamation came from Donna Isabella's father. The old man was looking behind them and speaking rapidly, angrily, to his daughter. Silver turned and saw that smoke was billowing from the upper storeys of Government House as if from a dormant volcano suddenly brought to life. Flint was on his way back, then! More smoke was rising from the huddle of wooden buildings facing the harbour. Soon Santa Lena would be like the dozen or so other towns that had fallen into Flint's hands – gutted, defiled and, finally, destroyed.

If he meant to set the young woman and her father free he must do so now! The wind was blowing great billows of smoke across their path, shrouding them from sight. Silver untied Donna Isabella's hand and led her quickly away from the harbour towards the burning houses opposite; her father stumbled behind them, coughing as the smoke burnt his lungs.

They passed between two blazing buildings. One, Silver saw, had been a ships' chandler's, but the door was broken down and the window shutters hanging awry; a huddled figure lay face-down in the doorway, his left arm twisted and broken across his back.

Further off there were more wooden buildings, beyond them a scattering of Indian huts, and then the encroaching brushwood and jungle. That, no doubt, was where a good many of the surviving inhabitants of Santa Lena would be found now, crouching in the undergrowth hoping to escape detection.

Silver quickly walked a score more paces. Then he stopped and said to the woman, 'Go towards the jungle. You will be safe there.'

Why did she hesitate? Her father was already making rapid progress away from them. He said, more roughly, 'Go now! Do you want to be killed?'

What was this? She was clutching at his shirt front, weeping and talking; talking so fast, in fact, that he could barely understand her meaning.

'I will come with you. Yes, I will come with you to the ships! You are the captain. And strong. You will protect me. Serve you. Yes, yes, I will serve you. Truthfully!'

Shaken, Silver said, in English, 'No, it won't do, miss. Now, get you gone!'

Clearly understanding him, the woman said, 'Yes, I *will* come. My mother is dead, back there. My father, well,' she shrugged dismissively. 'My husband died three years ago. The fever. This place. I hate it! I will come with you. Be your woman.'

She wept, and without thinking Silver enfolded her in his great arms. Here was a pretty pickle! How could he take her aboard? Flint would never stand for it. Nor would Billy Bones, as like as not. He'd have to kill Flint first. Kill him for this unknown woman. And the plate treasure lying there, waiting to be carried off and divided out! He'd look a proper fool! Maybe Flint would kill him first anyway. Then there was Annette. Of course, she was a long way off. The dons! There might be a pack of frigates bearing down on Santa Lena at this very moment! Trapped in this narrow harbour with nothing but the jungle and savage Indians at their backs. A fine way to end!

He was aware that the woman's tears were soaking through his shirt front and trickling down his chest.

'Enough! Be gone!' he said. Suddenly he hated her as well as pitied her. He took her by the shoulders and, turning her in the direction taken by her father, pushed her after him. A cloud of smoke surged round them, momentarily hiding her from his sight. Silver heard her cry out as he plunged back through the smoke towards the harbour. Whether it was the cry, so wretched and forlorn, or the stench of burning, he never knew, but suddenly he felt shaken and cold and ill.

23
❦ The Taking of the Treasure ❧

Billy Bones shook his fist at Silver as the latter ran along the quayside to where the *Walrus* had been tied up. Her gangplank was thronged with buccaneers struggling to load the plate treasure as speedily as possible. Silver saw with delight that a number of Spaniards were also engaged in the work, driven on by Job Anderson with blows from a hand spike.

Why was Billy in such a tantrum then? So far the venture was paying off handsomely. Silver paused to draw breath. All around him was activity and, in a way, order. He shook his head and began to walk, not run, towards the *Walrus*. To his dying day, he thought, he'd never fathom how the dons left Santa Lena so wide open to attack with all that silver and gold there for the taking. Maybe it was just rank inefficiency; after all, the Viceroy of New Castile hardly ever seemed aware of what the Viceroy of New Spain was up to; and in some ports Spanish warships lay unemployed, with no crews to man them, while buccaneers played havoc throughout the Main. It was a ramshackle system all right, far too ready to coast along on past glories, and only rarely able to take a firm grip on the present.

As Silver approached Bones he noticed Tom Morgan some way off, squinting at him over his shoulder. He called out, 'Ahoy there, Billy! This is what I calls shipshape and Bristol-fashion, my old son!'

Billy said angrily, 'You'd best step inside the captain's cabin, Barbecue. I've a word or two to say to you!'

As soon as they entered Flint's unkempt and rum-stained cabin Bones turned on Silver, his nut-brown face contorted with rage.

'Where's them hostages Tom Morgan tell'd me of? And where's Flint, God damn him! And you, you been playing the fool with some hidalgo's daughter I hears. D'you reckon this loot's going to float out to sea by magic, draw'd by angels a-flapping their rosy wings? We'll miss the tide if we don't get the treasure aboard within two hours. That Frenchy ship alongside us is already busting at the seams with gold. Her captain's stuck to his duty like a man. And her quartermaster too, I shouldn't wonder!'

'Belay there, Bill! You trying to blow me out o' the water with one broadside? Let's take it shot by shot. 'Twill be clearer then I reckon.'

Bones nodded coldly, and Silver continued, 'First off, Flint'll be here directly, though whether he'll be sober is another thing entirely. Next, I've not been idle. Pew and me took that fort, and cleared your way to sail in here as if 'twas Madagasky itself. As for the hidalgo's daughter, why bless me if she didn't hand over the keys what opened the storehouse. D'you reckon she'd have done that without me sweet-talking her a bit? Well, you got any more complaints, Billy boy? Speak up, if you've a mind!'

'Where's that dago woman now?' asked Bones roughly. 'And her father? How d'you know we won't need 'em as hostages if the dons cut up rough? Or as guides, even? Who are you to let 'em go? I'm mate and sailing master, Flint's right-hand man you might say, and I don't hold with let-ting 'em go. You've gone too far, John Silver, and you may lay to that!'

He still seemed beside himself with rage, Silver noted. He said prudently, 'You're right, Billy. I sees it now. You're a man o' vision, as I've always said. But the truth is th'old man was near to dying, and his daughter out of her mind – raving something terrible, she was! I didn't reckon they'd be much use to you or the cap'n in that state. For all I knows they're dead now, the pair on 'em.'

There was a lengthy pause. At last Bones said, with

deliberate diction, 'God damn you, John, for a smooth-tongued rogue. I can't make head nor tail of you, and that's a fact.' He looked into Silver's eyes and then said softly, 'There are times when I curse the day I ever quit Connecticut.'

'Don't say that, Billy! Why, we'd all be sunk without you! Look, you've set me to rights, you have. More'n that, anyone can see with half an eye you're worn out with frettin' here by yourself. Now I'm here, and I'll get that treasure stowed away in no time. You leave it to Long John, my boy!'

There was a commotion outside: cursing and ragged snatches of song. 'Flint's back, I reckon,' said Silver wryly. 'All the more reason to put our backs into it and clear the loot.' Bones nodded, and stooped to examine a chart lying on the table.

As Silver went out onto the deck, bellowing orders, Flint stumbled past him, accompanied by Darby McGraw, and singing as lustily as if belonging to some satanic choir.

Watching the faithful Darby tugging Flint aft, Silver considered the situation he now found himself in. Flint was once more becoming a slave to rum, and seemed able to hold less and less. If Flint should die of drink, as was more than likely, then the leadership of the buccaneers would lie between him and Bones. Did Billy feel this too? Was that why he had flown off the handle a while back? Trying to put him in his place, by the powers! Well, that wasn't so easily done. He was a damned sight sharper than Billy, that he did know. Stronger too. Stronger and sharper! That's what counted. He'd keep an eye on Master Bones. Before, they'd mostly acted together, and agreed on policy for much of the time. Now things might well be different. Maybe he couldn't trust Billy any more, nor Billy him.

So, at the moment of their greatest triumph, Silver's friendship with Billy Bones was blighted, and a mistrust sprang up between them which was to have the gravest of consequences in the unfolding of this story.

Not that Long John had much time to ponder over such matters at Santa Lena. There were the treasure ships to be unloaded first. Of the seven transports, only four had any quantity of treasure aboard. Doubtless the dons had plann-ed to bring more silver and gold from inland before the con-voy set sail; there was also the contents of the storehouse which Flint had rifled. Still, the haul was a staggering one, and Silver laughed with pure pleasure when he saw it.

Counting the treasure that had already been loaded aboard the *Jean Calvin*, the pirates had seized a hundred and ten bars of gold, over four hundred silver bars, and fifty-three bags of minted coin; then there were two baskets of jewels, some beautifully worked weapons, and the rest of the plunder from the storehouse. It was greater wealth than any of the buccaneers had imagined ever existed – let alone that it should be gathered together in one place, and theirs into the bargain!

Getting it aboard the *Walrus* was no easy matter. Even men as strong as O'Brien staggered under the weight of two silver bars. In the end it was done, but Billy Bones had missed his afternoon tide and the sun had been set some three hours before the last item was packed below hatches.

Flint had sobered up by then, and had taken to passing among his crew claiming every credit for the raid and regal-ing any that would listen with tales of his prowess and presence of mind. For the most part, the buccaneers slept like dogs, exhausted by their labours and little caring for Flint's ravings.

Shortly before dawn, Silver sent word to Pew and Israel Hands to bring back their men from the fort. They arrived within half an hour, and shouted for joy when they saw the booty below the *Walrus's* decks.

What was left of Santa Lena smouldered and glowed in the early morning light as the *Walrus* took the tide out to sea. She cleared the bar adjacent to the fort with her customary dexterity and was soon in open waters. The Frenchman sailed twenty minutes later, the idea being that the two vessels would tag along together till they could find a suitable spot to anchor and share out the treasure.

Whether the captain of the *Jean Calvin* had any plans to give Flint the slip once he was out at sea we shall never know, for as his vessel crept out past the fort two of the dons' cannons opened up. Israel, it seemed, had failed to spike all the guns before he left. Maybe he had been at the Spaniards' wine store, for the buccaneers manning the fort had soon consumed every scrap of food and liquor in sight.

At any rate, the Spanish gunners were able to fire roundshot after roundshot into the heavy-laden and slow-moving Frenchman. It was the first real bit of fight that the dons had showed since the fort and Government House had been taken; but it was a telling cannonade all right – at point blank range. The *Jean Calvin* lost her mizzen mast within five minutes, and the main topsail yard went crashing down soon afterwards. By some miracle she managed to pull clear, painfully and slowly, like a London cripple escaping from the stones of marauding urchins.

Once the *Jean Calvin* had made her escape, Flint sent off Bones and Silver in the *Walrus*'s long-boat to see the extent of the damage. Silver waded through the carnage aboard the French vessel: the dead and dying were jumbled together in unsightly heaps, and blood and guts were spattered everywhere. The French captain breathed his last shortly after Bones and Silver climbed over the side, and a good half of his crew were dead or else on the way to Davy Jones's locker. Those French pirates that had survived were either struggling to rig a jury mast in place of the lost mizzen mast, or below decks desperately pumping out the water that was pouring in through a brace of holes below the water-line.

Silver soon set the half dozen of the *Walrus*'s crew that

had accompanied Bones and him aboard at work baling out the Frenchman's hold.

It was not long, however, before Billy Bones drew him aside and said, 'Barbecue, things can't go on like this. I propose we takes over this 'ere vessel. If we don't the loot'll be on the sea bed afore nightfall.'

'And what d'you think French'll say to that, Billy? A bow and a smile and a "*merci beaucoup,* Cap'n Flint", eh?'

Bones scowled. 'I'd cut 'em down soon as say "knife", I would, just so long as we kept the treasure safe.'

'Them's dainty sentiments, Billy, and I won't deny the outlook's as dirty as the belly of a Cheapside whore when the fleet's in. I don't fancy a pack o' dago frigates bearing down on us, by thunder! But these French lubbers have been with us hand and glove in this 'ere enterprise. Seems to me we should be assisting 'em, not cutting their throats like so many porkit pigs!'

'My, ain't you the sperrit o' mercy, John Silver,' Bones said derisively. 'You took the wrong course as a gen'leman o' fortune, I reckon. Bein' an angel is more in your line o' duty; Flint's sentiments is the same as mine on that score, as well you know.'

'Billy, you're a tougher nut than me an' that's a fact! And you've a way with King George's English as is wonderful to behold; for a Yankee born and bred, at any road. But speaking of Flint recalls me to my duty. We'll put it to the cap'n, eh? He's a way o' seeing things clear as daylight when he's sober. We've tangled hawsers, you and me, Billy, maybe the cap'n can cut us free.'

So, leaving a handful of buccaneers aboard the *Jean Calvin* to work at the pumps, Bones and Silver rowed back to the *Walrus* a few cables away to the stern.

Flint hummed and hawed when he heard how things were aboard the Frenchman. Then he withdrew to his cabin, 'To think it over, peaceful like.' His deliberations were hardly peaceful, for he spent a good quarter of an hour yelling blue murder at Darby McGraw who, being dumb, was hard put to answer back.

At any rate, it was while he was closeted with the only human being he ever really trusted that Flint took the fateful decision to head for Kidd's Island. There, he argued, they could patch up the Frenchman properly, if that proved possible, and decide what to do with the treasure crammed into the holds of both ships.

Now Kidd's Island was named after the famous buccaneer who had used the place for careening his vessels. Flint had taken to bringing the *Walrus* there from time to time to do likewise. It was an isolated scrap of land, well removed from the main trade routes in the Caribbean and thus ideally suited as a pirates' hide-out or resting place. Apart from some wild goats, there were few animals on the island, though tropical birds screeched among the trees and great, brightly-coloured butterflies fluttered over the foliage. Below the strangely shaped hills, of which the tallest was named the Spy-glass, the land was, for the most part, wooded. Throughout much of the island the air smelt sweet enough, but here and there a rank bad odour arose from swamps and marshy land – fine breeding places for fever and pestilence.

The *Walrus* sailed into North Inlet towing the stricken French boat behind her. An examination of the damage she had received soon confirmed Flint in his judgement that she should simply be beached and left to rot.

But first the Frenchman was stripped of all plunder and valuables, and these were brought on shore. The *Walrus,* too, was unloaded in preparation for careening, and the plate treasure stacked neatly into gold bars, silver bars and coin; there was also a considerable cache of arms, some of it beautifully fashioned and studded with jewels.

While the men worked at the task of scraping the barnacles and weeds off the *Walrus*'s bottom, Silver took Flint aside.

'Cap'n,' he said. 'You've pulled a capital trick, you have. I never see'd a smarter man than you, and you may lay to that. But we're in a pretty mess now, I reckon. If we stow the loot from the Frenchy in the *Walrus,* together with all our treasure, her timbers'll open up in the first heavy seas we meet. And talk about heavy! Why, the dons could over-haul us in a rowboat with the weight we'll be a-carrying.'

'Well,' said Flint morosely, 'one way we can lighten the load is to throw them damned Frogs overboard, and we'll have their loot an' all.'

'Fair do's, cap'n,' said John, 'they led us to Santa Lena, and there ain't too many of them left now.Why, even their cap'n went and snuffed it in that cannonade, as well you know. No, what I propose is this, we'll bury most of the treasure here, and then come back with two or three fine vessels to ship it home leisurely-like.'

'Ah,' said Flint, 'and only you'll know where it's hid, I'll be bound. You'll be steppin' up for cap'n next, I shouldn't wonder!'

Silver struggled to mask his irritation, and eventually said blandly, 'Why no, cap'n. That ain't my way at all. 'Tis only right you should bury the treasure, with maybe half a dozen to give you a hand. We'll let the men draw lots for it tonight. But first, with your permission, I'll put the plan to the lads for their approval.'

So that night, as the buccaneers sat beside their open fires hungrily devouring portions of roasted goats' flesh and swallowing mouthfuls of rum, Silver harangued them.

It was a marvellous oration – a mixture between a hot-gospelling sermon and a high-court judge summing up an intricate case. Of course, a good number of the buc-caneers were openly hostile to the notion, men like George Merry who would have strangled their own mothers rather than see them make off with twopence, but Long John argued them down.

His final words were among the most telling. 'You've

done us proud, lads!' he cried. 'And, by thunder, the cap'n, God bless him, means to do proud by you. We don't want to see you boys strung up by your thumbs in a dago's torture chamber while some monkish devil chops off your privities! Even you, George Merry, don't fancy that, I reckon. No, we wants to get the loot safe home, even if it takes a bit longer. That way you'll be rolling in carriages in Hyde Park, or nicely shacked up in Madagasky with ten wives a-piece. I puts it to you plain, lads, 'tis the only way!'

Well, that was it. The great majority of the men agreed with John's arguments, and proceeded to draw lots for the risky business of helping Flint to bury the treasure.

At last it was done. The six men chosen to go with Flint stood in the firelight, not altogether certain that luck had been on their side. Meanwhile, a score of the buccaneers, supervised by Billy Bones, packed the gold bars, nearly half the silver bars, the coin, and the choicest of the arms into stout packing cases. The remaining silver was to be stowed aboard the *Walrus*. Pew gazed longingly at the chests, aware that some seven hundred thousand pounds' worth was contained in them.

At first light, the treasure was loaded into two of the larger ship's boats, which settled perilously deep into the water under the weight. Then the burying party rowed off, Flint with his hand on the tiller of the long boat, and a tall, cheerful, yellow-haired man named Allardyce in charge of the other. As the little procession made its way out of the North Inlet, Long John Silver turned briskly towards the watching buccaneers.

'Well, lads,' he said with a fine show of bluff goodwill and confidence. 'It's up to Flint now. Our fortunes is in his hands. So let's get th'old *Walrus* spick and span, and back in the water. Then we'll get the rest of the bar silver aboard and be ready to make off just as soon as Flint and th'others get back. Come now, step to it, and we'll be back again a-rooting out that loot afore six months is past!'

24

❧ *The Loss of the* Walrus ☙

W hen the burying party had left, the rest of the buccaneers finished the work of making everything
ready for sea. Then they lounged upon the *Walrus*'s deck or
wandered into the woods and glades of the island.

Silver, shunning the idle drunkenness of the men lolling
aboard the *Walrus,* made several forays into the island,
though never straying too far from the anchorage lest Flint
should return and cast off straightaway. During one of
these trips he inspected the blockhouse and stockade which
Kidd's men had built twenty years before, and noted that
its timbers were still in good order. On another occasion he
climbed Spy-glass Hill, accompanied by Job Anderson and
the deferential Ben Gunn – who had been brought along to
carry the muskets and provisions; from the Spy-glass, John
could look south to Haulbowline Head and Mizzenmast
Hill and south-east towards Skeleton Island.

But Flint and the treasure were never far from his
thoughts. Had he been a fool to trust Flint and the burying
party with the secret of where the cache was hid? Why, no,
there was some security in numbers. If six men knew the
spot, then surely not all of them were likely to try and cheat
their messmates? Still, the prize was enormous, more than
seven hundred thousand pounds, enought to tempt the
Archbishop of Canterbury to mortal sin.

He could see that others, too, shared his anxieties. Billy
Bones drank more heavily than ever, bawling out scrappy
choruses of 'Fifteen Men on a Dead Man's Chest' until the
parrots took flight and whirled and squawked above the
trees. Israel Hands kept his sensitive ears cocked for the
sound of an approaching boat, and Pew pulled on his long

white fingers until the joints cracked.

At last, on the fifth day, at about ten o'clock in the morning, there was a great commotion upon the *Walrus*'s quarterdeck.

The smaller rowboat was approaching. Soon the pirates could see that it bore but one man, pulling clumsily on the oars; otherwise the boat was empty.

They strained to make out the identity of the lonely oarsman, shading their eyes from the sun. Suddenly Pew cried, 'It's Flint, by thunder!'

'Flint,' said Israel. 'That's no surprise, is that.'

'But where's the others?' said Billy Bones. He leant heavily on the taffrail as if trying to make out the whereabouts of the missing men.

'We'll know soon enough, I shouldn't wonder,' said Silver grimly. Then, to Bones, 'Has Flint drawed a map o' this here island, Billy? And if so, where be it?'

'There's no map as I know of,' replied Bones. ' 'Tis all in his head, I reckon.'

'We'd best keep his head on his shoulders then,' said Long John.

By now Flint had drawn alongside the ship. He tied up the boat to a line cast down to him by Black Dog, and then hauled himself painfully up the side.

There was quite a reception committee awaiting him when at last he staggered on to the deck, his breeches filthy, his shirt ripped open as if by a wild beast, and a bloody scarf swathing his head.

John Silver drew on his pipe and blew a cloud of smoke towards the swaying figure that looked for all the world like a lost soul but recently escaped from the Eternal Pit.

'Why,' he said affably, as if asking the time of day, 'where be the others, cap'n?'

Flint glared at him, his face drawn, and full of hatred.

'Dead!' he rasped. 'Every man jack, and damn them to hell fire, traitors all!'

And with that he stumbled aft towards his cabin, with Darby McGraw clucking round him in alarm.

Silver and the other Lords, as you may imagine, followed hard behind McGraw. They entered Flint's cabin in time to see him collapse onto his bunk, blood still seeping from a huge gash in his skull.

'Rum, Darby,' said Flint feebly. 'Fetch aft the rum.' And with that he fainted away.

Bones fiercely slammed the cabin door in the faces of the mob of buccaneers who were crowding round to catch a glimpse of Flint.

'Well, mateys,' he said. 'I ain't going to let old Flint daddle me out o' my dollars. That island's nine miles by five if it's an inch. If Flint goes below hatches we're done for. How'll we ever find the spot?'

'Easy now, Billy,' said Long John. 'First things first, and duty's duty. Israel, get that swab of a Yankee surgeon down here smartish. He can spout some Latin and open a vein in Flint's arm all at the same time. Job, get back on deck an' tell that rabble to stop their bleating. Tell 'em the cap'n's on the mend already. Issue 'em with an extra tot of rum a piece, an' all.'

Anderson turned heavily to go. 'And, Job!' called Silver. 'If George Merry or any other likely lad begins a-speechifying and a-crying cheat, you tell 'em to step along to me or Gabby here. That should shut their traps, by the powers!'

'Right you are, Barbecue,' replied Anderson. 'But Flint don't look on the mend to me. At death's door more like.'

'Job,' said Silver. 'Thinking's my job, an' Billy's too. Yours is hollering, I reckon, so sharp about it.'

As Anderson left, Silver said to the other Lords, 'We'd best quit Kidd's Island for New Providence. There'll be bloodshed and mutiny here and 'tis safe enough there now, I fancy. Pipe the hands to weigh anchor. There's an ebb tide and a fair breeze. Me and Billy'll stay and tend old Flint, and nurse him back to health, God bless him!'

Pew, Israel, Black Dog, Tom Morgan and the rest shuffled resentfully at this. Silver turned on them in one of his rare shows of fury. 'Get out, you lubbers! Or I'll see the colour of your insides one by one!' he cried.

When they had left, he bent down to look closely at the wound on Flint's head. Darby McGraw was already wiping away the blood with a wet towel, and weeping tears of anguish.

Silver straightened up. 'Billy,' he said. 'We've got to get Flint to cough up where the cache is hid. You've a fair hand for drawing, you have. Sketch us a map of the island, and when Flint comes round he can mark a cross on the chart, just for you and me.'

At that moment the Yankee surgeon, Adams, came daintily into the cabin, carrying bandages, a bleeding bowl, a lancet, and other tools of his trade. Long John nodded meaningfully to Bones, and watched, while the movements of the ship indicated that she was already making out to sea.

The *Walrus*'s voyage to New Providence was little short of a nightmare for John Silver. Flint raved and cursed in his cabin, these bouts being encompassed by lengthy fits of unconsciousness. Try as he might, John could never get him to concentrate his mind for long enough to mark upon the map the place where the treasure lay; not that Flint would have willingly divulged the information to Silver in any circumstances. The crew, moreover, were restless and querulous – reluctant to obey orders and sluggish in their duties. Clearly they felt they were about to be defrauded of their share in the Spanish treasure buried upon Kidd's Island, and even though Billy Bones reminded them of the thousands of pounds' worth of plunder, including the bar silver, in the *Walrus*'s hold, they were not appeased.

It was small wonder, therefore, that the whole ship's company should be caught napping. The *Walrus* was skirting the Florida Cays, barely two hundred and fifty miles from New Providence, and boldly flying the jolly roger. Silver was in Flint's cabin, trying to coax some coherent speech out of him. He had spent many fruitless hours at such work since they had left Kidd's Island, and this was probably the prime reason why discipline among the crew had slackened.

Be that as it may, there were no look-outs posted, and the deck hands were lying in slovenly groups, dozing or throwing dice.

Indeed it was the helmsman who saw the danger first. He spun the wheel violently, swinging the *Walrus* round to starboard, and shrieked, 'There's a dago galleon a-closin' in on the port bow!'

Silver let Flint's hand fall from his grasp so abruptly that the knuckles banged noisily on the cabin floor boards. Within seconds he had burst out onto the quarterdeck, where Bones soon joined him and clapped a telescope to his eye.

'Pray God she's not an armed galleon, Billy,' he said. In Caribbean waters the Spaniards had latterly replaced a good many of their armed galleons with the faster hunting frigates. If the galleon bearing down on them carried only a token number of guns they were safe, given good luck and a steady hand at the wheel, for, despite the plunder in her hold, the *Walrus* could outsail so ponderous an enemy.

Bones swore brief and hard. 'She's armed all right! Two tiers of guns, God damn her! Forty guns each side o' her!'

Israel Hands approached them, shaking his big shaggy head, as if he hoped to spill the rum out of his ears. He had caught Bones's last words. 'Forty guns!' he said, his voice muffled, 'she'll blow us out o' the water straight off, by thunder!'

John Silver seized him by the dangling lobe of his right ear: 'You stow such talk, Israel! Your head may be fuddled with grog, but that don't signify much. Use your eyes, you swab, sight your guns! Get below!'

Where was the galleon now? She had altered course to cut off the *Walrus,* and, whether because she had more canvas aloft or because the wind was favouring her more, the gap between the two vessels was steadily closing.

Those buccaneers that were sober enough to stand had already been kicked to their posts. Frantically they put on more sail. It seemed of no avail – the galleon closed in upon them, like doom.

Pew licked his pale lips. ' 'Tis no good,' he said to Silver, his voice for once devoid of bitterness. ' 'Tis like a cloud a-blottin' out the sun. We're for it now, John.'

A cannon was fired below decks.

'Israel's trying a long shot, I see,' said Bones grimly. 'Much good will it do us.'

More shots came from the gun deck. But still the galleon came on unharmed.

'She's waiting till she's close enough to fry us,' said Silver calmly, but then he roared to the buccaneers on the maindeck, 'Sharpen your cutlasses, shipmates, we'll be in among them dons in a brace of shakes. We'll carve 'em up, by thunder!'

The galleon slowly drew level, with her rows of gun ports gaping ominously open.

'Why don't she fire?' screamed Black Dog amidships.

As if in perverse response the *Walrus* fired her port-side guns in a flurried succession of explosions.

Almost simultaneously the galleon rolled to port. Two score puffs of smoke spurted from her starboard side, and within seconds the full force of her broadside whined and smashed into the *Walrus.*

Smoke shrouded the two vessels, but aboard the *Walrus* the violent rending of her timbers and the pitiful cries of the wounded told a terrible tale.

As the pall of smoke cleared, her decks looked like a slaughterhouse, and a great hole had been punched in her port bow above the waterline.

Upon the quarterdeck Billy Bones grasped the wheel, his cheek bleeding from a wound as neat as a sabre cut, the helmsman dead at his feet.

To his left a roundshot had carried away a section of the taffrail before ploughing up splinters from the deck and bounding into the sea. But in its progress it had struck down both John Silver and Gabriel Pew.

Silver lay unconscious, his left thigh smashed just below the hip, the whole limb merely held together by scraps of flesh and the torn leg of his breeches. Two yards from him, Pew moaned horribly, clawing at the bloody holes where flying splinters had torn out his eyes.

Elsewhere, men lay broken and bleeding where the roundshot and cannister had knocked them down like skittles. There is no doubt that if the Spaniard had brought another broadside to bear, the *Walrus* could never have survived and the secret of Kidd's Island would have vanished for ever. But this was not to be the case, for grievously as Flint's crew had suffered, by a miracle no substantial damage had been done to the ship's masts and rigging. The Spanish galleon, however, had been less fortunate, and Israel's ragged broadside had carried away her foremast and bowsprit. So, though she could still be steered properly, she began to fall behind the *Walrus*.

Slowly, painfully, with Billy Bones urging on the surviving buccaneers, the *Walrus* pulled away from the Spaniard – whose captain, no doubt, stamped and cursed in impotent rage as he saw his quarry, and his prize money, elude him.

Within four hours of her brief but terrible encounter with the galleon the *Walrus* had shaken off her crippled pursuer. Billy Bones stood at the wheel all this time, his hard, brown face as immobile as an old oak figurehead in a Biscay squall. He was never the laughing type, was Billy, and he had little enough to laugh at now, by God, as he steered the *Walrus* due east towards New Providence. Close on a hundred buccaneers were dead, or so near to hell-fire as made no difference. Of the rest, a bare two dozen had escaped injury of some sort, and a good many were maimed as seriously as Silver and Pew.

Israel Hands had emerged unscathed from the galleon's broadside. He came to Billy Bones at irregular intervals, each time bearing some further detail of the losses suffered by the *Walrus*. In this way, Bones learnt that Job Anderson and Tom Morgan were hale enough among the Lords; even Black Dog, who had lost two fingers on his left hand to a whirling fragment of bent iron, was capable of carrying out his duties – though with much whining and complaining. Of the deck hands, George Merry's sneering tongue was as active as ever, and O'Brien, Dirk Campbell and Ben Gunn were fit for action, though the latter's nerves had been rendered more ragged than before and he had taken, unaccountably, to talking fitfully of cheese, and in particular of the toasted variety.

Bones cursed when he knew the full extent of the casualties. 'Here I am, come through earthquakes and Yellow Jack, an' all, and as near as that' – snapping his rough fingers – 'to rolling in luxury like a king, and damme if we'll ever hobble home to New Providence at this rate!'

'Well, I'm here to do me duty, Bill,' said Israel Hands.

'You're a good cool gunner, Israel,' said Bones. 'But you ain't much of a seaman, neither. There's Flint aft, a-raving and a-singing when he don't swoon away. Pew's lost his deadlights, and Barbecue's left leg ain't all that it was, says you. That makes me captain according to my reckoning, seeing as how I don't choose to stand for election, things being what they are.'

Israel said 'There's none hereabouts as'll go against you, Bill.'

'No,' replied Bones. 'Maybe not. Leastways not now Long John's been cut down to size.' He squinted ahead. 'Israel, I ain't touched more'n a drop o' rum since we quit

Santa Lena, and bless me if it ain't the water of life to me, but is that sails ahead on the starboard bow?'

Hands clambered into the mizzen shrouds, peering at the horizon. 'By gum, Bill, you must have smelt 'em! Two sail ahead, as right as rain. 'Tis likely they ain't enemy though.'

'We've two dozen men fit for duty, matey. Not enough to furl the sails if we runs head-on into nasty weather, let alone man the guns in any proper fashion. So I says, every ship on the water's our enemy, by thunder! Them sail yonder is athwart our course to New Providence. Damme if I'm giving 'em a chance to sniff my stern. I'm off on a different tack. It'll be dark within the hour. We'll give 'em the slip easy then.'

'We can't go back, Bill. Anyroad, the breeze ain't favourable. Where you aiming for, then?'

'Savannah, matey. We'll strike northwards. It's a longer haul, but a safe one I reckon.' And with that he began to alter the vessel's course, shouting orders to the pitifully small handful of buccaneers upon the maindeck.

As the *Walrus* headed northwards, shrouded in darkness, the Yankee surgeon, Adams, worked feverishly upon the wounded stacked in the forecastle. It was a proper hell-hole in there and no mistake, what with the ship pitching, and the wounded shrieking and rolling on to each other. How Adams saved the men he did was little short of a miracle, for he was obliged to work in stifling heat with the lanterns fluttering and the light uncertain. Hitherto the buccaneers had mocked Adams, laughing at his prim ways and calling him 'Missy' behind his back; but there were none to mock him that night. He looked more like a horse-butcher than a college-educated gentleman – blood smeared all over his apron, his saws and scalpels stained and reeking.

Black Dog, being classified as 'walking wounded' – despite his protests that he was near to dying – was seized by Adams to act as his medical assistant. This was a grand-sounding title all right, but the work was hardly dainty, for

Black Dog spent his time scraping splinters and fragments of grape-shot out of a variety of limbs and torsoes, and sewing up gaping flesh wounds with a coarse black sailmaker's thread.

Pew was among the first that Black Dog attended to, timorously washing his scarred forehead and rubbing a salve around his empty eye sockets. Then his sightless brow was bandaged up in a length of blue cloth torn from an old shirt, and he was dumped in a corner of the forecastle where he alternately cursed his ill-fortune and moaned pitifully for food and drink.

Adams spared little time on those whom he considered too grievously maimed to survive the night; such unfortunates were dragged onto the upper fore-deck and left to die amid the flying spray and the sharp gusts of wind that beat across the *Walrus*'s prow.

It was some hours after the *Walrus* had shaken off her Spanish foe that Adams laid a hand on the stricken quartermaster. Long John winced as the surgeon probed his shattered thigh and awoke from the feverish sleep that had hitherto dulled his senses.

Bending over John's sweat-stained face, Adams said in his high-pitched, careful, New England brogue, 'Mr Silver, it's my decided opinion that I must amputate your left leg, close to the hip.'

Silver shook his great fair head. 'Ampytate my leg! There's no man living as'll do that, by thunder! I'll not be a cripple, begging in the gutter, sponging for scraps. It'll mend as like as not. I know you surgeons, Latin by the bucketful! You can't rest content till you've carved up a good seaman or two to see if his innards is like what it says in the books!'

The surgeon said, 'If we leave that leg on you'll be dead within a week, Mr Silver. Your femur is smashed into particles, and you have lost too much blood. I fear I can smell an infection in the flesh already. Have you ever seen gangrene, Mr Silver? In Boston I once removed a quart of maggots from the leg of an old ruffian who thought he knew better than the surgeons; 'twasn't a pleasant sight to see him die. What say you, Mr Silver? I ain't got time to discourse on this matter. You can live, maybe, or die as sure as fate.'

Silver glared at him. 'Take it off, Adams. I never know'd you was such a man for argument, and you may lay to that.'

It needed four of them to lift Silver's huge frame onto the bloody trestle that served as Adams' operating table. There was, it seems, nothing prissy about the surgeon when it came to amputation. A folded leather belt was thrust between Silver's teeth as he lay on his back; Black Dog reluctantly leant on his shoulders to pin him to the table, and Adams set to work. So badly damaged was Long John's thigh-bone that there was hardly any need to use the saw upon it. Adams' main task was to cut through the mangled tissue as expeditiously as possible, and to staunch the rush of fresh blood.

He was a brave man, was John Silver, and never braver than when he felt the sharp edge of Adams's knife; he twisted his head from side to side, and clenched his great hands till the nails bruised the palms, but he never once cried out. Not, that is, until the stump of his leg was plunged into boiling pitch to cauterise it. Then he gave a bellow which shook the rafters above him. Adams gave a thin smile and said triumphantly to Black Dog, who had near-enough fainted away, ' 'Tis healthy to hear a man holler so, Mr Dog. If his lungs be that powerful, he has a fighting chance of recovery, I do declare!'

So it was that John Silver lost his left leg. It is worth recording that he nearly lost his life at the same time, for he straightway contracted a fever, a sort of ague, that shook his whole body till his teeth chattered in his skull. Black Dog did his best to nurse him back to health, mopping his

burning, streaming face, and pouring drops of rum down
his throat whenever he had the chance and Adams
was elsewhere.

Who can say what terrible events and base treacheries
would have been averted if Long John Silver had died
aboard the *Walrus?* The lives of a good many true men
would have been spared for one thing, though some rogues
would very like be living yet and continuing to plague decent, ordinary folk.

Be that as it may, Silver did not die, though for several
weeks he lay between life and death, as weak as a lamb and
barely knowing where he was.

While John struggled to survive, Billy Bones put into
Savannah in the new-founded colony of Georgia. It was a
wise decision, since Flint had once, with an effort, in-
gratiated himself with the Governor, a pompous and dis-
honest man called Bondhead, during his earlier raids upon
the Florida coast. Anyhow, the *Walrus* limped into Savannah, and Billy went ashore with a chest of silver to sweeten
Bondhead's temper. The upshot was that the *Walrus* was
allowed to anchor off Savannah, and the noble Governor,
who was always looking for ways to line his own pocket,
even at the expense of his master King George II, went so
far as to send his personal physician aboard.

For three weeks the *Walrus* lay off Savannah, for all the
world like a hospital ship. During this time a good few of
the crew that were fit, and those that had mended, flitted
off, either to find berths on other vessels or to try their luck
in the colony itself; those with enough sense took a silver
bar or two to help them on their way.

Flint flitted off, too, in a manner of speaking, for one
night he died, after screaming an oath that might have set
the harbour waters boiling. Billy Bones was at his side as
he finally set sail for the Inferno. No doubt it was then that
Billy learnt the whereabouts of the buried treasure on
Kidd's Island, for no sooner had he placed penny-pieces on

Flint's eyes, and called in Tom Morgan as a witness, than he cut out a hefty portion of the loot from the hold and made off.

Almost as if he sensed Bones's treachery, Silver rallied the same day, and, propped up in a cabin corner below the poop deck, questioned Tom Morgan closely.

'I see'd Flint dead with these here deadlights, John,' said Morgan. 'Billy took me in, like I said, and there he laid.'

'And where's Billy now, Tom Morgan? Take your bearings. No one's a-pressing of you. 'Tis a rare pleasure to hear the way you spit out the words, one after t'other, like. Why, you makes talking sound like music, and no mistake.'

Morgan said, uneasily, 'Billy never telled me where he was a-goin', John. He ups and he says, "Matey, I'm a-castin' off. Tell Barbecue, if he lives, that I've done him good and proper, for I've got a map what is as pretty as a picture. He'll know what I mean," says he.'

Silver pulled himself up into a sitting position. 'Know what he means, the swab!' he roared. 'I know what he means right enough. He's got Flint to tell him where the treasure's hid! Marked that map an' all, I'll be bound! By the powers, Tom Morgan, 'tis lucky for you you weren't hand in glove with Billy, for I'd have your hide for it, cripple though I am!'

He fell silent for a moment or two, gasping for breath. Then he said, more calmly, 'Tom, you never had much to spare when it come to brains, I reckon. But you've a way with wood as is a treat to behold. Cut me a crutch, mate, as 'ud do any gentleman o' fortune proud. Bring Gabby Pew here by the hand. And Black Dog, and Israel, and any others o' the old gang that ain't yet slipped their cables. Tell 'em I've shook off the ague. I'll soon be a-raring to go. Billy had best look out, for I'll track him down if I has to hop all the way on one leg!'

By the next morning, Silver was fully in command of the remnants of Flint's crew, and already using his freshly-fashioned crutch with great dexterity. As soon as he could, John sold the *Walrus* to a grasping local merchant called Oglethorpe, and supervised a share-out of this money and of the remaining treasure. Then, with near enough two thousand pounds in his possession, and with Gabriel Pew as a grateful dependant, he got himself aboard a sloop bound for Jamaica, serving as ship's cook.

Already he was formulating his plans. He would bring Annette from Jamaica, leaving his stripling sons to manage his affairs; then he would make for England. There he would settle in a likely seaport, invest his money, and lease a property. Bristol seemed as good a place as any, though his parents he guessed were long since dead. From this base, he would continually watch and listen for any clues that might tell him of Billy Bones's whereabouts. Why, Billy himself might turn up in Bristol sooner or later – most seamen seemed to do that. An inn, that would be the best: a vantage point near the waterfront where seamen would come and go, and tell their tales and blab and gossip.

25

❦ The 'Spy-Glass' Inn ❧

John Silver was indeed a remarkable man, despite his infamies. Consider his circumstances in the year of grace 1754: although in the prime of his manhood, he was crippled for the rest of his days; he had worked tirelessly and intelligently to secure the plate treasure for Flint's crew – now the main part of the cache was buried in some unknown spot on Kidd's Island. True, there was a map marking the place, but Billy Bones had it safe in his keeping. Where was Billy? That was the riddle that cried out for an answer. Find Billy, get the map from him by fair means or foul, and return to the island to pick up the plunder – this became the overriding ambition of Silver's life.

But Long John was never one to rush things. Although plans for the recovery of the treasure continually fermented in his brain, though he relived again and again the brief tragedy of his maiming aboard the *Walrus* and repeatedly reminded himself of the injustice of Bones's treachery, he remained for a time outwardly calm – content, even.

Pew, who accompanied him on the voyage back to England, failed to comprehend his apparently imperturbable, even passive, outward show.

As the ship at last neared Bristol after a storm-tossed crossing of three and a half weeks' duration, Silver led Pew onto the foredeck to take the air.

Turning his head from side to side, Pew sniffed the breeze hungrily, then held out his long, pale hand as if to feel the texture of the atmosphere. His empty sockets were now shielded by a thick green eyeshade fastened to his head with a length of twine.

He said sourly, ' 'Tis the smell of England right enough:

dank and cold.' He sniffed again. 'I can't catch the scent of Billy's trail, though, John. I reckon you're plumb wrong to hope to find him here.'

'Gabby,' said Silver. 'You rest easy on my account. I've not come back to Bristol to fret over a swab like Billy. Great guns! I've a fair bit o' blunt stowed in my old sea-chest below these boards. And a bit more I put aside with my missus, years afore this. No, my son, it's the easy life for me as soon as ever we docks.'

'I'd like to get my hands on Billy!' Pew said. 'I'd tweak his Adam's apple, by the powers!'

'Well now, Gabby, you was always one for a bit o' sport. But you're a rich man now, on your own account. Twelve hundred pounds! Shiver my sides, you can live like a lord in Parliament on that.'

There was a silence for some moments, then Silver continued, 'Supposing, after a while, I gets a hankering to see my old mate Bill? Well, what better place than Bristol to get wind of him? 'Tis a bustling place is Bristol – why, after London 'tis far and away the biggest city in the whole country, as well you know. Its docks is packed full of all manner of vessels from every quarter of the globe. I'd wager that if I was to sit upon the quayside for just one day I'd hear some item of news concerning a seaman as was knowed to me.'

Pew said, 'And I'd wager one o' these new, queer ten pound notes folks is a-talking about that you could sit there for a six month and hear not a scrap about any of th'old gang.'

'Gabby,' replied Silver, 'all this is talk. I ain't the one to work myself into a lather over Billy Bones. No, I'm a-going to sleep soft and eat dainty when I'm ashore, and so will you, my son, if you get your bearings set straight.'

With that he began to talk animatedly of what he could see as the vessel worked her way along the Severn estuary, towards the city of his birth standing solidly amid green hills.

Soon after settling unobtrusively in Bristol, Silver learnt that both his parents had indeed died some years ago. Of his two sisters, one had perished during a smallpox epidemic and the other had married an East India Company clerk and had settled at Fort St George, near Madras. He also discovered, much to his satisfaction, that his brief service with Captain Hawke during the War of the Austrian Succession entitled him to a free Royal pardon for crimes committed before the outbreak of those hostilities.

So it was with a relatively clear conscience that he was able to buy the lease of a bright little tavern, close to the docks, and with a street on either side of it. When he moved in as landlord the first thing John did was to rename the inn the Spy-Glass – no doubt in remembrance of that hill far away on Kidd's Island which, for all he knew, harboured Flint's buried treasure.

The Spy-Glass with its light, low rooms and sanded floors was much patronised by seamen, for John Silver kept a good board, and a hungry man could eat a supper of veal cutlets, pigeon, asparagus, lamb and salad, apple pie and tarts for a mere six pence. The liquor was undiluted and the beer flowed freely. The inn was kept spotlessly clean; and warm, too, in winter, for he regularly bought several tons of coal freshly mined in Somerset by rough gangs of men brought down from Northumberland.

Silver soon established an enviable reputation as an honest, hardworking, scrupulous landlord; he became a sub-postmaster, too, and a staunch supporter of the Tory cause at election time. In short, Flint's old quartermaster transformed himself into a veritable pillar of the local community, and the Spy-Glass inn was a beacon light for those drawn towards fair-dealing and hospitality of the rare, old-fashioned sort.

This was all to Silver's purpose. Money-making was not his chief concern, for he was, by the standards of the day, a rich man, and had put substantial sums, in both his own and his wife's name, into a number of the new-fangled banks that were then springing up in provincial towns. But if profit was not his chief objective, respectability was, and he pursued this aim with all his characteristic guile and singlemindedness.

Within two years John Silver's position in local society was secure enough to allow him to unmask, little by little, his grand design to track down Billy Bones and crown his career with a successful swoop on the treasure of Kidd's Island. So while he played the part of an affable, courteous and good-humoured landlord, he was for ever sifting through the rumours and yarns of his customers, his ear cocked for a clue that would unravel the mystery of Bones's whereabouts.

Soon he was sending his confederates hither and thither in the West Country, hoping that some stroke of good fortune would enable him to unearth the necessary clues. By this time he had gathered around him a number of the survivors of Flint's crew. Chief of these was Pew, whom John kept in his pay as an extra pair of ears. Although Gabby had brought back twelve hundred pounds from Savannah, in less than a year it had gone – after all, it is doubly tempting for rogues to swindle a blind man, even one as ferocious of disposition as Pew. In short, Silver rescued his old friend from the gutter, where he was nothing but a whining, cursing beggar-man at odds with the law.

Black Dog also ran errands for John, and kept his eyes skinned for Billy Bones. The Spy-Glass was the haunt of Tom Morgan, too, and Israel Hands, Job Anderson, Dirk Campbell and Michael O'Brien could all be found there on occasion. Even George Merry had been known to partake of Silver's hospitality, though he was liable to spit out the last dregs of his mug of ale and pronounce it no better than rat's vomit.

So Long John sat, like some brooding, cunning spider, at the centre of a web specially and painstakingly spun to catch Billy Bones. Patiently he waited at the Spy-Glass Inn; patiently, but hungrily, and anxiously. As the months passed, and then the years too, his patience became flimsier and flimsier, his hunger more predatory, his sense of loss more overwhelming, his anger at Bones's treachery more difficult to contain.

For all his steady surveillance, precious few clues came his way – though now and again he caught a snippet of gossip that seemed promising. He became pretty sure, for one thing, that Billy had slipped into the colony of Maryland after he had quit Savannah, and had later sailed from Baltimore to Nova Scotia. He knew, for another thing, that his quarry had bobbed up later in Calcutta at the time of Robert Clive's conquest of the Nawab of Bengal and his French allies. That had been 1757. But then for three years he heard nothing. In the autumn of 1760 the boatswain of a Liverpool packet swore that a man answering to Bones's description, scarred cheek and all, had sailed with him as second mate aboard a slaver bound for the Bight of Biafra. Two years later came word that Billy, befuddled with rum, had been heavily fined by magistrates in London for being drunk and disorderly in Threadneedle Street. So at least he was back in England; and, it seemed, having failed to collect the treasure from Kidd's Island.

Three months after Silver received this piece of intelligence, Michael O'Brien brought him real hope. It was late one November evening when O'Brien strode noisily into the bar-room of the Spy-Glass, knocking over an unoccupied bench and treading heavily upon the hindquarters of a spotted whelp dozing upon the stone-flagged floor.

Long John was closeted in a side room, wreathed in clouds of tobacco smoke, and astounding the parish beadle with the vehemence of his denunciation of footpads and highwaymen – in particular the notorious Maclaine and his predecessor Dick Turpin.

As soon as word was brought that O'Brien wished to see

him, Silver ushered the beadle from the room, pumping his hand and earnestly thanking him for his uplifting conversation.

O'Brien's story was like meat and drink to Silver, who put on and took off his old cocked hat at least nine times as he lapped up the information. At last he said, 'Michael, I'll keep you in rum to your dying day, bless my buttons if I won't! At the sign of the Star and Anchor, you say? A man by the name of Bones! With a tarry pigtail down his back, and an old sea-chest with him. Just stepped off the London coach, has he?'

'Now see here, Michael, watch this!' So saying he drew out his claspknife, and taking a scrap of yellow parchment from a nearby drawer he cut out a circular piece as neat as a newly-minted crown.

'Matey, get along to the kitchen. Ask my old gal for the ink pot and a sharp quill. Tell her it's for business.'

O'Brien was soon back. Silver took the pen and wrote carefully upon the disc of parchment. Then he swung himself over to the fireplace and, with his forefinger, scraped some soot off the inside of the chimney breast. Returning to his place on the oak settle, he carefully smeared the soot over the reverse side of the disc.

He handed the circle of parchment to O'Brien. 'Go along to our pal Billy. Give him this. He'll know the black spot when he sees it.'

O'Brien frowned and turned the disc from side to side. At last he said, threateningly, 'There's writing on it. What's it after saying? Holy Mother of God, it might say "Billy, cut O'Brien's throat," for all I know!'

'And it might say "Billy, off with ye and strangle the Bishop of Cork," an' all,' replied Silver mockingly. 'Michael, my lubber, you're a-fretting too much, you are. 'Tain't good for your brains. 'Twill addle 'em, and you may lay to that.'

As O'Brien shuffled angrily, Silver continued calmly,

'Howsoever, I'm not the man to trick his own messenger. Long John'll play straight with you, my lad! The writing says "By noon". Then there's my mark on it, "J.S.", as clear as print. 'Tain't much of a message, you'll be a-thinking, Michael. But dear old Billy'll get the drift of it straight off, by thunder! Off with you! And be back here directly!'

Silver settled down to await O'Brien's return. We shall never know the private agonies that he endured while he waited, alone in the side room, the fire burning cheerfully at his right hand. The minutes passed; five minutes, then ten, then thirty. Silver lit his pipe, picking up a red-hot coal from the fireplace with the brass tongs, and drawing greedily upon the tobacco.

Forty-five minutes. Fifty. An hour. A few late carts and carriages passed by the Spy-Glass, their iron-shod wheels scraping on the cobbles, their horses' hooves ringing out. What was that? A raucous commotion from the bar-room; shouting mingling with the singing, then the sudden sound of oaths and protestations.

The door of the side room flew open. There was Black Dog, his tallowy features twisted with fear. O'Brien was leaning on his shoulder, gasping for breath, his frock-coat torn and his shirt front stained dark red with blood.

Silver hoisted himself into a standing position, as Black Dog let O'Brien tumble headlong to the floor.

Barely able to mouth the words, Silver said, 'What's this, you swab?'

O'Brien lifted his face from the floor and looked up at Long John standing over him and casting a gigantic, flickering shadow onto the further wall. He said, with half a sob, 'I saw Bill, in his room. Talking we was. Friendly, to be sure. Then I give him the black spot. By all the angels, he outs with his cutlass and gives me a cut across me left shoulder. Then suddenly 'twas all dark, like the grave, by God!'

Silver said, slowly and with some effort, 'The grave is

where you belong, by the powers. You fool! So you let him
go. I've a mind to stove your skull in with this here crutch!'

At this, O'Brien groaned and rolled onto his left side,
clutching his head with both hands.

Ignoring the groan, Silver said, 'And when you opened
your eyes again he was gone? That's the size of it? Blast
you!'

O'Brien groaned again, in assent.

Long John turned away from him without a word, and
shouldering aside Black and Job Anderson, who stood gaw-
ping at the scene, made his way down the passage and
began to pull himself up the stairs, painfully, like an old
man.

Billy Bones's escape from the Star and Anchor in
November 1763 weighed heavily upon John Silver's spirits.
For two weeks afterwards he scarcely spoke to a soul, and
even then with none of his customary good-humour and
civility. He grew listless, and took to brooding by himself in
the kitchen corner, barely noticing what was going on
around him. He drank more heavily than at any time in his
life hitherto, but the liquor dulled his senses rather than
enlivened them.

Thus he sat, hunched in his high-backed wooden chair,
while the months passed, and still there was no word of
Billy Bones. It is possible, indeed, that he might have suffered a steady decline in his health, a decline that would
have taken him to the grave as surely as consumption, con-
vulsions or malignant fever, but for news Black Dog
brought him in the winter of 1764.

According to Black Dog, a mate of his from Plymouth
had heard tell of an old sea captain tucked away in a lonely
inn on the south Devon coast. The old ruffian, so Black Dog
heard, was mighty partial to his rum, and when deep in
drink roared out all manner of sea-songs and shanties –
including 'Fifteen Men on a Dead Man's Chest'!

Silver drew Black Dog into his kitchen as soon as he

heard these particulars; he was almost beside himself with suppressed excitement.

' 'Tis fair promising, is this,' he said. 'Where do you say this seaman is sityated?'

'All lonely like,' replied Black Dog. 'A country inn, the Admiral Benbow by name. The lubber in question keeps hisself to hisself. What's more, he's main feared of a seafaring man with one leg. Who'd that be, do ye reckon, John?'

Silver laughed in relief, smacking his right knee. 'It's him, by thunder! Billy, my boy, we're on your tail at last.'

'Now, see here,' he said, animated, but suddenly serious. 'This won't do. Black Dog, step over to Mr Blandly's office next to the Old Anchor and tell him I wants to hire a lugger – the price he sets don't signify. Then get me Pew, Job, Johnny, Dirk and any of the old gang, and bring 'em here. Smart about it, you swab!'

Within half an hour Black Dog had gathered up the buccaneers that Silver had named, and four more besides. John gave them their orders.

'I knows the place. There's nought but a hamlet near. You'd best land at Kitt's Hole, and sidle up to the inn secret like. Then you tips Billy the black spot, and when his time is up you snaffles his sea-chest and let him go hang!'

'John,' said Black Dog timorously, 'I ain't tipping Bill no black spot. He'd hack me head off, soon as look at me, let alone the black spot.'

'You were wrong named, I reckon,' said Silver contemptuously. 'Yellow Dog'd suit you better.'

'Hold hard, Barbecue,' said Pew, his head tilted to catch every word. 'Let Black Dog talk to Billy first, make him see the error of his ways, you might say. If that's no go, then tip him the black spot.'

'And who's the lubber to do that?' said Silver.

'I'll do it, John,' said Pew, fingering his great green eye shade. 'I'm not afraid of Bill, nor never was. And when I gets to thinkin' of all them doubloons and dollars I lost my deadlights for I'd tip Satan hisself the black spot if needs be.'

'Gabby,' said Silver. 'You're a man, you are!'

And so it was that the little gang of buccaneers, led by blind Pew, worked their way in a hired lugger to Kitt's Hole in January 1765. There, as you know, their luck deserted them, Black Dog fled from Billy Bones's cutlass, and Pew was ridden down four days later and killed by Supervisor Dance and his companions. The rest, being too stupid or too cowardly to hunt down Billy Bones's sea-chest, slipped back to the lugger and returned to Bristol.

Long John gave them a rare roasting when they returned, sheepish, and without the chart, to the Spy-Glass inn.

'Call yourselves buccaneers?' he roared. 'Why, gals in muslin dresses would have done better! There was but one real man aboard that lugger, and him a blind man too, tap-tapping with his stick while you swabs skulked and trembled. Poor dead Pew, you weren't fit to lift the hem of his sea-cloak, and you may lay to that! You ain't got heads on your shoulders, boys, you've got plum-duffs instead. If so be I should ever run short of roundshot again, and the dons a-pressing in, I'll load the cannon with your skulls – you'd never know the difference!'

Job Anderson spoke up in a shame-faced sort of way. 'Easy, John,' he said. 'We leaves the thinkin' an' such to you, but you wasn't at Kitt's Hole, more's the pity.'

'Pity!' cried Silver. 'I'll pity you! There's enough treasure on Kidd's Island to make nabobs of us all, every man jack! We'd be as rich as Robert Clive, we would, as rich as Croesus!'

Dirk Campbell said, uncertainly, 'I never sailed along o' this 'ere Creesus, Long John, but there's one item we ain't had a chance to speak of yet.'

'Speak away, my lad,' said Silver menacingly.

Dirk said, 'As the lugger pulled away from Kitt's Hole, this grand fellow, Dance, he yelled at us, threatenin' like,

"I'll have Squire Trelawney and the law on your backs, you scoundrels!"'

'Trelawney,' said Silver thoughtfully. 'I knows that name.'

He hopped over to the corner of the kitchen and fed a tit-bit to his caged green parrot, which he had now, with a touch of malice, re-christened 'Captain Flint'.

'Ah, yes,' he said softly, as if to the bird. 'Trelawney. He's the squire in them parts. Why, he has the Parliament seat in his pocket for the Tory candidate – I knows that. And bless me if he ain't a pal of our friend Blandly across the way, though Blandly twists him something terrible whenever they does business.'

He turned back to the buccaneers and smiled. 'Boys, we've a chance. A mighty slim 'un, but a chance all the same. I mind that Blandly once telled me how this fat calf Trelawney's always a-hankering after a life at sea – "noble work afore the mast", an' all. Well, if he's nosed around and lighted on Billy's map, and being the usual type of country squire, by which I means greedy and pig-headed, 'tis odds on he's heading for Bristol at this very minute!'

This short speech caused something of a stir among his audience.

Silver went on, 'Blandly'll do anything for money, seeing as how he's got a stuck-up missis and four stuck-up daughters all a-crying for the moon. So, I'll make him a handsome gift o' gold, and tell him to give me the nod if this here calf Trelawney comes a-mooing to buy a ship and hire some old salts. Then I'll step up to the squire, and touch my forelock, all respectful like, and show my ampytated leg – lost in the service of my country – and offer him my assistance and advice. I'll drum up his crew for him, by thunder!'

At this he threw back his head and laughed his great, ringing laugh.

'D'you reckon it'll work, John?' said Anderson doubtfully.

'Work?' said Silver, wiping the tears from his eyes. 'It'll work all right, or I'm a Dutchman. Patience, my boys, that's what you need. And a spark or two a-kindling up here,' and at this he tapped his forehead knowingly.

'Now, you lubbers, out o' my way! I've got customers in the parlour and my good name to think on. You leave it to old John, my sons, and he'll see you right, by the powers!'

Off he went, swinging skilfully on his crutch, to move among his clients, slapping them cheerfully on the shoulder and jesting with them in high good humour. And it was in similar mood that I, Jim Hawkins, cabin boy, found him on a bright morning early in March in the year of 1765.